P.S. You're the Worst

An Enemies to Lovers Romance

Jane Anthony

Jane Anthony Author

P.S. You're the Worst

ISBN: 979-8-9872621-2-2

Editing by:

Candace Royer

Jenny Sims, Editing4Indies

Cover Design:

Kate Farlow, Y'all. That Graphic

For...

The man I devoted my entire life to: You're the fucking worst. I hope your balls shrivel up and fall off.

Playlist

"Different for Girls" – Dierks Bentley/Elle King
"Black Sheep" – Dorothy
"Wicked Game" – Stone Sour
"Royals" – Lorde
"Undo It" – Carrie Underwood
"Gunpowder & Lead" – Miranda Lambert
"Mama's Broken Heart" – Miranda Lambert
"What Hurts the Most" - Rascal Flatts
"Till There's Nothing Left" – Cam
"Before He Cheats" – Carrie Underwood
"Redneck Woman" – Gretchen Wilson
"Numb" – Lincoln Park
"Here's to Us" – Halestorm/Slash
"Friends in Low Places" - Garth Brooks
"Crazy Bitch" – Buckcherry
"The Sex is Good" – Saving Abe
"Dirty Little Thing" - Adelitas Way
"Casual Sex" – My Darkest Days

"Fuck Away the Pain" – Divide the Day
"Dirty Little Girl" – Burn Halo
"White Trash Millionaire" – Black Stone Cherry
"Anymore" – Haley Hoffman Smith
"Smooth" – Florida Georgia Line
"Rewrite the Stars" – Zac Efron/Zendaya
"This is Me" – Kesha
"Bad Reputation" – Joan Jett & the Blackhearts

Chapter One

DARLA

RAIN PELTS ON THE roof of our trailer in a rhythmic pattern. Unusually cold for Texas, I pull my robe tighter and cinch the thin satin with the sash, slamming my foot on the vent. A desperate puff of heat dribbles out. A death rattle.

"Fuckin' piece of shit," I grumble under my breath.

The kitchen connects my room to the living area. I step out slowly and reach for the kettle on the stove. Mom doesn't bother to look up. Her fried hair is all you can see of her curling above the back of the lounge chair that separates the space between us. A burnt-out cigarette dangles from her spindly fingers. Believe it or not, she used to be almost pretty. Now she's half a corpse staring at the television as my tea boils.

I hear the toilet flush seconds before the accordion door slams open. The hair on the back of my neck rises along with my shoulders as Ray shimmies past. His finger hooks on the edge of my robe. Luckily, I'm quick and grab the tie before he pulls it open. "This little thing is almost see-through," he grumbles.

"Get the fuck away from me." I elbow him off, and he stumbles back.

"Hey," he snaps, his furry fingers taking hold of my bicep. The stink of booze wafts off his breath and permeates his ratty ribbed tank. He wrenches me closer as the lights go out.

A gurgled gasp escapes my mom as the three of us are drenched in darkness. "What happened?" As my eyes adjust, I see her stumble to stand and stagger toward us. "Didn't I give you money to pay the bill?"

The sound of her voice loosens Ray's hold. Just like the time he "accidentally" found himself in my room instead of hers. "I must've forgot."

"Forgot? What'd you do with my money?" she slurs, pulling open the dead fridge. Glass bottles ting together. She takes the vodka from the shelf and thumbs open the cap. "Can't even pay a fuckin' bill. Lazy, good for nothin'—"

Ray's open palm comes down on the back of her head. She lurches forward, catching herself on the counter. "Who you callin' lazy, bitch?"

She lashes out and pounds on his thick chest. This is where it starts. They'll brawl in the dark, and tomorrow I'll go down to the electric company and pay the stupid bill to have the lights turned back on.

If I don't get out of Hell's Bend, I'm going to end up just like my mother—drunk and old before my time, with a piece-of-shit husband who offers nothing except leering eyes and a disgusting beer gut that hangs beneath his sweaty shirt. She threw her life away, and I'll be damned if I follow in her vodka-soaked footsteps.

I flop on my bed and open Tinder on my phone. I'm starting a new job tomorrow. The responsible thing to do would be to stay in and rest, but I'm not in the mood to sit in the dark listening to them bicker all night. Maybe I can find a guy to offer a distraction from this hell on earth I call my life. Worst-case scenario, at least a free meal.

I swipe left on any guy posing with a fish or a deer carcass. I never understood why men do that. Do they think dead animals are some kind of weird aphrodisiac for women? Because I'll tell you right now, I don't need to know about it unless it's on my plate.

Left on Mr. I'm Standing Next To My Mom to Show How Sensitive I Am.

Left again on Mr. This Is a Close-Up Photo of My Junk in Sweats.

Left on Mr. Your Profile Pic Is Clearly Ten Years Old.

Left on Mr. I Don't Need a Guy with Nicer Eyebrows Than Mine.

I'm about ready to give up when I finally land on a worthy contender: Dylan, 23. Long blond hair and soulful eyes, he stares up at me with a lazy grin cocked on his handsome face. His profile doesn't say much, but that doesn't matter to me. I'm not much for talking anyway. He looks like a badass. I've always been a sucker for a tough guy. Someone who will keep me on my toes and fight for what he wants. That kind of broody arrogance makes my panties damp. I get off on the chase. What can I say? I'm a little fucked up.

I sweep my finger to the right and smile when the app tells me we've matched. A chat window opens instantly.

Dylan: Hi.

I bring my knees up and lean the phone against my thighs.

Me: Hi.

Dylan: How are you?

I hate these monotonous chats. I doubt this guy gives a shit how I am. Why bother asking? Get to the point and shut up. But I play it cool and respond like I have a little class.

Me: Fine, thanks. You?

Dylan: Alright. Can't complain.

I roll my eyes. This guy has the conversational skills of my grandpa.

Dylan: What are you doing?

Me: Nothing. Sitting at home.

My stomach rumbles. I press my palm to my belly button to calm it down when his next reply comes in.

Dylan: Do you want to meet for a drink?

Me: Sure.

We exchange a few more messages and decide to meet at a bar over in White Tail Creek. The only bar in Hell's Bend is The Great Notch Inn, and aside from the fact that I work there, my fake ID wouldn't get past Cindy Wilder anyway. I grew up with her son since preschool. The aforementioned "tough guy" who used to rile me right the fuck up . . . until he took off with that fucking East Coast Barbie. But I digress.

That's one of the things I hate most about living here. Everyone knows everything. There are no secrets in a small town.

I get myself ready by candlelight, then steal Ray's keys (my truck needs gas) and head out the door. I weave through frigid drops falling from the sky. My damp skirt sticks to my thighs in the dusty old cab of his Ford F150. I start it up and ease through the trailer park, swiping the condensation off the windshield with my palm before hitting the road.

Slater's Mill is a little place off the beaten path. A converted barn that arcs up into the clouds and thumps with a thick bass I feel pounding in my chest as I go inside. I shake my hair out with my fingers, trying my best to rejuvenate my rain-wilted curls as I slide onto a barstool.

"What can I get ya?" The bartender meanders over and throws a coaster in front of me.

"Tequila."

His heavy brows pull together. "You got ID?"

I roll my eyes, then dig through my bag to find my wallet. Butterflies swirl in my gut. I hand over the card, and he holds it out, squinting to see the tiny lettering in the dark. A few seconds later, he gives it back with a curt nod, then wanders off to make my drink.

"Darla?"

When I turn toward the sound of my name, my heart fucking stops dead. Long blond hair frames his steel jaw, his eyes piercing in the neon lights. A hard-core mix of silver and leather wrap his wrist as he extends his hand. "I'm Dylan."

Fuck yes, you are.

"Hi." I reel in the stupid grin splitting my face. He looks like a rock star with all ripped denim and long chains over his tight black tank. Usually, you meet a guy on Tinder and he looks nothing like his photo.

Either they're older than pictured or clearly photoshopped. But this guy went the other way. Photos don't do him justice.

He nods his chin toward the glass as the bartender sets it on the coaster. "What are you drinkin'?"

"Tequila."

He lifts a brow. "I'll have the same," he orders, waving his hand between us. "And start a tab."

His tongue slides across his perfect, plump lips, and I find myself thanking a God I was starting to doubt existed before he showed up. He doesn't even need to talk. I could look at him and fall deeper into lust the longer I sit here.

"So where're you from?" he asks. I hate the usual first-date chitchat. Where're you from? What's your major? What do you do for fun? Blah, blah, blah. It's all so benign and boring. I want to jump past all of that and get into the meat and potatoes of a person. Don't tell me what you do for a living. Regale me with stories of the most embarrassing moments of your life. The nitty-gritty details that make a person who they are. I may bluster like a violent wind, but deep down, I'm looking for the same thing any other young person is looking for. A connection.

"Hell's Bend."

I almost see him scowl, but like a true gentleman, he holds it in. I don't blame him. It's a blight on this great state. A white-trash mecca where hope goes to die. No one leaves Hell's Bend. It's quicksand under our feet. The harder we run, the faster we sink.

Without breaking eye contact, I run my tongue across the back of my hand. With my skin still wet, I sprinkle it with salt before licking it again and slamming the shot. The initial sting burns my throat. I close my eyes to stave off the onset of tears, but the lime wedge gnashed between my teeth helps me recover quickly. This ain't my first rodeo.

Dylan grins at my temporary distress. "Nicely done."

"Thanks." I giggle.

He throws his drink back as if it's water, skipping the ritual.

"Impressive. Do you have other talents, or is drinking with a straight face all you've got in your bag of tricks?"

A laugh rumbles in his chest, dark and rich. "You'll find out in due time."

Heat pools in my gut. "Can't wait."

He gestures to the bartender to bring another round. "Let's try it your way this time." He brings my inner wrist to his mouth and suckles it between his lips. Teeth scrape against my sensitive skin, sending mini shock waves of excitement straight to my core. He salts the spot, then tongues it off in a sensual circle. "Mmm," he says, tipping his head back to empty the glass, then reaches for the fruit.

"You keep doin' shit like that, I'm not gonna make it home."

His gaze darkens. "I'll take care of you. Don't worry."

My chest tightens. I like him already.

A beat of silence sits between us before he picks it back up. "These dates are the worst, aren't they? I've never been great with small talk."

"Me neither."

"Can we skip all that and hang out like regular people?"

Did I say like? Scratch that. I think I'm in love. "Definitely."

Easy conversation flows back and forth. We gravitate toward each other like magnets being pulled together. I'm not entirely sure if it's the tequila or him, but I feel lighter than air. The weights that shackle me to the ground have broken open, and I'm legitimately happy for the first time since . . . God, I don't even know when.

A lineup of empty glasses and bitten limes litters the bar. Unfortunately, what goes in must come out. I slide off the barstool and stumble the minute my feet hit the floor. Dylan grabs my arm to steady me.

"You all right?"

"I gotta pee."

A crease forms between his brows. "You gonna make it?"

I peek up under my lashes. "You wanna come?"

"Yeah." He searches the space for the bathroom signs, then takes my hand to lead the way.

"You're so sweet," I slur like an idiot. Rarely do I let my guard down this much. A girl's gotta be careful who she chooses to sneak into hidden corners with, but something about him makes me feel safe.

And let's face it, a little horny.

"You're sweet, too." He stops outside the ladies' room door and tugs me against him before I can enter. I let out a gasp, but his lips are on mine before I have time to come up with a witty response.

The room spins as my eyes flutter closed. I allow his hard body to pin me to the wall. I'm dizzy. Drunk on the remnants of tequila on his tongue as it glides against mine in the dark alcove. The music thumps through my veins. I lose myself in his mouth and allow myself to be carried away at the moment as he leads us through the door. His groping hands explore my body, the mixed scents of citrus and spice driving me wild.

"You're so hot," he mumbles between kisses.

"So are you."

We stagger into a stall and fumble for the lock. Before I realize it, I'm on my knees. Did I fall willingly, or did he push me down? But when I tilt my head back to question, the look on his face steals my breath. A halo of blond hair cascades around his beautiful face like an angel. He peers into my soul with a haunting stare that tethers me to the filthy floor at his feet.

"I want this," he mumbles, undoing his belt.

With the pad of his thumb, he traces my lips. I suck it in, then let it out slowly, holding his gaze as he falls against the metal wall.

When he drops his fly, I notice a small tattoo near the base of his shaft. A permanent kiss on the outskirts of the shaved patch of hair. I press my mouth against it, then make a small trail to his thick erection before letting it slide against my tongue.

He groans. I pull him into my throat, milking his cock with my mouth and hands. The guttural sounds radiating in his chest make my pussy wet. There's nothing else like it in the world. A concert of grunts competing with the busy bar outside the door, the idea that we can get caught any time makes this tryst hotter.

"That's it, baby. Take it all the way."

The alcohol numbs my gag reflex. I take him deeper, letting him tangle his fist in my hair as he finishes without warning. I swallow his cum and fall back on my haunches.

"You're something special. You know that?" He tucks himself back into his pants and readjusts his belt. "Do your business. I'll pay the tab, and we'll get outta here."

The second he's gone, I relieve my bladder and wander back out to the bar, but there's no sign of him anywhere. I move toward the door, but the bartender's gruff voice stops my flight.

"Hey! You gonna pay this tab?"

I spin on my heel. "You mean the guy I was with didn't pay for it?"

"He said he was closing it out, then split."

Rocks tumble in my gut. "There must be some mistake."

"No mistake, sweetheart. He came back, downed another top-shelf tequila, then walked out the door. Now, I don't care who pays it, but I'm gettin' my sixty-five bucks."

"Sixty-fi—" I drop my head into my hands, staving off the nausea beginning to build. That son of a bitch. The taste of his cum still lingers on my tongue. I slam down my debit card and pull out my phone, then load the dating app to tell him what an asshole he is, but my blood boils me sober when I realize he blocked me.

That motherfucker.

"Thanks for the shitty tip," the bartender snaps.

I turn and flip him the bird as I walk out the door. My instincts are usually better than this. I can spot a loser from a mile away, but this guy somehow flew under my radar. He played me for a sucker. Literally.

All I can say is Lord help Dylan, 23 if I ever cross paths with him again.

Chapter Two

DARLA

THE WROUGHT-IRON GATES OF the Red Drum Country Club loom over the hood of my rusted truck. I made it here by the skin of my teeth, no thanks to the hangover still burning behind my eyes.

Member parking slopes off to the left where valet attendants wait to take their BMWs and Mercedes to the tree-lined lot. Staff parking veers to the right, a small square of sun-soaked concrete with dumpsters dotting the parameter. It's a living metaphor. The dividing line between two very different towns that started as one.

With less than roughly a thousand combined population, Hell's Bend and Red Drum are both small communities in Nowhere, East Texas. Dots on a map. Everyone knows the large cities. Say the name Texas, and thoughts immediately jump to huge metropolitans like Houston, San Antonio, Dallas, or Austin, but what people fail to see are the tiny territories shoved between. Towns like ours. Secrets hidden in small corners of the Lone Star State. We're the dirty socks under the bed in an otherwise clean room.

But our similarities end there. When the towns were established in the late eighteen hundreds, Red Drum and Hell's Bend were a single city. A railroad stop en route to the first post office in the area. Back then, the main source of income was farming. With the addition of the railroad, they could ship crops across the countryside, but they only grew in a small section of town. An imaginary line cut straight down the middle, one side rich with flourishing greens, the other nothing but barren dirt. Fast-forward to 1925, and the land was cut in half. Two mini towns were left — one that thrived and one that didn't.

It's feast versus famine. We are the children of the hungry, forced to watch our wayward half get fat on our losses. Someday, I will cut the wheel and park in the shade, but for now, I lift my face to the sun and soak its heat, for the day's light is one of the few things in life we're given for free.

I pull into an empty space near the recycling bin and scurry in through the back entrance like a dirty little secret. Light pixies dance before my eyes as my vision adjusts from the brightness outside to the dimness of the employee lounge. I search for the card marked *Darla Burke*, then slide it into the time clock, but the sound of my name steals my attention before I get the chance to slide it back into the rack on the wall.

"Hey, Shy," I reply.

A flush grows under her freckles. "There you are. You're almost late."

"Almost late? Isn't that the same as on time?"

She rolls her eyes. I love Shyanne, but she's as stressed as a hound dog during a fireworks show at all times. Girl needs to relax before she piddles on the shitty linoleum. "Try to be a little more on time tomorrow." She reaches into the small closet and pulls out an apron. "Today, you are my shadow, got it?" She steps closer, wrapping the ties around my waist, then twists the knot in the front. "Just follow me around, and I'll show you what to do."

"Okay."

She steps back with a sweet grin. "You're gonna do great."

I pull a breath into my lungs and let it out slowly. "Thanks again for gettin' me this job."

"Of course! You're gonna love it here. Everyone is real cool." She pauses to secure her hair around a scrunchie. "Except for those damn customers."

I laugh, but my chest tightens. It's never something I would admit aloud, but I'm a little scared. Keeping my mouth shut was never something I excelled at. It's one of my less attractive qualities, but I know Shyanne went out on a limb to get me this job, and I don't want to do anything to screw with her credibility. She needs this job every bit as badly as I do, if not more. Her folks ain't worth a shit, and she has a kid at home to feed.

"So the first thing you'll do when you come in is check the side work chart. Eddie, the manager, assigns the chores on a rotating schedule." She gestures to a whiteboard tacked to the wall. Names of the staff are scrawled in blue ink down the side with the list of duties at the top. She makes a sound in the back of her throat. "We're setting today."

"They don't have people to do that for us?"

A snort-like chortle pops in her nose. "Wouldn't that be nice? They don't wanna pay extra salaries, so the waitstaff is also the cleaning staff during the day. Bussers work the dinner shift. Fun times."

The doors that separate the workers from the guests are propped open. Bright sunlight floods in from the floor-to-ceiling windows, highlighting yellow arches over the hardwood floor. Beyond the glass, miles of green as far as the eye can see. Golf courses are such a waste of land. Four miles of terrain wasted on old men with too much money trying to get a ball in a hole.

"Mornin', Rex." She pokes her head behind the wall of stainless steel, the wisps of her ponytail falling to the side. "This here's Darla. She's the new server startin' today." She pulls me in closer to make introductions. "Dar, this is Rex, the head cook. Stay on his good side, or he'll burn your toast."

A deep rumble of laughter rattles Rex's wide chest. "I burnt her bread once, and she's never gonna let me live it down." He reaches out his hand. Warm and thick, it encases mine like a blanket. "Welcome to Hell's Kitchen."

I lift a brow, but he goes back to stocking his station while Shy and I get to work. She runs through the first shift routine of making coffee and setting tables. "The club restaurant is open for lunch and dinner, and each shift requires different settings. They both start with a plate in the center with the napkin fanned over the top, salad and entrée forks on the left, spoons and knife on the right." She sets all the silverware as explained, making sure to set the knife beside the plate with its blade facing in, "for safety" she says, although if you're enough of a dumbass to cut yourself on a butter knife, I'm gonna go ahead and say you probably deserve it.

"They really need all this shit to eat?"

A humorless laugh blows from her nose. "Girl, we ain't even got to the glasses yet."

My jaw drops. "I'm never gonna remember this."

The edge of her lips lifts in a lazy smirk. "I thought the same thing at first, but it's second nature now. You get used to it."

We meticulously set each table in time for the main doors to open. Shyanne offers a raised arm wave to the hostess on the other end of the room. A girl who graduated from Hell's Bend High a couple of years before I did—I think her name is Jess—waves back.

In the back, Shy points out other waitstaff members, but no introductions are needed. Rex's joke finally makes sense. Everyone who works back here comes from Hell's Bend. We're the folks slingin' the hash and pourin' the drinks. It's literally *Hell's* Kitchen.

Little by little, the customers arrive. Slow at first, then all at once.

I tail Shyanne around the place and back again as fast as my legs can carry me. Take the order, drop the order, bring the order. *Smile, smile, smile.*

The hostess peeks around the corner. "Shy, just sat Governor Masters at table twelve."

Arms full of dishes, she whips her head toward the table. "Shit. Darla, take their drink order while I drop these off."

Without waiting for a reply, she scurries into the dining room while I stand there like a dope. *Where the fuck is table twelve?* "Over there." As if reading my mind, another server—a Mexican guy named Angel who graduated in my class—points at the table where a handsome older man sits.

I pull a breath into my lungs and saunter out. "Hi, I'm Darla. Can I get y'all somethin' to dr—"

The wind leaves my body before I can get the final word out. I lift my gaze and lock on a set of blue-gray eyes that I haven't stopped thinking about for the past twelve hours. Sitting at the table with his hair pulled into a tidy knot at the nape of his neck and his broad shoulders cloaked in a crisp button-down shirt is *Dylan, 23.*

"Drink?" I force the question from my dry throat, staring into him hard, but he averts his gaze as if last night never happened. If we were anywhere else, I would sock the son of a bitch right in the nose, but I bite my tongue and control the feminine urge to scratch his eyes out right here at the table. He's not worth getting fired over, especially not on my first day.

"Darla. You must be new." The governor's statement steals my attention. I paste on a smile and nod, afraid of what will come out if I open my mouth. If I bite my tongue any harder, I'll end up drawing blood. "My wife and I will have sweet tea. Son?"

"Arnold Palmer."

The same voice that tickled my spine last night now sounds like nails on a chalkboard. He's the governor's *son*? That tidbit of information may have been more useful to me yesterday. Then again, yesterday he was someone else entirely. A delectable rock god, dripping with sex. Today, he looks like all the other buttoned-up, stuffed-shirt *Chads* who have marched in and out of this joint all afternoon. Talk about a one-eighty.

With a tight-lipped grin, I turn on my heel and march off to the kitchen to fetch their drinks. If I were a vengeful woman, the bastard would be getting more than lemonade in his sweet tea. Good thing for him I'm a fuckin' lady.

"How'd it go?" Shyanne's voice drifts in from behind.

I glance over my shoulder as I reach for the pitcher. "What do you know about the governor's son?"

She slides a drink tray on the counter in front of me. "Not much. I know his family is powerful, and he's being groomed to follow in his father's footsteps. They come in here a lot. Mrs. Masters is one of those ladies who never speaks. The husband always orders for her. It's weird."

A *hmpt* sound dies on my tongue.

"Why?" she asks.

I fill three tall glasses with tea to keep my hands from shaking as I tell her the quick version of last night's events.

Her eyes widen. "Dylan Masters? No way."

"I'm telling you. It's him." He can wear anything he wants, but I will never forget those eyes as long as I live. The way they smoldered down at me from his towering height as I took him in my mouth; the explosion inside those blue-gray orbs when he came. A girl doesn't forget something like that.

Or the fact that he left me with the bill.

Shyanne starts toward the tray, but I stop her. "Can I bring these to them?"

"Sure, go ahead. I'll be right down to take their order."

I slide the tray onto my upturned palm and hold it steady with my free hand as I turn toward the dining room. Pulling a deep breath through my nose, I move toward the table at a brisk pace. A fake smile stretches my lips. Dylan's gaze rises to meet mine as I lift the first glass from the tray. The loss of its weight knocks the whole thing off balance, and it wobbles on my open palm. I lean to my right as if I'm trying to catch it, but in reality, I'm aiming it where it needs to go.

Directly onto Dylan's lap.

I fake a gasp for effect. "Oh my gosh, I'm so sorry."

Ice scatters at my feet as he jumps to his. I pull my lips between my teeth to keep from grinning like a fool as he stares at his Dockers in shock.

"Let me go get you a towel."

His fist wraps around my bicep as I turn to scurry away. "This is going to take more than a towel, you clumsy idiot."

His mother interjects. "The girl is new, Dylan, bless her heart. Couldn't we give her some grace?" But the old man's scowl matches his son's. Family dynamic at first glance: men are assholes; women are ignored. Perhaps I dodged a bullet after all.

My chest rises. "Do you need me to show you to the bathroom?" Disdain drips off my voice like the tea from his shirt.

He captures me in his heated gaze, its crystal blue darkening to a stormy shade of gray. "I can find it on my own."

He drops his hold and steps around me as I stand there feeling victorious. "I'll get someone to clean this up," I say, turning back toward the kitchen.

Shyanne stands with her arms crossed over her chest.

"What?" I ask with a flair of innocence. "It was an accident."

Another lazy grin tugs on the corner of her mouth. "You're unbe-lievable."

"Please, a lap full of sweet tea is a small price to pay for my dignity."

"Fair enough. Mop's in the back room." She waves her arm in the direction as if ushering me off.

I quickly clean up the mess, and by the time he returns, it's almost as if it didn't happen, save for the light-brown stain soaked into his fancy clothes.

True to her word, Shyanne handles the table without me while I check on her other guests. It isn't long before the lunch rush begins to dwindle. Keeping busy is good like that. Time flies when you aren't looking.

With a moment to breathe, I duck into the alcove near the ladies' room, but a strong hand takes my arm. "I should get you fired for that little stunt you pulled."

Goose bumps prickle my skin. I wrench from Dylan's grip. "You threatening me?" I poke my finger into his hard chest. "You should be kissin' my boots for not announcing to the whole damn dining room what a real piece of shit you are."

The set of his jaw tightens, making it appear razor sharp. "Do you have any idea who I am?"

"Yeah. You're a dipshit stalking in dark corners like some creepy-ass villain. Last I checked, plying girls with booze, then eliciting sex bor-ders on rape."

He juts his chin out, the breath blowing from his nose like a heavy wind. "And you're a low-rent bar whore from nowhere. No one in their right mind is going to believe you over me, so you better think long and hard before you open your mouth about what did or didn't happen last night. As far as I'm concerned, you're just another poor server spreading lies in hopes of a handout."

I even my voice to a controlled tone. "Well, as far as I'm concerned, you're nothin' but a bad memory. So don't worry, your precious reputation is safe. But believe me when I say your actions will come back to bite you in the ass someday, *Dylan, 23*. What happens in the dark always comes to light. Remember that. Now, if you'll excuse me, I have to get ready for another shift. I suggest you march your ass out of my restaurant before I do somethin' I regret." Spinning on my heel, I slam the butt of my palm into the ladies' room door and leave Dylan in the past where he belongs.

Chapter Three

Darla

"Darla, darlin', I'll do another Bud and a shot of Jack when you get a chance."

I turn toward the sound of Garvin's gravelly baritone with a bemused smirk. "Sure thing, hun. Comin' right up." Reaching under the bar, I grab a fresh bottle and set it in front of him, then fill the shot.

The neon light behind the bottles shines on Garvin's bald head, illuminating the rogue strands of silver hair struggling to stay attached. He knocks back the shot and slams it on the counter. With a twinkling gaze, he pushes a wad of bills to the edge of the bar. "When you gonna make an honest man of me?"

I shake my head, biting back a smile. "Don't you already have a wife at home?"

He waves an arthritic hand with a scowl. "Ack. She doesn't get me the way you do."

"Brew's on me, Garv," I say with a laugh.

"You're an angel."

"Uh-huh." I take a five from the pile to pay for the shot and bring it to the register.

"Garvin proposin' marriage again?" Cindy slides a tray of clean glasses under the bar, then flings the fishtail braid off her shoulder.

"You know it."

"You'd prolly give the old coot a heart attack if you actually said yes."

I giggle. The Great Notch Inn is one of the oldest establishments in Hell's Bend. A framed article from its inception still hangs on the wall, a faded newspaper clipping with the newly built bar in the center of town.

Before the interstate routed drivers from one end of Texas to the other, they used to come through here to get to bigger cities. The Great Notch was a stop on their path. A place to rest and stretch your legs, sit on the covered porch away from the sun, and have a drink before continuing on your way.

Now it's a dilapidated structure held together with duct tape and a prayer from the family of termites that likely live in the log cabin walls. Yet it still stands, and it's the only bar in the town. When Cindy Wilder took over management a few months back, I offered to help her out. It's an easy job. Mostly old locals getting loaded on beer and whiskey, but after working at the restaurant all afternoon, my dogs are barking. I lean against the back wall with a yawn.

"Tough day?"

"Tough life," I reply.

"I dunno why you waste your weekends here. You should be out havin' fun, bein' young with other young people 'stead of here with these grody old-timers."

I click the tongue on the roof of my mouth. "You're not *that* old."

She snaps a bar towel in my direction. "I didn't mean me, smart-ass."

I let out another laugh. The sad truth is, I like it here. Cindy is more of a mother to me than my own mom ever was. When my mom was too drunk to get me from school, Cindy would take me back to her house and feed me dinner before dropping me home. The Wilder family never had much, but they always extended whatever they could.

Giving back this small amount is the least I could do. Besides, most of my friends scattered after graduation. I have no boyfriend, no prospects of a boyfriend—other than Garvin. It's nice to know I have someplace to be where folks are happy to see me. The Great Notch Inn is my home away from home.

"You hear from Jace lately?"

Cindy softens at the mention of her son. "Yep, he called this mornin' while Ellie was in school. He's doin' good. Workin', savin' to get their own place. He's tired of livin' with roommates."

"I bet."

It's hard to picture Jace Wilder shacked up in a minuscule New York apartment with a bunch of design students. I still can't believe he ran off with that East Coast elitist. Sure, she's pretty and all that, but I never would have guessed she'd be the one to domesticate *The Wild One*.

The woosh of the door pulls my gaze. A trio of guys strut into the bar and pull up seats at the end. My heart rate stutters. It's rare to see people under forty come in here, let alone a group of twentysome-things who don't look like they're from around here. Most of the hot spots are out in White Tail Creek, which is a thirty-minute drive from here. They must be lost.

"That's all you," Cindy says, lifting her palms in protest.

I take a deep breath and let it trickle out as I wander to their side of the bar. "What can I get ya?"

The dark-haired one with the perfect amount of scruff answers first. "You got any IPAs?"

I raise a brow, wondering if he's serious. Clearly, this isn't that kind of establishment, but his Yankee accent confirms what I originally thought. "Domestic beers only."

He purses his lips. "I'll take a Mic Ultra, a shot of Jäger, and your phone number."

Without missing a beat, I chuck a thumb over my shoulder. "Sorry. I'm already promised to Garvin."

"Tough break, Xan," his friend quips, shoving him in the shoulder before turning his attention to me. "Just set us up with a tab." He throws a credit card on the worn-out bar, the name Richard Masters III glimmering in the light.

"That yours?" I ask, choking on the irony. This trio is clearly not from around here. What are the odds that these three are any relation to the Masters family of Texas? I mean, I've never been good at math, but I doubt it. It has to be a coincidence.

He rests his forearm on the counter beside it. "Who else would it belong to?"

"I mean no disrespect. Most people pay with cash, is all, and you look kinda young to be carryin' around a black card."

"Listen here, Ellie May –"

"Whoa. Settle down, Rick." Xan steps between his friend and me. "It's all right. We'll pay in cash."

Now I'm sure Masters is universal for "asshole." Richard, Rick, whatever the hell his name is, swipes up his card and stands down. His friend extends his hand. "Alexander Masters. You can call me Xander. This is Rick and Aiden."

"Darla." An olive branch, I suppose.

My interest in pursuing a conversation with these chumps hangs by a cheap thread. I set out to fill their order and walk away, but the one called Aiden pipes up first. He lifts the bottle and scowls. "No draft?"

"Word of advice. Never order draft beer in Texas."

He cocks his head. "Why's that?"

"Bottle does double duty. It's both drink and weapon."

Laughter erupts, but it's hardly a joke. Pilsner glass ain't gonna do shit if you should ever find yourself in a bar brawl. Yankees best be warned if they're gonna hang around here.

Xander speaks next. "I can already tell you're gonna be heaps of fun."

With a strong sigh, I peer down the length of the bar to see if anyone else needs my attention. The three guys huddle in the corner, but snippets of chatter catch my attention. Something about *D* being on his way. I don't know who D is, but if it is who I think it is, I'm going to lose my shit fast as fuck.

"So, Darla, what's fun to do around here?"

"Besides cow tipping," Rick says between fits of obnoxious laughter.

Ignoring him, I answer, "I guess that depends on your definition of fun."

"What's *your* definition of fun?" Xander's dark gaze sparkles. He cocks his head, holding me with his stare as I try to come up with a response that will allow me to politely walk away, but when the door opens a second time, it steals the breath from my lungs.

"D!" A chorus of throaty voices announce as my nightmare comes full circle.

Dylan, 23 in the flesh for the second time today.

Of course.

"Another round, Dar," Xander orders, but my feet remain glued to the beer-stained floor. Why is this happening to me? What sort of carnage did I inflict in a past life to deserve this fucker popping up at every turn? I must have been some sort of evil dictator. Never in my life have I seen him before, yet here he is for the third time in twenty-four hours.

Dylan's quick glance becomes a double take. Light flashes in his eyes before going dim behind fluttering lashes. I stand like a stone waiting for him to acknowledge me, but he ignores my presence and turns back to his friends as if I'm not even here. "'Sup, guys?"

A hearty band of hellos circle as I set up another round. This time, when Dylan drops his credit card, I accept it without hesitation.

"Darla." Xander's voice rings out. I lift my head as he slaps Dylan on the back. "Dylan, Darla here was about to give us the inside scoop about what the locals do for fun."

I try on a sweet smile, laying into the Southern Belle routine as thick and saccharin as syrup. "Between moonshinin' and trips to the Piggly Wiggly, we like to open fire on those who done us wrong, then soak in the blood of our enemies."

Dylan chokes on a cough, but Xander's beaming grin stretches from ear to ear. At least someone thinks I'm funny.

"Where're you from, darlin'?"

"Red Drum," Dylan utters.

"Mmm." I lean on the bar with both elbows, gently squeezing my cleavage together as I slant toward Xander. "What about you, cutie pie? You from Red Drum, too?"

"DC," he replies with a cocky grin.

I catch Dylan's smoldering stare from the corner of my eye. His jaw set, his nostrils flared. Something about me flirting with Xander has him feeling some kind of way. I'm not sure what, but I'm having far too much fun watching him stew.

"Whatcha doin' all the way down here?"

"We're helping our uncle out with his political campaign."

I raise my brows. "Politics, huh? My, my, my, aren't you just full of sweet surprises?" I rest my chin on my fist and trace my pointer finger around Xander's knuckles. "If you ever need a break from your dear ole uncle, you know where to find me." I push back and saunter away to refill drinks down the line, but I feel eyes boring into my back as

I go. Glancing over my shoulder, I expect to find Xander's hard stare watching me walk away, but I'm shocked to find it's Dylan's. With a wink, I turn away, feeling vindicated yet again.

"Take my word for it, cuz, you don't want to consort with Hell's Bend trash."

My expression hardens as I whip toward the sound of Dylan's announcement. "I'm sorry, sugar, I think I misheard you. Would you mind repeatin' that a little louder for the rest of us to hear?"

"Pretty sure you heard me just fine." He takes in the last swallow of beer and slides the empty bottle toward me. "Now be a good girl and get me another."

Chills break on my skin, but my blood boils beneath. I may have to kiss ass over at the club, but this is *my* turf. "How about I smack that smug smile off your face instead?"

A degrading laugh blows from his nose. No one laughs at Darla Burke. I don't know who this guy thinks he is, but I get the feeling he's due for an ass whoopin' of epic proportions. I ain't above kicking his pansy ass all the way back to Red Drum. He *and* his cousins, if that's what it takes. I advance, ready to make good on my promise when Cindy's arm hooks around my waist. "There a problem here?"

Lucky for him, her presence throws a little ice on my fire. "Nothin' I can't handle."

She nods but doesn't leave. Instead, she takes it upon herself to snatch up another bottle and sets it on the counter. "Why don't you boys finish up here and be on your way?"

"We're not looking to cause any trouble, ma'am. We'll behave," Xander says.

"Fine. Y'all need anything else, let me know. Darla's goin' on break."

"I don't need a break," I argue, but she just lifts her hand and points at the back room. Discussion over. Cindy Wilder has spoken.

A gleam of superiority rolls across Dylan's smug face. With an incensed eye roll, I duck under the trapdoor and free myself from the confines of the bar. Yellow light shines on the dingy walls of the back room office. I drop into the seat behind the desk and let my head hang off the back. The past twenty-four hours have been something of a nightmare, but it's almost over. Tomorrow is a new day. Things can only go up from here.

Little did I know how wrong that statement would turn out to be.

Chapter Four

DYLAN

"Bitches be crazy," Rick murmurs into the mouth of his beer bottle.

Xander snickers. "This place is lame anyway. Where's a guy gotta go to meet some chicks around here?"

"Depends on the kind of chicks you're looking for," I reply.

He lifts a dark brow. "The kind that say yes."

My chest tightens. Darla is definitely the kind of chick that says yes. It didn't take much to get her on her knees. A few drinks, an attentive ear, and she was pecking corn like a hungry chicken. She was damn good at it, too.

The girls from our social circle are bred differently. They're looking to settle down, get married, and have two-point-five kids in front of the fireplace on the Christmas card. There's no fun there. Dating a debutante is a job. Blow jobs come with strings. If you get a Red Drum girl's lips on your dick, you better expect to be walking into a jewelry store the next day. Not Darla. A few tequilas and the girl guzzled my cock like it was her job. I swear, my soul almost left my body.

But I never expected to see her again.

I mean, it was fun. She's hot, but let's be honest here . . . she's a server. Call me what you want, but I'm the governor's son. Soon, the president's. I can't be alley-catting around with the help. It's a tale as old as time, yet still juicy as a Georgia peach. My political career will be over before it even starts.

My brain knows that. However, that little fact didn't stop the chain reaction of feelings that ricocheted through me watching her all up on Xander's junk. Why do I care? I was done with her anyway. Yet, for some reason, the way she smiled at him made me see red. That could only mean one thing.

I gotta get the hell out of this bar and into someone else.

"There's a nightclub in White Tail Creek we can check out."

"Perfect. Settle up, and let's get out of here."

I crane my neck to get the other bartender's attention as some old guy comes rushing through the door, screaming like a banshee.

"Darla, you thievin' bitch, you can't hide from me!"

The patrons barely register, as if this is a common occurrence around here. The older chick runs out from behind the bar as the man stomps farther inside. "Ray, dontcha come in here hollerin' your fool head off like some kinda lunatic."

"Get outta my way, Cindy, before you get hurt," he growls.

My stomach churns. Darla pokes her head out from the back room door. "Go home, Ray."

Red-faced and raging, he attempts to sidestep Cindy, but she's surprisingly strong for a relatively small woman. "Not until you give me my money back!"

Darla rolls her eyes. "You ain't nothin' but hot air with a whiskey stink, you know that?"

"And you ain't nothin but a freeloadin' thievin' bitch!"

Who the fuck is this guy?

I hear Aiden make some kind of joke about being thankful for his beer bottle, but I'm too busy watching the scene unfold to pay any attention.

"Is that the only insult you can think of, Ray? Surely you can do better than that, you drunken piece of shit." She digs into her pocket, then slams a wad of crumpled bills onto the counter. "There's your stupid money. Don't you ever come here hootin' and hollerin' like this again."

"Consider yourself lucky that hollerin' is all I did." He swipes the money off the counter and squeezes it in his sweaty fist.

"Don't threaten me, old man."

She turns to leave, but he yanks her by the hair. "I'll show you old man."

She stumbles back with a yowl, reaching for her scalp. "Let me go, you fucker!"

Veins pop under his skin, his lips curling over his yellow teeth. "I've had just about enough o' your sass, little girl."

Don't get involved.

Don't get involved.

Don't get involved.

But my feet move of their own volition. It's as if my body became separated from my brain. I see it unfolding, but I can't do anything to hold it back from inserting myself into this disturbing domestic dispute. I find myself stepping between Darla and Ray. "Listen, man. I don't know what went down between y'all, but maybe this isn't the best way to handle it."

Of course, my attempt to mediate doesn't affect Ray in the slightest. His fist tightens as he pulls her closer. "Next time you steal from me, I'm gonna take it outta your ass."

With a grunt, she jams her elbow in his soft belly. The minute his grip loosens, she twists away and snatches a dirty knife off the counter. "You touch me again, and I'll cut your damn heart out."

Ray's glare burns through her. Blood rushes my ears. I don't know anything about this girl, but I'm pretty sure she seems crazy enough to do it.

"You got your money, man. Why don't you just get outta here?" I advise.

"Who asked you, asshole? This don't concern you."

Behind me, my cousins attempt to coax me back, but I lift my palm to quiet their persuasion. I'm in this now. I intend to finish it.

"Oh, but it does. You see, my cousins and I are trying to catch up over a few drinks, and your childlike outburst is ruining my buzz. So you see, I find this very concerning. Not to mention how classless it is storming in here waving threats at women."

"Darla ain't no woman. She's a cheap slut like her mother." He jabs his fist in my direction, but clips my shoulder instead. I barely move. Meanwhile, he stumbles backward as if his old man punch has a kickback.

I chuck a laugh over my shoulder as if making a joke, then whip back and nail a punch square in his jaw. He flies into an empty barstool and sinks to the floor. "This is no way to talk to a lady." I grab him by the back of the shirt and drag him to his feet. "Now say you're sorry."

"I ain't apologizing to no one."

I wrap my free hand around his neck. His legs flail, but I'm far too tall for him to achieve footing. "What was that? I didn't hear you."

"I'm sorry," he croaks.

"Good. Now that we've settled that . . ." Tightening my grip, I stalk to the door as Cindy pulls it open. "Sleep it off, and next time try talkin' to Darla with the respect she deserves." I hurl him onto the porch where he falls like a sack of potatoes. "And stay outta this bar."

A few hoots ring from beyond the slumped shoulders of The Great Notch patrons, but my gaze zeros in on Darla's blanched expression. "No need to thank me."

Her jaw drops. "Thank you? I ought to be kickin' your ass! I coulda handled Ray. I didn't need you gallopin' in here on your fuckin' white horse to save me."

"That's not—"

"Save it, dude." She throws her hands in a huff. "I ain't no one's charity case. I can take care of myself."

My momentary rush of adrenaline wanes, leaving nothing but anger stewing in my gut. "Hey, I didn't mean to cause shit between you and your sugar daddy or whatever. I was just trying to help."

She throws her head back with a laugh, then advances toward me with a razor-sharp glare that could cut glass. "Sugar daddy? First of all, Ray ain't got no sugar. Second, he's my stepdad, not my lover. And third, if I didn't have to charge sixty-five bucks to pay for the drinks last night, I wouldn't have had to steal it from him to fill my truck with gas. So, no, I won't be thankin' you anytime soon."

She moves in dangerously close. The sweet smell of her perfume brings lurid thoughts rushing back. I force myself to concentrate on her words instead of her killer rack pressed against my chest. I back into the bar with nowhere else to run. "I'm sorry, I—"

"You should know better than to go stickin' your nose in places it don't belong. I had it handled. Do I seem like a wilted flower to you? Do I look like the kinda girl who can't handle a dipshit like Ray? All ya done there was make shit worse for me."

Her tongue-lashing hurts worse than cat-o'-nine-tails. I'm bleeding out all over her knockoff Cavender boots. When a lady's in trouble, you're supposed to help. Isn't that the rule? Chivalry and shit?

Then again, Darla isn't much of a lady. She's more like the feral raccoon my dad put down after tearing up the trash. My lips part, my brain working overtime to come up with a reply, but the first thing that comes to mind flies off my tongue with no regard. "That ain't my problem."

A humorless laugh ruptures between her lips. She steps back with a demonic grin, cracking her knuckles in her palms. "It's about to be your problem, rich boy. I've had just about enough of your shit."

"Grab the bottle!" Aiden yells.

I pull in a deep breath and blow it out hard. Is this white-trash bitch really planning to fight me? More importantly . . . am I above hitting a girl?

But Xander jumps in before I have the chance to find out. "We'll cash out whenever you're ready."

Darla spins in a huff and ducks back under the bar. She grumbles something under her breath as she snatches my card from its temporary glass home and stalks to the register. Moments later, she drops a receipt and a pen in front of me. I scrawl my name without looking and tuck my card back into my pocket.

Once outside, I feel as if I can breathe. "My car only has two seats. Y'all have a rental or something?"

Rick snorts. "Wait until you see the car they gave us." The alarm chirps when he presses the key fob. It echoes through the open space as our feet crunch under the gravel. The lights flash on a Mercedes Benz A-Class. "This is what passes as a luxury vehicle around here."

"Be thankful you didn't get a pickup truck," I grumble, falling into the passenger seat. I tap the address in the GPS as we roll out of the lot.

Xander laughs. "Man, that may have been the hottest girl I've ever seen. I'm definitely going back there before I leave."

"Too hostile for my blood. She's liable to bite your dick off," Aiden adds.

"I like that. She had that dirty, sexy, slut vibe. Like she'll fuck you to the brink of death, then resuscitate you just so she can do it again."

"Enough," I snarl between gritted teeth.

A line forms between Xander's brows. "What is your problem tonight?"

Heat prickles my skin. I roll the window down, hoping the fresh air will wane the riot in my chest, but it doesn't help. What *is* my problem? I wasn't planning on going back for sloppy seconds, yet the idea of Xander picking up where I left off fills me with the urge to kill.

Of the three, Xander is the one most like me. Not only are we the same age, but we've always had this love-hate relationship between us. We live in a constant state of competition. If he thought for a second I had an inkling of feeling for Darla, he'd work overtime to get her into his bed first. "The girl is a trashy barmaid. She's probably slept her way through that dumpster of a town. Take my advice and move on."

My chest tightens as the words leave my lips. Remorse. That must be what I'm feeling. It's like naming a cow before sending it off to the slaughterhouse. I've gotten to know her a little bit, and I regret my actions. Full disclosure, I intended to pay the bill, but when I saw her coming back, I knew I had to get out of there fast. I didn't realize that leaving her the way I did would result in her having to steal from her violent stepfather. That has to be what's bothering me. There's no chance in hell that I'm . . . jealous?

Fuck that. No. I don't get jealous. Girls like her are a dime a dozen. Pretty, poor, looking for a way out of a shitty situation. She's one in a long line of many.

"Jesus, how far away is this place?"

As far away from Hell's Bend as I can get. "Cool your jets, Xan. We're almost there."

Silver moonlight glints off the rows of cars parked behind The Rusty Nail. We pull into a spot and tumble out, ready to continue our night of debauchery. Part of me wants to drive back to Hell's Bend and finish what I started, but the piece drenched in reality knows that would be a mistake. She's as psychotic as she is beautiful, a lethal combination that would ruin my family's name in ten seconds flat. I am expected to find someone who comes from a family as rich and powerful as my own. My path was written before I was born, and it doesn't include a boisterous blonde with a venomous gaze and lips like poison. She's a loose end. A closet affair. The kind of girl you defile in secret, then go home to missionary with the wife, and I hate her for weaseling her way into my head the way she has. She has no right to be there.

I stuff my hand in my pocket and feel the receipt crumpled at the bottom. I pull it out and glance at the numbers before tossing it in the trash. A flush heats my skin. Xander may have gotten in the way before our fight grew out of hand, but Darla got the last laugh regardless.

Down at the bottom, above where I scrawled my name, is a sixty-five-dollar tip.

Chapter Five

DYLAN

"Hi. This is Dylan calling on behalf of the Republican Party for George Masters. If you have a minute—"

Click.

I take a deep breath and blow it out hard. "Nobody wants to talk to me," I announce to no one in particular. I'm sour today. Telemarketing is not my job. I was hired to be the fundraising director which, in layman's terms, means I manage the day-to-day operation of the fundraising team, not sit here like a peon making the calls myself. I should be on the golf course schmoozing the big bucks out of heavy hitters, but we're short-staffed. This is what happens when you rely on volunteers instead of actual workers. I get stuck doing their job.

All around me, variations of the same speech whisper from their individual quadrants. Naturally, my father decided to have his campaign headquarters on home base to drive the idea of "small town every man." The Hub, as he calls it, is on the ground floor of an empty office building that went out of business two years ago. It seemed like the perfect spot since it already had cubicle spaces and a big office with a wall of windows right at the front so her majesty has a view of everything happening. In addition to all that, he also has a satellite office in Austin when he's out there seeing to his gubernatorial duties. It's a tight ship.

I stand suddenly, my chair rolling backward. Xan looks up over the makeshift cubicle. "Where're you going?"

"Coffee break."

A wry grin tugs the corner of his mouth. "Was this field trip approved by Gang-Grein?"

I roll my eyes. Campaign Director Liz Grein is a bitch in high heels. It's no secret that she disapproved of me being given this job. Putting funds in the hands of someone still wet behind the ears is "too big of a risk," but I've grown up playing this game. Politics is in my blood. My great-great grandfather was Red Drum's first mayor, and it trickled down from there. My granddad was a legal aid to the chief justice, my uncle sits in the Senate, even my mother's father worked as a speechwriter. My entire lineage has been linked back to the founding fathers. She calls it nepotism. I say it is a birthright.

"I've been making calls for the past four hours. I need a coffee before I go insane."

"You going to Countryside?"

"You want something?" Normally, I'd tell him to come with me, but Xan is no longer welcome in Countryside for messing around with the girl behind the counter. He's been here a handful of weeks and has already screwed around with more girls than I've been with all year. I swear, he'll shove it in anyone. I suppose that's the freedom of knowing you aren't sticking around. A few months from now, they'll be gone and long forgotten, but seriously, the guy's gotta stop shitting where he eats.

"Get me a scone."

I push in my chair and head toward the exit when I hear a grating voice behind me. "Day isn't over yet, Masters."

I turn on my heel. "I'm taking a break, Liz."

"Elizabeth," she spits.

"Sorry, *Elizabeth*. Don't get yourself all twisted in a panic. I'm running out for coffee, and I'm coming right back."

Her nostrils flare as wide as dinner plates. I guarantee she could fit highlighters in there. "Ten minutes. And I want a large hazelnut latte."

"Yes, ma'am." I take long strides toward the door to avoid anyone else placing an unoffered order. I'm not a waiter.

Darla.

Nope. Not thinking about her. I wasn't thinking about her in bed, and definitely not in the shower. She didn't pop into my head on the car ride over, either . . .

After the second week, I'm this close to going insane. It seems I'm thinking about her even when I'm *not* thinking about her, but it's all a glamour. She got one over on me, and it annoys me to no end. It doesn't help at all that she's beautiful. Well, in a dirty kind of way at least. I mean, she's not ugly, that's for sure. And I already have a thing for blondes, so that part is a given . . .

Okay, enough. I'm not thinking about her.

Not her eyes, or her tits, or her tight ass in those painted-on jeans she likes to wear, and I'm certainly not still fantasizing about her lips sliding over my cock as I cross the road.

The scents of coffee and sugar fight for control inside the tiny café. Countryside Cravings has been the place to go since I was a burgeoning teen. It's no surprise that there's nothing to do around here. When we weren't drinking beers in the woods or sneaking off to house parties when the folks were away, we were sitting tailgate in the lot of the coffee shop. Starbucks and Dunkin' can't hold a candle to it. It's the best café this side of Texas.

The cute brunette smiles as I enter. At least, she was cute until Xan put his filthy hands all over her. "Hey there. The usual?"

"Yes. Plus a large hazelnut latte and whatever flavor scone you have on hand."

The sudden vibration in my pocket makes me jolt. I pull out my phone and stare at the incoming text from my sister.

> **Tara**: Have you talked to Mom today? I've been trying
> to call but she isn't answering. I'm worried.

I pull my brows together as I read the message, but the realization hits me like a punch in the gut. My gaze slides to the date at the top of the screen. How could I forget? I've been so wrapped up in the campaign and my cousins that it completely slipped my mind.

Today is the anniversary of Caleb's death.

I type in a quick reply and hit send.

> **Me**: I'm at work rn but I'll stop home and check. Let
> ya know.

I crane my neck and call out to the clerk. "Can I get a slice of cherry pie, too?"

She replies with a simple, "Mm-hmm," and finishes getting my order together. After settling the tab, I run back across the street and push through the glass doors with my hip. "I gotta run out again," I tell Liz as I set down her latte and Xan's scone.

She looks up under bare lashes. "What is it this time?"

"I gotta check on my mom." It's all the explanation I give before turning back toward the door. I don't have to explain myself to her. It's not like I can be fired. Besides, my family secrets are none of her business. If she wants to take it to my father, so be it. Let him spill the tea.

The ride home is quick. Cherry pie in hand, I let myself in through the front door. "Mom?" I call, but the only reply I get is my own echo reverberating through the cavernous space.

My heart rate picks up. Suddenly, I'm seventeen again, watching my mother slowly unravel while helpless to do anything about it. My father moved on as if nothing happened, but she couldn't. Grief is sneaky. A sound. A scent. A song. The smallest memory turns to tears on a dime. In order to avoid it, she withdrew into herself, a shell of the woman she was. Even now, six years later, she barely speaks unless necessary. In this family, it doesn't matter how you feel. It only matters how you look. On the exterior, she seems perfectly put together, but inside, she's empty.

"Mom?" I call again, traversing the ground floor before heading upstairs. Her bedroom door sits wide open, enough for me to see the sliver of light emanating from her closet. I pad through the space and peek inside. A large, tufted ottoman sits in the center surrounded by all her personal belongings, and teetering on the edge is her, head cocked, staring into nothing. "I've been looking for you."

She looks up as if surprised to see me. "Oh. I didn't realize you were home."

"I wasn't." I force a lighthearted smile on my face. "I brought you a cherry pie. Your favorite."

With a tight-lipped grin, she stands. Touching my cheek as she passes, she saunters from the room without a response. I follow her to the kitchen, still holding the pie like an idiot. "Have you eaten anything today?"

She lifts her hands in a dismissive wave. I set the container on the table. "Come sit. I'll get you a fork." I wrap my hands around her slim shoulders and usher her to the table.

"What did I do to deserve such a sweet boy?" she asks as she sits.

The corners of my mouth turn down. I'm far from sweet. I'm

simply all she has left. She doesn't deserve any of this. I pull a plate from the cabinet and a fork from the drawer and walk them over. "You want coffee, too?"

She nods.

Anger bubbles up inside me. This should be my father's job. He's supposed to be the one pulling her out from under these manic episodes instead of throwing drugs down her throat and fleeing off to Austin. She needed therapy. She needed time to grieve. But instead, she was made to force a smile and go on living the life my father expected after seeing her son lowered into the ground.

It wasn't fair.

I make quick work of putting together her coffee and bring it back to the table to sit beside her. "Are you all right?"

Another wave of her fingers. "Stop doting. I'm fine."

We've never been an affectionate family. I can count on one hand the number of times my father hugged me. It's not something we do, but that isn't how my mother was raised. My grandparents were wholesome and loving. Mom grew up in an environment where she was adored only to end up in a house where she merely exists.

I rest my hand on her forearm as she tastes a small forkful of pie. She sets the utensil down and lays her hand over mine. "This is good. Thank you, Dylan."

Familiar warmth settles up my arm. I used to compare her hugs to a furnace; her kisses all but seared my skin. She would joke that she ran hot, but I know it's simply because she has a warm heart.

"Tara has been trying to call you."

"Oh. That's nice."

I cock my head to catch her empty gaze. "She's worried about you."

She slides her arm out from under my grasp. "She doesn't need to worry about me. I'm the parent, and she's the child."

My hands ball into fists. I lean back in my chair, drawing in slow, steady breaths. "Where's Dad?"

"He had to go to Austin. He did say he'd be home for dinner."

Grinding my jaw, I hold in the string of curses building on my tongue. *Restoring the values of the American family.* What a joke. His entire campaign is built on lies. If only his voters knew what a dumpster fire of a husband he is. At times like this, I feel the urge to use my registration list to warn people against him. It's a fun fantasy, but one I'd never actually fulfill.

The truth is, for all my bluster, I'm as bad as my mother. My entire life is an act, my persona merely a put-together version of the chaotic me that lives deep inside the sub cockles of my heart. It's bullshit. My entire family hangs by a thread, secretly terrified of the stiff wind that could make it snap. It's an illusion. Caleb was the only one with the balls to be his true self. I hated him for it, quietly envious of his indifference. I can't *not* care. I don't have that gene inside me. I desperately need to make those I care about happy, even at the cost of my own peril. Caleb made himself happy, then left the rest of us to clean up his mess.

I sometimes wonder if I'll ever stop being angry.

"We should get out of this house and do something. Maybe hit a movie?"

Gray eyes snap to mine, twins in different faces. For all intents, I look like my dad. Both Tara and I were cut from the Masters's cloth. Same blond hair and straight sloped noses; long legs with an athletic build. Caleb was darker like our mother, but when it came to our eyes, our father was the outcast. It's the only physical trait my mother gave me. "I'm sure you have other things you'd rather be doing."

I lean in, touching her arm again. She isn't wrong. I've not been a good person, a good son. I'm a ball of rage wrapped up in designer clothes. I'm more like my father than I care to admit, but her silence cries so loud it's deafening. She needs someone to show her she isn't alone. She isn't the only one who feels Caleb's absence. She doesn't have to suffer in silence. "There's no one else I'd rather be with today than you."

She responds with a smile that doesn't reach her eyes. "I would like that."

Chapter Six

DARLA

BODIES GRIND ON THE dance floor, writhing and swaying to the infectious beat. I link arms with Shy and drag her to the second-floor bar. Usually in places like this, people congregate on the first level. The second floor is generally reserved for those with bottle service. The assumption is that getting a drink upstairs is easier because all the action is happening on the floor below us.

Of course, there are exceptions to this rule.

I lean my elbows on the bar, hopelessly trying to gain the bartender's attention. Behind me, Shy's shoulders clench, her thin arms tight against her sides. If anyone needs a night out, it's Shy. Lord knows I love her to death, but the girl is wound so tight if you stuck a lump of coal up her ass, she'd have a diamond in two weeks. It's a product of her upbringing.

At times, I wonder how we're even friends. Shy is the exact opposite of me. She's the calm to my storm; the sweet smile to my angry scowl. She's been fucked over, dragged up from pillar to post, yet still came out on the other side grinning like a damn fool. Some may find her inspiring. Others could call her a doormat. I guess it depends. I tend to be more of a glass-is-half-empty kind of person. When shit goes south, I've likely already prepared to tuck and roll.

"Another week down," she muses.

"Another week closer to death," I joke.

A laugh dies in her throat. "I think that's what I love about you most. Your positive attitude."

"Well, I'm positive this guy is ignoring me. Hey!" I shout, but the bartender rushes past me at least half a dozen more times before making eye contact. "Two beers," I shout, holding up two fingers in a V.

I've been begging Shy for a girls' night out, and after the week I've had, the timing is perfect. Seven consecutive days as a server feels like a year. From the outside, the job appears easy. A person asks for something, you go get it, but anyone who's walked a few laps in these ugly-ass orthopedic shoes knows it's so much more than that. It's a juggling act. Ten tables, ten families, ten chances to get reamed out for the smallest screwup. These folks don't fuck around. Every mistake I make is another percentage off my tip. I swear I see them doing the math in their heads, trying to work out whether or not my service was worth 20 percent of the fancy overpriced lunch I set in front of their fat faces. At least tending bar at The Great Notch is easy enough, but working this hard will make me gray before my time.

With a curt nod, the bartender meanders down the line. I lean in closer to Shy. "You gonna talk to anyone tonight or nurse a beer and slink home with nothing between your legs but your tail?"

A line of wrinkles forms on the bridge of her nose. "I don't slink. I have obligations at home."

"C'mon, girl. We could both use a little fun in our lives. You especially."

A wounded look crosses her freckled face. "What's that supposed to mean?"

I offer a sidelong glance. "You know exactly what it means."

Shyanne is no stranger to the burn. The only guy she's ever been with fled the scene before the sheets were dry. Hunter took more than her virginity. He stole her spunk.

She meets my stare but quickly looks away as the bartender returns with our drinks. I slide a ten across the bar, but he slides it back. "From the guy at the end." He throws a thumb over his shoulder, and my good mood evaporates like smoke.

Xander lifts his hand in a two-fingered wave, then disappears into the crowd only to reemerge before us like magic. "Fancy meeting you here."

"Charmed, I'm sure." I bring the free beer to my lips, trying not to make it obvious that I'm searching the crowd for signs of Dylan. For the thousandth time this week, I curse myself for letting that man roll across my thoughts. He pops into my head at the most annoying moments, which lately means all the time. Amazing how he can still aggravate me when he's not even around.

"He's here somewhere," Xander answers without being asked.

I open my mouth to announce I'm not looking for *him*, but he looks right past me and zeros in on Shy. "I saw you from across the bar, and I thought to myself, that girl looks totally lost."

She lifts a brow. "Huh?"

A lazy grin rolls across his face. "Xander Masters." He taps the bottom of his bottle against hers. "Cheers," he says before taking a swig.

"Thanks?"

"Don't worry, I'm not trying to pick you up. Darla and I go way back."

A wry smile tugs at her lips. "Is that so?"

"Yeah, like a week," I interject.

A gleam shoots across his gaze as he tips his head. "It's been more than two."

I roll my eyes. "Thanks for the drinks. C'mon, Shy. Let's go dance."

"I'm good."

I stare at her hard, but my unspoken plea falls on deaf ears. I'd hoped she'd find someone to light a little fire under her apathetic ass, but not him. Anyone but him. The guy may as well have *fuck boy* tattooed across his forehead. Not that I'm one to talk, but her taste in men is god-awful.

"I'm not so sure about that."

"She looks good to me," Xander replies.

Even in the dim light of the bar, I see the flush sweep across her cheeks. This is not what I expected. The last thing Shy needs is another hit-and-run, but who am I to spoil her fun?

"How long are you guys planning on staying in town?" I ask. It's not a completely innocent question. A part of me wants it to be known upfront that he won't be here for the long haul, but the more selfish part hopes that without the goofball brothers dragging him around, Dylan will stop randomly showing up at my haunts.

"Open ended."

"Hey." The voice floats in over the thumping bass to caress my ear.

I turn toward the sound and lock eyes with the beautiful boy towering over me. "Hey, yourself," I reply with a half grin.

A dimple sinks into his cheek when he smiles. He brushes a lock of dark hair off his forehead, and my stomach twists. I dragged Shyanne out with the hopes she'd find a guy to help her get over Hunter, but maybe finding someone else is good advice for us both. I need to cleanse myself of douchebag Dylan and get his taste off my tongue once and for all.

"You want another drink?" he asks.

"I was actually just about to head to the dance floor." I back into the crowd, wagging my finger for him to join me. He follows my lead, and the music takes hold. My hips sway to the beat, my heart keeping time with the pounding rhythm. Cute Boy slings his arm around my back and tugs me against him. The hard shell of his body molds against mine, the smell of sweat and cologne and sex tethering us closer. I didn't get his name, but that's all right. Some boys are meant for fun, and others are meant for something more. The way he's staring at me with hunger in his eyes tells me he's the former.

But a flash in the back of the room steals my focus. It dulls the sound, mutes the lights, yet somehow ignites a spark to my ever-present hatred.

Sweat forms across my collarbone. I suck a breath deep into my lungs, but it only forms a shallow pant that makes my head spin.

In the shadowy corner, a leggy blonde inches closer to the guy beside her. It shouldn't affect me the way it does. It shouldn't make my jealousy bleed across the sticky floor for all to see, but I can't reel it in. In a room full of people, my gaze zeros in on *him*.

Chapter Seven

DYLAN

HEAVY BASS THUMPS IN my chest. The neon lights swirl in my alcohol-soaked brain, making my head spin. I lean back on my chair and scowl at the flowery scent of the girl beside me. Her lips move, but I can't hear what she's saying, nor do I care to. She's a tool. A pretty blonde to counteract the one who keeps sliding uninvited into my subconscious. She's giving me all the signals—a flirty smile, a lingering touch, a leg crossed dangerously close to mine. I could easily take her out of here. All I have to do is say the word, yet I don't think I want to. And that's the issue plaguing my mind as she blathers on and on about I don't know what.

What the hell is stopping me?

Xan and his brothers paired off hours ago. I'm the only one left. Last man standing. When she leans closer, the tickling hair against my cheek brings me back to my present state. What was that again? Oh yeah, drunk, horny, and pissed.

"Do you want to go somewhere and talk?" she says with a hopeful smile. For a split second, I think *screw it*. May as well fuck out whatever seems to have me stuck in my own head, but the second I lift my gaze toward the dance floor, the word seizes in my chest. I've made a grave error. I took my eyes off the prize for a split second and found myself pulled into her radar.

Fucking *Darla*.

Her name rumbles on the edges of my wasted subconscious, and there she is. Light hair tangled up in a mess of waves that tumble down her back. Waves that my fingers ache to get lost in.

Why is she here?

Doesn't she know she doesn't belong?

In my club? In my head? Anywhere near my heart?

That fucking girl is a plague.

My cock twitches for the first time in four hours, but soon my need is succumbed by the rage building inside me. *Who the hell is she with?* His hands on her body, her legs twined with his. My grandad always said that a drunk man's words are a sober man's thoughts. The smart thing to do would be to ignore her and jump in a cab with the girl next to me and fuck her until her screams drown out the sight of Darla on the dance floor, but I can't. I'm a fly caught in her web, and she's the black widow who wants to destroy me.

"I think we've talked enough." I push to my feet as she stammers behind me, and I don't look back. With far too many shots of Jäger eating through my stomach walls, I stumble into the throng of people to find the bar, but the floor opens beneath my feet.

Images of her on her knees flash in the blink of the neon lights. The way her eyes begged as they looked up through mascara-caked lashes. The way my cock brushed the back of her throat as she swallowed me down with greed. Whether I intended to or not, I marked her that day, and nobody touches what's mine.

I pry her apart from the dancing douchebag. "What are you doing here?"

Her perfume wafts into my personal space—fruity, floral, and crisp. It makes me wonder if her skin tastes as sweet as it smells. A few more drinks would have me sinking my teeth into her neck to find out. Lucky for both of us, I still have my wits.

She narrows her gaze, cupping her jutted hip. "In case you failed to realize, this is a public place. I can be here if I want, with whoever I want."

The lilt in her words comes out like a melody. I remember it from the other night. The more she drank, the more her accent slid out, slow and sensuous. Strange how different things are on either side of the imaginary line that divides our worlds. Dropped G's and drawn-out drawls have been bred out of us a long time ago, but slipping off Darla's lips, her twang floats into my chest like a love song.

The guy she's with lifts his palms and begins to back away. "We were just dancin', guy. No worries."

The razor-sharp edge of her stare makes a divot in my chest. A series of expletives and girlie grumbles dapple her lips, but I can't hear over the thumping bass as she stalks back to the bar. I follow and find Xan talking to some cute redhead I almost didn't recognize without her dorky waitress outfit. "This club is beat. Let's go."

Xan turns with a lazy grin. "You have somewhere better to be?"

"Home."

A laugh bubbles from his lips. "Right. Do you know Shyanne?"

"We haven't officially met. Dylan, right?" She offers her hand, and I begrudgingly take it. "Certainly, you remember Darla."

My gaze slowly slides to my left. "Hi," I grouse.

She flips her hair off her shoulder and turns her head just so. My mouth goes dry. Wait a second. Is she *ignoring* me? Fuck that. Girls don't ignore me. Darla may be tough, but I have yet to meet a mare that can't be broken.

"Weren't you the one who extorted sixty-five bucks from me last week?"

That gets a rise out of her. "Extorted?"

My heart slams against my rib cage so hard I can hear it. Her outrage makes my dick hard. Anger and lust are two faces of the same coin. The madder she is, the more turned on I get. "Oh, I'm sorry. Is that too big a vocab word for your basic education? *Extortion*. It means to obtain from a person by force, intimidation, or illegal power."

She scowls. "I know what it means, dipshit. And I didn't do no such thing. I simply took what I was owed."

Xander and the waitress seem to be hitting it off; Rick and Aiden are nowhere to be found. The way I see it, I have two options. I could call an Uber and get the fuck out of here, or I can hang out and be civil.

Then there's the third option.

I lift my drink to my lips and seal the final nail in the coffin. "I didn't realize you charged for your services."

Her body snaps to attention. Shoulders back, chest out. She's poised to fight, and I'm ready to fuck. "What the hell did you just say to me?"

"You heard me."

"I've met plenty of assholes in my day, but you take the cake."

I step forward, invading her personal space. "I take the whole bakery, baby."

The fire inside her sparks. Meeting my stare, she tips her head back, her eyes sparkling in the neon overhead. "I ain't your baby."

"Not yet." I throw the last of my drink back and slam the empty glass on the bar. "You wanna get out of here?"

Darkness creeps over her expression, but the eyes don't lie. The color explodes in bright blue beams before going dim. "There ain't enough booze in the world that could make me fall for your bullshit again."

A wry grin tugs the corner of my mouth. Something about knowing how much she hates me makes my cock twitch. She's feisty. I like that.

I don't usually go back for sloppy seconds, but I'm ready to break that rule just this once. "I'm willing to test that theory." I wave the bartender over and order two shots of tequila.

"Make it four," Xander adds.

"Make it none," she spits.

The bartender pauses for a beat. I lift four fingers to finalize my order. "I don't remember you being this big of a killjoy last we met for drinks."

"I don't remember you being this much of a douchebag, so we're even."

The bartender sets up four shots on the bar. Xander, the redhead whose name I've already forgotten, and I lift our drinks and wait. Darla rolls her eyes with a sigh before sweeping up the tiny glass but doesn't bother to toast. She sucks it back, then slams it on the bar facedown.

"That's it. I'm outta here."

Her friend lifts a brow. "Already? This was your idea."

Darla's gaze slides my way before snapping back to her friend. "I've had a few bad ideas recently."

Xander interjects. "We could all go somewhere quieter?"

"I'm up for anything," the redhead continues. "I have until one."

A lazy grin tugs at my lips. "You still got a curfew, Red?"

Her mouth bows downward. "Don't call me that."

"Okay." We all whip toward Darla's sudden shout. "You guys enjoy your evening. Thanks for the drinks." She gives her friend a stoney look. "You ready, Shy?"

"Well . . ." She chews the edge of her cheek. "I have the key to the restaurant."

Xander's jaw drops, and he hangs his arm over Shy's shoulders. "Can we get into the pool through the restaurant?"

With a small grin, she nods.

"Yes. Let's do that." Xander starts to move, dragging Shyanne with him.

"Shy, wait . . . This is a bad idea," Darla stammers after her friend, but Xander's already worked his magic. He's like catnip. Pussy throws itself at him with little effort on his part.

Deafness falls in the parking lot. I breathe in the country air and let it out slowly, letting the lack of sound wash over me until Xander breaks the spell. "Shy's gonna take us all in her car since she's the most sober."

I follow the crowd to a white Dodge Neon with a red door and a dent in the fender. "Are you fuckin' serious with this?" I ask Xander.

His eyes widen as he shrugs. Of course he doesn't care. He isn't the one with something to lose. Being seen in this pile of shit is no skin off his nose. He's here under the guise of my father's campaign, but in reality, he and his idiot brothers are dicking their way south. No way am I leaving him with both of them, alone and wet and buzzed on tequila.

"Oh fuckin' hell," Darla cries beside her friend. She wrenches open the back door and climbs inside. In the war between good and evil, temptation reigns king. I saunter to the back door and peer inside before ducking in. Darla's sitting bitch, one long leg on either side of the console and pressed up against a baby car seat.

The heat from her thigh radiates against mine as I drop in beside her. "Did you steal this, or what?" I ask as Shyanne turns the key.

"Nope. This baby's all mine. Don't be jealous now." She lets out a playful giggle as she pulls away from the lot.

Meanwhile, the hate radiates off Darla in waves. *Don't worry, Dar, the feeling's mutual.* I'm only here to finish what we started. And make sure Xan doesn't make a play for them both.

Twenty-five minutes later, we're veering through the wrought-iron gates of the Red Drum Country Club. The hair on the back of my neck rises. This is where the elite come to unwind, but for me, it's an act of flagellation. My entire life I've been told to stand straight, tuck in my shirt, speak when spoken to, be pleasant, be funny, be charming . . . be what they want you to be.

In other words, be anybody except for the person I am.

My given name is a noose around my neck. I've spent so many years being who they want me to be that at this point all I am is numb.

We tumble from the car one by one. Shyanne whispers, "Hold up a sec. I gotta disable the alarm." She disappears into the back door of the restaurant, then steps out a minute later with an ear-to-ear grin. "We're golden."

"Are you sure we aren't gonna get caught?" Darla asks.

Shy offers a dismissive wave. "Nah. Long as we don't leave a trail, we'll be fine."

Xander slips his arm around her waist and jaunts into the unlit building as if he owns the place. Darla follows, but not before whispering, "This is so fuckin' dumb," beneath her breath.

The light of the full moon shines on the still water like a spotlight. The quiet serenity wraps around me, the scent of chlorine mixed with the night. The girls sit on the edge and soak their legs as I drop on a lounge chair inside an open cabana. I hated this idea at first, but in the solitude of the darkness, I give myself permission to drop the mask and just . . . be.

"Let's get this party started." Xander's voice breaks my Zen. I look up to find him at the brim of the pool with a bottle of champagne in his lifted hand.

Shy blanches. "Where did you get that?"

"I grabbed it from the bar."

"You have to put that back. Swimming is one thing, but they'll notice that's missing when they take inventory."

But Xander's already peeled back the foil before she finishes her statement. The pop echoes around us. "Ooops. Too late now." He tips his head back and takes a long swig from the bottle before letting it drop between his fingers. "Bein' bad feels pretty good, huh?" He dangles it before Shy, as Eve offers the forbidden apple.

She looks up with a scowl but brings it to her lips. A petite belch escapes her throat, and the girls giggle.

Yes, even Darla. She fucking giggles, and the sound hits the tip of my dick like lightning. I bend my knee to hide the budding erection taking shape, but all bets are off when she pushes to her feet and pulls off her top.

A black bra cups her tits, the plunging lace contouring around each perfect mound. The pants go next, and what do you know, the panties match. If I've learned one thing over the years, it's that girls don't bother with matching undergarments unless they plan to be seen in them. In other words, she came out tonight with a purpose, and that purpose was to get laid.

She dives into the pool. Enveloped in blue, she kicks her legs and swims across the bottom before bobbing back to the surface. Xander follows, though his cannonball is far less graceful. "You comin' in?" he calls to Shy.

"I'm okay here." She takes another drink and sets the bottle between her thighs, wringing its neck with her hand. Darla swims over and stands in the shallow end. I can't hear what the girls say next. A quiet exchange, I assume Darla coaxing Shyanne into the pool, because she takes the champagne as Shy scrambles to her feet and slowly starts to undress. But I'm not looking at her. I'm too busy watching the way Darla's throat moves as she takes a strong pull from the bottle, then licks her lips.

"You comin' in, bro, or what?"

I roll my head across the cushion to look at Xander. "Nah. I'm good." It's a half lie. The truth is the idea of getting wet beside Darla pulls all the blood away from my brain. She did that shit on purpose, and I'm playing right into her hand. I'm dizzy with desire. Swooning from the idea of owning her smart mouth for a second time. I want to make her beg, want to hear her unraveled moans whisk across the night sky as she comes apart, but it's a long game. The phrase "all is fair in love and war" exists for a reason. Darla has already dropped the most destructive bomb in her arsenal, and I am about to try every tactic in the book to win, no matter how dirty. I'm simply biding my time.

It isn't long before the bottle's empty and the noise of splashing dwindles to the soft sounds of whimpers emanating from the corner of the pool. Soggy footsteps approach. Darla drops into the seat beside me with a huff. "Looks like your boy went for it."

"Please tell me they aren't fucking in the pool. My family swims here."

A breathy giggle falls from her lips. "Nah. Shy wouldn't screw a guy she just met. She ain't like that." She suddenly straddles the lounge and leans toward the end. "But maybe give them some privacy," she mumbles before pulling the string on the curtain. It flutters closed like a butterfly wing. Copying, I tug on the other side, and both curtains meet in the middle.

Enclosed in the dark, I hear her breath blow in and out. She's quiet for so long I can't help but ask the question, "Are you asleep?"

"No."

"You can talk to me, you know."

A band of moonlight streaks in from the opening at the top of the cabana. It's just enough to make out her profile, but it highlights the gleam in her eyes as she turns to look at me. "I have nothing to say to you."

"Well, I have nothing to say to you either, but we're trapped here until my cousin is finished with your friend, so we may as well make the best of it."

"Of all the people in that club, it had to be your fuckin' cousin."

I narrow my gaze. "What's wrong with my cousin?"

"The only reason I even agreed to come out here was to make sure Shy doesn't get fucked over by Johnny hormone out there. He may have her all wrapped up in a purty bow, but the reality of it is, you people don't give two shits about anyone but yourselves."

"You don't even know me."

"I don't need to know you. I know your kind. You're all alike."

"Oh, and you think being poor somehow makes you a better person?"

"Well, I'm certainly more appreciative. I bet you don't even know how to boil water. You'd fuckin' starve if not for people like me bringin' you the food you eat with your silver spoon."

"Wow. And you have the nerve to get mad at me for generalizing? You're just as bad."

"You know what? Forget you. This is why I didn't wanna talk to you in the first place. Clearly, you don't listen."

I sit up and kick my legs over the side. "I'm listening, but all I'm hearing is a lot of *poor Darla*."

She mirrors my stance, her knees brushing mine. "Let's get something out in the open. You might think I'm trashy, but in my neck of the woods, I'm the girl next door. I work hard, I play hard, I love hard, and I thank the good Lord above every day for the blessings He's bestowed upon me, so don't you dare accuse me of feelin' sorry for myself thinkin' I want what you got, 'cause all the money in the world can't buy you class."

My lips part, but no words emerge. I'm choking on the hate, drowning in the lust. She pushes to her feet, but I jump to mine and take her by the arm. Her chest heaves, brushing mine with each deep breath. I can't help myself. I can't stop the want flooding my veins as she stands before me, trembling and damp. I only wanted to keep her from leaving, but I can't stop pulling her in the moment we touch. My opposite hand plunges into the wet tendrils tumbling down her back. It all happens so fast I've little time to consider the consequences. As soon as my lips touch hers, I know I've made a mistake I cannot come back from.

A shallow moan leaks off her tongue as I coax her mouth open with mine. For a split second, she melts in my arms. I feel her body loosen before tightening back up as she breaks us apart. "You asshole," she growls, but advances on me, her teeth tugging my lips and her hands in my hair. "How dare you kiss me without permission?" Her words escape on a wanton breath. I attack her neck with my teeth. Her body arches, her leg wrapping around my waist for support. "I should fucking kill you right now."

I direct us to her lounge—the very one where she reprimanded me for being a terrible person—and push her down. "This doesn't have to mean anything." I slide my fingers through my hair and secure it with the band around my wrist. "You can go back to hating me in the morning."

"I hate you right now."

"Good." I crawl onto the lounge and run my tongue over her lace-covered nipple. Her head falls back, a breathless pant fluttering to the sky. I take it as an invitation. Venomous feelings aside, she wants me now, and that's all I need to know.

I fumble with my pants, but she wraps her fingers around mine, slowing my pace. "Go down."

A disgruntled grumble rumbles in my chest. Foreplay is for people who like each other. That's not what this is about. This is about cold, hard, necessary roughness. A fuck fueled by spite and anger. Skin slapping, hair pulling, fuck her out of my system so I can finally move on sex.

But she shoves me with her feet as she thumbs her panties off her hips. Gotta hand it to her, she's a girl who knows what she wants and isn't afraid to ask. I lean in to push the headrest down. She falls back with a gasp. I sit up on my haunches and slip her panties past her feet, then fling them aside. I brush my palms down her inner thighs, pushing them apart. Saliva builds on my tongue. I lower my head to nip at her folds before going in for the kill. I feel her anticipation beginning to grow as my tongue traces up one side and down the other. Her hips buck, but I hold them steady. I'll give her what she wants, but it won't come easy. I'll tame this brat one taste at a time.

"Oh my God, just do it already." But the slight giggle twisting with her rasping breath tells me she loves it. The tease, the torture, the act of bringing her to the edge until she's trembling beneath me, boiling over with a need that makes the whole thing that much hotter.

"You'll wait like a good girl till I'm ready."

Another exasperated growl, and I smile against her skin. I'm about ready to give in when the light glints off something inside her. I pull her apart with my thumbs to look. "What the fuck is that?"

She pushes to her elbows. "That ain't somethin' a woman wants to hear on the verge of being eaten out."

I cock my head. Two little metal balls sit perfectly at the peak of her cunt. I touch one with my thumb, and she shudders. "Holy shit, your clit's pierced?"

She starts to push herself up. "I knew this was a bad idea."

"No." I press my palms to her shoulders. "It caught me by surprise.

I can work with this."

I'd love to say I'm not intimidated, but I've never met a woman this sexually fierce. She owns her pleasure, and it's the hottest thing I've ever seen in my entire life.

"Does this hurt?" When I gently flick the lower ball, she quivers ever so slightly. Okay, I'll take it back. *That* is the hottest thing I've ever seen in my entire life.

"No."

"What about this?" When I massage it with the pad of my thumb, she lets out a hiss that I feel in my dick.

"I can finger myself." She drapes her leg over the arm of the lounge, her big eyes pleading. "Please don't make me beg for it." The vulnerability in her voice shakes me to my core. Darla oozes confidence from every pore. Helpless is not a word I would ever have associated with the callous bitch lying before me, but it's the way she says it. As if she hates herself for wanting something, for wanting *me*. It's the same way I feel about her, and the lust is paralyzing.

I flatten my tongue and lick a straight line from her asshole to the balls of wonder at the apex of her thighs. She drops her head back, but remains on her elbows. "Fuck yes," she pants.

Lifting her opposite leg, I rest it over my shoulder. She's open for me, a feast of sweetness dripping with my own saliva. A single taste has me ravenous for more. I want to tongue every fucking inch of her. Watch her squirm under my touch until there's nothing left but a wasted pile of whimpers and moans.

I grab her ass to pull her in closer and flick her tight bud again. She clenches, but the sound she makes urges me to keep going. I play over her pucker again and again until her hand comes to cup her mound. I smack it away as if she's a toddler going for a cookie.

"I wanna come."

"I'm in control. You don't come until I say you can."

"Fuck you."

I lift my head just enough to let my gaze skim up her body to the raging pulse in her neck. Darla and I are walking a fine tightrope between love and hate. One wrong move and we both crash to the ground below. May as well test the waters before taking this further. "Shhh . . . The next time you open that pretty mouth, mine stops. Okay?"

She pauses for a beat before eeking out a small, "Mm-hmm."

"Good girl."

In the gray light, I see her lips curl into a grin. Holy shit . . . do my eyes deceive me? Darla's a sub. My mind begins reeling with possibilities. She's a lion in public, but a pussycat in bed. Her bluster is bullshit. Her body is mine, and I'm going to defile it however I see fit until that sweet pussy begins to purr.

I plunge into her depths, coming up to slurp the ball into my mouth. She vaults off the lounge. I throw one arm over her hips to hold her down. With my other hand, I press against her tiny back hole.

"Oh fuck. Fuckfuckfuckfuck," she pants as I broach the opening and push inside. She has a filthy mouth, but she knows what she likes. I finger her ass in and out as I tug on her clit with my lips. She rips at my scalp and pulls me closer. The band snaps. My hair unravels across her lap the same way she unravels against my face.

She's almost there. I add a digit to her sodden pussy. It clenches as I work both holes, tonguing her clit like its candy. Her cursed chanting switches to a chorus of "don't stop" over and over. Her thighs tremble; her muscles tighten. The tiny cabana fills with her keening cry. Her pussy clenches. A squirt of sugar lands on my tongue, but that's not the end of it. Her release puddles beneath us. I've been with my fair share of women, but I've never experienced anyone come with this kind of explosive fervor. I continue going, and so does she, a staccato of orgasms dripping off her hot cunt like rain.

Then, without warning, she pushes me off.

With her palm over her face, she gasps huge gulps of air. "Dammit. That was some of the best head I ever got. Thanks." She kicks her leg over me and gets to her feet.

I pull my brows together as she dances around trying to pull her panties up wobbly legs. "Wait. Where are you going?"

She shrugs. "Give a girl a second, will ya? Don't be so fuckin' eager." She parts the curtains, then disappears through them.

I lie back on my lounge chair with my head on my forearm. Darla's taste still sits on my lips. I savor it like a snack, letting it seep into my mouth. When my gaze wanders to the wet spot on the chair beside me, my ego soars. That's a lot of cum for one little girl. I thought this would get her out of my system, but to my chagrin, it only made me want her more.

Fuck.

When the curtains open again, I'm ready for round two—cock meets cunt—but my erection wanes when Xan bursts in. "Thought you'd be halfway to pound town by now."

He purses his lips. "Nah, she wasn't DTF. I ordered an Uber. Let's get outta here."

I lift a brow. "Just because you struck out, we both gotta go?"

He side-eyes me. "They're gone, bro."

"What do you mean they're gone?" I sit up with wide eyes.

"Darla came out, told Shy it was almost one, then ran out of here like she was about to turn into a pumpkin."

My heart pounds against my ribs. That bitch ditched *me*? No fucking way. Girls do not ditch Dylan Masters.

"You sure she isn't coming back?"

"Nah, they're gone. She even locked all the doors and pointed out a crick on the fence for us to squeeze through." He rolls his eyes.

Heat roils up my neck. I pull my phone from my pocket to call her, then realize I'd never actually gotten her number. A bell goes off in my mind. *The dating app.* I pull up my legs and rest my forearms on my knees as I tap the icon and wait for it to load, but when I move to my messages, my heart sinks. I forgot I blocked her.

My thumb hovers over the unblock button. Is this really something I want to pursue?

Heck yes, it is.

Without a second thought, I compose a message.

> **Me:** Who the fuck do you think you are ditching me?

I sit for a second, awaiting a reply. When the message dots jump, so does my heart.

> **Darla:** Got what I wanted. I suppose this makes us even.

Anger burns me up inside. I feel the flush roll across my cheeks and forehead as I try to maintain my composure. Did she plan this? Did she make a point to get me to go down on her just so she could dump me afterward?

The sound of her screams still echoes in my head. I thought I hated her before, but the malice is a weight on my chest. I gulp for air, but I can't get enough in my lungs to satisfy the ache building inside me. I let my guard down. I let her seep inside just enough to give in to the want, but never again.

Chapter Eight

DARLA

"TABLE SIX!" JESS'S VOICE echoes over the sound of rushing water beating against the dishes.

Shyanne pulls a steaming tray of coffee mugs from the dishwasher and rests it on top of the nearby stack with a grunt. "This one's yours."

"And the hits just keep on comin'," I say as I saunter through the double doors.

The lunch rush has waned, the usual din of chatter now reduced to a faint hum. I reach into the pocket of my apron to pull out my pad as I move toward the table, but the smile falls off my face when I see *him*, once again, sitting in my section.

My lady bits tingle. It's been close to a week, and I still feel him, his face pressed up against my skin as he tongue-fucked me into oblivion. At the time, I thought it was a great idea. Get him back for what he did to me, but the sober light of day tells another story. One where I'm still just a server forced to put up with his bullshit.

But the biggest kick in the crotch is that a piece of me still wants to get to know him. Of course, there's also the part that wants to grind onto his lap, but that other tiny fragment is the most concerning. I mean, sex is sex. It's easy. What is it about Dylan Masters that makes me want more than his dick?

"Hello," I greet, resisting the urge to shake off the chills creeping down my arms.

Governor Masters looks up from his menu. "Hello, Darla."

"Hello, sir. I'm startin' to think you're sittin' in my section on purpose," I reply with a flirty wink, meanwhile I'm dying inside. My gaze flicks to Dylan for a split second before jumping back to his father. "Can I get you something to drink?"

"Sweet tea for my wife and me."

"Same," Dylan orders. "And bring out a basket of bread, too."

I make sure I've turned away from the table before rolling my eyes. I make quick work of filling their drinks and preparing the basket. The quicker I get them served, the faster they can leave. Dylan Masters is a mistake that continually comes back to haunt me. He's like herpes with no chance of remission. An itch I can't seem to scratch.

I set their drinks on the table and place the bread in the center. Dylan reaches for a slice immediately, then snaps his hand back with a sneer. "It's cold." My lips part, but no words escape as he scowls up at me and barks, "If the bread isn't warm, the butter won't spread efficiently."

Is he seriously mansplaining bread to me?

Heat rolls up my face as I reach for the basket, wishing it was the knife instead. I pull in a calming breath, reminding myself that I'm at work. Is watching him bleed worth losing my job? I'll get back to you on that one. "I'll take care of that right away."

"It should have been done right the first time."

I scurry into the kitchen. A growl escapes my throat the minute the doors close behind me. I ball my hand into a fist as I slam the loaf into the toaster. "If the bread isn't warm, the butter won't spread," I mock. "I hope you burn your tongue on it, you elitist prick."

"What did that bread do to you?" Rex muses from behind the heat lamps.

"Fuckin' customers, man."

Deep laughter rumbles in his chest. "That's why I stay back here."

"Lucky you." I fling open the door and throw the warm loaf back into the basket. Seconds later, I set it in front of Dylan. "I hope it's warm to your liking."

He picks it up and hands it back to me. "Now try it again without the attitude."

Wow. He is cruisin' for a bruisin', but I clench my teeth to keep my smart-assed tongue hidden inside. The customer is always right at the Red Drum Country Club. "I'm sorry, sir."

"Better. I'll have a grilled chicken Caesar wrap, with fries well done." He looks up from under his light lashes and adds, "That means crispy. Not burnt."

My hands tremble as I scrawl the order on the pad. It's all I can do to keep myself from jamming a butter knife into his eye socket right now. This motherfucker thinks he can talk to me like this and get away with it—and worst of all, he's right. While I'm on the clock, I belong to him and every other idiot patron of this bullshit restaurant. If I want to keep this job, there ain't a damn thing I can say to any of them.

After taking the rest of their order, I find a corner of the kitchen to let my frustration fly. They should install a punching bag back here. That way I can pretend I'm driving my fist into Dylan's stupid face over and over until his damn fries are crispy enough.

"Order up!"

I grab the plates and bring them down. "Is there anything else I can get for you?" I ask.

"No, we're great," Governor Masters replies.

Dylan's lip curls. "Ketchup."

Shit. I was so busy talking to Rex that I forgot to fill the stupid condiment cup. Whatever happened to bottles on the table? Is that too simple a concept for folks around here? It's ridiculous.

I run back like a good little helper monkey and return with Dylan's precious ketchup, only to find his scowl deepening. "You call these crisp?" Hot oil still glistens on the golden french fry in his hand.

Deep breaths, Darla. Deep breaths.

I can't believe I let him see me naked.

"I can have the chef throw them in a few more seconds if you'd like."

"Forget it." I pause for a moment to make sure he doesn't have anything else to bark at me before I go, and he doesn't miss the opportunity. "I've definitely tasted worse."

I suck my bottom lip into my mouth and bite down hard. Was that supposed to be a shot at the other night? Please, he loved it as much as I did. "Enjoy your lunch," I grumble before rushing back into the kitchen.

"Has anyone ever successfully gotten away with murder?" I shout to no one in particular.

Shy wanders from the back. "Who are we murdering today?"

I run my fingers through my hair, loosening my ponytail. "I don't think I can keep working here, Shy."

Her eyes widen. "What? Why?"

I lock on her moss-green gaze. "Two words: Dylan fuckin' Masters."

"That's three words," she says with a wry grin. "And no one told you to fool around with him again."

"Your logic is unhelpful."

"I know seeing him is hard, but work is work. You can quit if you want, but we both know you need this job."

"Again with the logic." I pout. "Why do you have to be so damn right all the time?"

She winks. "I'm older and wiser."

A laugh bubbles through the anger. "I'm not sure those two whole years really make that much of a difference."

"You'd be surprised." She peeks through the doors behind me. "Now, do you want me to check on the table for you, or can you manage to separate work from your personal life?"

I blow out a hard breath, rubbing the tension from my neck. "I can manage. I don't like it, but I can do it."

"That's my girl." She offers a tap on the shoulder for support. "I'm always here if you need me."

"Thanks." With a sigh, I turn on my heels and breeze through the doors, but my empowerment slips the second I see his face. Why does he have to be so gorgeous? Hot is one thing, but Dylan is far beyond hot. He's . . . beautiful. Even with his hair slicked into a knot at his crown and the stupid polo shirt hiding his lean build, he's the most beautiful man I've ever seen in my entire life.

The only other guy who came close was Jace.

It's yet another thing I hate him for. Making me feel things I don't want to feel every time he looks at me. I refuse to offer my heart to another asshole with a pretty face.

"How's everything over here?"

"Delicious as usual," Governor Masters replies. He folds his napkin and sets it beside his empty plate. "I'd love a cup of joe when you get a chance."

"Coming right up. Anything else?"

The wife chimes in. "Coffee for me as well, please, dear."

"You got it." I start to leave, but Dylan's voice stops my retreat.

"Can I get this wrapped?"

I turn back to find a single bite of Caesar wrap left on his plate. This is, of course, another round of mental manipulation by the master himself, but Shy's words wash over me. *Work is work. Leave my personal life at the door.* "No problem." I take the plate and saunter back into the kitchen.

After packing what's left of his majesty's lunch, I fill a tray with cream, sugar, and three mugs, then grab the coffee carafe on my way back out. "Here you go," I croon, placing it in front of him with a cheerful grin. "I brought you a cup in case you wanted coffee, too, hun."

I fill the cups and tuck the tray under my arm to pull the bill from my pad. "I'll take this whenever you're ready."

The governor sets his credit card on top of it. "Thank you, Darla."

How is it that a man so polite has a son that's such a raging-ass hat? I grace him with another grin and scurry away. Safe in the kitchen, I run his card. After a quick exchange, the Masters family wanders out, and I can freely breathe.

I grab a bin to bus the table and start piling the dirty dishes inside when I notice Dylan's sunglasses still sitting in the corner. Silver-toned square, with a gradient tint. I lift them up to read the label. Versace, of course. I tuck them into my pocket to finish my work when I hear the sound of a man clearing his throat behind me.

"Those are mine."

A knot forms in my stomach. I glance behind me as if his presence at my back doesn't have a profound effect on my knees. "I wasn't planning to steal them." I pull them from my pocket and hand them back.

He tucks the arm into the V of his shirt. "Good. I'd hate to think you're a thief, too."

I roll my eyes with a sigh. "Well, you got your precious sunglasses. Enjoy your afternoon."

I turn to retreat but his hand closes over my bicep. "I left them on purpose."

"Testing me now?"

He steps closer and locks eyes with mine. "I wanted a reason to come back and talk to you."

My heartbeat slows. I force my drooping shoulders back, refusing to let him get to me. "Don't you think you berated me enough?"

Hurt flashes in his steely gaze. It's like the sky before a heavy spring rain. A hint of blue struggles to break through, but all it does is brighten the gray from beyond. It's a color that suits him. Hard, yet behind the stark exterior lurks a brightness so profound it's scared to emerge.

"You took the wind outta my sails the way you ran out on me the other night."

I shrug. "You said it yourself. It meant nothing."

His nostrils flair. "If you say so."

My patience wears thin. "What do you want, dude. An apology? Forget it. I don't have the energy to fight with you right now."

I turn on my heel but, for the second time today, his voice stops me in my tracks. "What time is your shift over?"

My mouth goes dry. I lick my lips in a desperate attempt to build up moisture, but it's no use. "A few minutes," I reply without turning around.

"I want to take you out."

Glancing over my shoulder, I search his face for signs of mockery, but all I find is a vulnerable stare looking back at me. "You come in here, treat me like shit on your shoe, and now you want to take me out?"

"Yes."

Wow, he's bold. "Sorry. I got work tonight. Go find someone else to screw with." I turn forward and don't bother looking back until I've reached the kitchen. When I peek through the double doors, he's still standing there awaiting my return.

Old-school country croons from the jukebox in the corner of The Great Notch Inn. I hum along to George Strait as I wipe down the bar for the last time tonight. Cindy sits on a barstool counting the till. "Pretty good take for a Sunday."

"Yep. That new TV really draws a crowd on game night." When the heavy doors slide open, I immediately call out, "We're closed," but my heart begins to pound when I see Dylan standing there. Freshly showered, his light hair hangs over his shoulders, still slightly damp. It waves at his temples, then falls into a frame around his perfect face. "We're closed," I say again, but my voice sounds hollow in my chest.

"I didn't come to drink."

I swallow hard, the lump in my throat steadily growing the longer he stands there. Weeks of going back and forth have left me on the losing end of this battle. I'm tired of being angry. "I'm closed, too."

Cindy's stool screeches against the floor. "You all right, Dar?"

"Yep. Ima go finish taking inventory in the back."

I breeze into the storeroom and lean against the desk. Seconds later, Cindy emerges. "You wanna tell me what's goin' on?"

"There is nothing to tell."

Ever the mother, she purses her lips and crosses her arms over her chest. "You wanna try that again without the lie?"

I break into the entire story, starting with the disastrous first date and ending with today at the restaurant. Cindy sits emotionless and listens until the moment I come up for air. "So you're into the guy, and you're terrified he might be into you, too."

I pinch my brows together. "How do you deduce *that* from everything I just told you?"

"Darla Burke, I've known you since you were knee-high to a bull-frog. You used to chase my Jace 'round the playground. I didn't know if you wanted to kiss him or kill him, but I'm pretty sure it was both." She pulls herself up on the desk and crosses her legs. "The worse he treated you, the harder you fell. Now I can't imagine all that's changed so much, has it?"

Staring my boots, I shuffle my feet. "Jace was different. He and I were on the same playin' field."

A knowing grin tugs at the corner of her mouth. "You sayin' that guy out there is somehow better'n you? You cut that out right now. Don't ever let some ding-dong make you second-guess who you are, Darla. You are young and beautiful and can have any guy you want."

I look up and catch her dark gaze. "Couldn't have Jace, though, could I?"

"Ima tell you somethin' I'll deny sayin' later. You were too strong for my baby. Jace needed Ellie. He needed someone soft to buff out all his hard edges, someone who let him feel like he's in charge. That's not you. It'll never be you." She drops her hand on top of mine and curls her fingers around it. "I'm not sayin' to let the guy push you around. I'm just sayin', maybe stop pushin' back so hard."

"I don't know."

"Well, you'll figure it out in your own sweet time. But maybe cut out the sex stuff for a while. Confuses the brain."

A nervous laugh flies off my tongue. "Maybe you should start. How long's it been, anyway?"

"Bless your heart." She clicks her tongue against the roof of her mouth and pushes to her feet. "Now scoot. My bed is callin' my name, and I can't wait to get home to it."

"Alone?"

She points at the door. "Go on."

My stomach sinks when I see Dylan gone. It's for the best. Maybe Cindy is right. The guy has all my feathers ruffled to the point where I'm confusing sex and lust from hate and passion. It's stupid.

Feeling better after our chat, I grab my bag and head outside, but it all floats away when I see Dylan sitting on my truck's tailgate. "Didn't I tell you to leave?"

"Didn't I tell you I wanted to take you out?"

"You don't hear the word 'no' a lot, do you?"

"I was taught to go after what I want."

"Funny. I was taught how to aim a shotgun to kill in one shot."

He tips his chin, ignoring my snide comeback. "When's the last time you ate?"

I shrug. "I had some peanuts during my shift."

"I mean a real meal."

"Who are you, my mother?" I shoot, rolling my eyes.

"Let me at least buy you breakfast."

My stomach growls on such perfect cue like it's a fucking romcom come to life. "Fine."

I wrench open the door, but he pushes it back with his hand. "I'll drive."

Looking up into his face, I inwardly chastise myself for the smallest amount of excitement that swims in my stomach. "Long as you know I ain't gonna fuck you."

"Not tonight." He turns on his heel and moves toward the sports car parked at the end of the lot. I follow as he pulls open the passenger door. "What are you waiting for?"

Stunted by intimidation, I stand in awe. The yellow glow of the streetlight beams across the gleaming finish. Charcoal gray, with a silvery sparkle and black painted pinstripes across the hood. It's hard and sleek and as sexy as he is. I slide into the buttery leather enveloped in a fragrance I've only heard about in movies: new car scent. He slams the door and jogs to the other side.

"This is a nice car," I say as he turns the key. The engine roars, then settles into a low growl as he moves the stick shift. The internal vibration rumbles up my legs. I shift in my seat trying to avoid the pulsing sensation in my undercarriage, but it's hard to ignore.

"It's more than nice. It's a hand built GT500 Shelby Mustang with a Ford Performance V8 and a Procharger F1-R supercharger built on a '67 fastback chassis."

I lift a brow. "Didn't take you for a car buff."

"I'm not. It's just *this* car."

I roll my eyes. Men get so goofy over four wheels and an engine. It's a mode of transportation meant to get you where you need to go. The rest is ego.

We ride mostly in silence, the radio filling the cab with rock 'n' roll. He lifts his phone from the console and offers it in my direction. "You can put on anything you want."

"Nah, this is fine. Believe it or not, I love this song."

He chucks a glance toward me before staring back out onto the road. "You know Stone Sour?"

"I don't live under a rock, dude. Plus this is a remake of an old Chris Isaak song. It's been around a while."

"You just struck me as more of a country girl."

"I am. But this country girl likes a lot of things." When he moves the shifter again, the sordid memory snaps like a rubber band. I cross one leg over the other, stifling the heat building between my thighs. The pointed tip of my boot touches the glove box. I stare out the window, hoping to hide the flush growing on my cheeks as I work to push the thought of his mouth from my head. "Where are we goin' anyway?" I ask, changing the subject.

"There's a little diner off the main road just past White Tail Creek that's open twenty-four hours."

"And there's a Waffle House six minutes from the bar. Why drive so far out of your way?"

He shrugs. "They make good biscuits and gravy."

"If you say so."

"Can you not put your feet on the dash?"

I uncross, letting my foot fall to the floorboard with a thump, but it exacerbates the damn rumbling below every time he shifts gears. Trying not to get worked up in his presence is impossible when I'm riding shotgun in a vibrator on wheels. Imagine how pissed he'd get if I left a wet spot on his precious seat? The thought makes me snicker.

Another round of silence falls as we finish our drive to the middle of nowhere. A lit sign with Boone's Diner written across it greets us at the edge of the parking lot. The place looks mostly empty, save for a scatter of patrons visible from the large windows. I step onto the gravel, letting my heel sink in as I push up from his beloved Mustang.

He holds the door as I enter the brightly lit space. It's small and dingy, with booths lining the windowed wall and a long counter stretching across the opposite side. Pink and silver, with a grayed-out floor that used to be white. I don't know what I was expecting, but this wasn't it. I guess I was anticipating something as bougie as he is.

I love it here.

Goose bumps prickle my skin as he rests his hand on the small of my back and leads me to the booth at the end. It's too possessive of a gesture. That's a move reserved for dates. I don't know what this is, but I sure as shit know it isn't a date.

The server in her pink uniform dress meanders over. Her salt and pepper hair is tied into a neat twist that creates a halo pinned in curls atop her head, but her face looks too young to be gray. This is me in ten years. Old before my time, working the nightshift at a roadside dive, then going home with about enough time to sleep and wash the sweat off before starting all over again.

"Welcome to Boone's! What can I getcha?"

Dylan looks at the placemat menu. "Um . . . I'll take a coffee and an order of biscuits and gravy with a side of grits."

She jots it on her pad, then looks at me next. "And for you?"

"A short stack with a side of bacon and a coffee too, please."

"Maple syrup or boysenberry?"

My stomach grumbles. I wasn't hungry back at the bar, but now that I'm here, I'm starving. I can't remember the last time I took the time to have breakfast, let alone a steaming pile of pancakes. "Maple."

She offers a curt nod and wanders off. A minute later she returns with our drinks. Dylan dumps some cream in his coffee and hooks his finger through the handle. "Damn that's good. Better than the shit y'all serve at the country club."

"Yet you come in every weekend."

"My parents . . ." He trails off with a head shake. "Lunch at the club is a tradition. He travels home from Austin every weekend to keep up the appearance of 'small-town family values.' Honestly, the place isn't that great."

"So tell your folks you don't want to go."

A jolt of laughter rattles in his throat. "I can't do that."

I cock my head. "You're a grown man. Why not?"

He takes a tentative sip and swallows slowly. "It's what's expected of me."

The spoon dings on the porcelain as I stir in a packet of sugar. "Do you always do what's expected of you?"

He looks at me as if I'm insane. "Yeah."

The return of our server brings our conversation to a momentary halt. The heavenly aroma that floats up the second she sets the plate in front of me makes my mouth water. "Anything else?"

"I'm good," I say, already reaching for the butter to slather on top.

"I'm Janelle. Holler if you need me."

"Thanks," Dylan adds.

The maple syrup pours slowly from the mini carafe and drips down the edge to pool on the plate. I run a piece of bacon through it, then stuff it in my mouth.

"You dip bacon in maple syrup?"

My gaze jolts upward. The second the food arrived, I forgot he was here. I was definitely hungrier than I thought. "Yeah, so?"

Lines form across his wrinkled nose.

"Never heard of maple bacon? It's a thing."

"A gross thing."

I purse my lips. "Salty and sweet, two things you don't think should go together, but they work so well. Like pineapple on pizza."

"Wow. You didn't tell me you were an all-out food criminal."

"Don't knock it till you've tried it."

"Hard pass."

"I thought you always did what you were told."

"Family, yes. Other people? No."

I cut my pancakes into quadrants, then lift a piece to my lips, inadvertently moaning from maple buttermilk orgasmic goodness. A lazy grin plucks Dylan's mouth. "Told you this place was good."

"I stand corrected. What is it with your family? Your folks seem pretty nice."

He covers his stuffed mouth, waiting until he's finished chewing to reply. "This conversation's a little deep for four a.m., don't you think?"

"Nope."

He lets out a sigh. "I'm the eldest son of three children, and my parents have expectations of me. My entire life I was told I would grow up and follow in my father's footsteps. That's what I am doing."

My expression falls neutral as I try to process what it must be like. "What if you don't want to follow in your father's footsteps?"

A humorless laugh bubbles up as he sips his coffee. "Doesn't matter."

"Well, that's kinda sad."

"Naw. It's just how things are."

I drop my hand over his resting on the table. It's warm and soft, the hands of a man who's never done a day of hard work in his life. "That isn't fair. You should be able to make your own future."

He slides his hand out from under mine and sits straight up. "At least I have a plan for my future."

Chills skitter up my arms and legs. "Was that a shot at me?"

"I'm just saying. You're, what, nineteen? You have the nerve to talk to me about my future while you waste your time working two menial jobs instead of going out to build one?"

I push my half-eaten plate up and lean my elbows on the table. "I was tryna be supportive, dick. We don't all have rich folks paying our way. I bet you went to some fancy Ivy League school on your parents' dime, right? Here you are with your baby-soft fucking hands giving *me* shit?"

He puffs his chest out. "I did. And I went to the school they told me to go to, chose the major they insisted upon, and as for my hands... only the right one is soft." He drops his left hand on the table. Soft palms give way to calloused fingertips. Before I have a chance to ask he explains. "Twelve years of guitar. Self-taught."

A slow smile stretches across my lips. "You wanna be a rock star, but daddy won't let you."

A line forms between his brows. "I don't want to be a rock star," he spits with a narrowed gaze. "I just wanted to learn to play, but my dad refused to pay for lessons. Said it was a waste of time and money that he could not support."

"But you did it anyway." He nods. "So why not bring that rebellion to the other parts of your life?"

He drags his hand through his hair, his Adam's apple bobbing. "So I assume you're working to save for college."

I snort. "I'm workin' to keep the damn lights on and, hopefully someday, get myself as far away from this hellhole as I can, while still being able to have a little something for myself on the side."

"What did you *hope* to do with your life?"

"You mean like dreams? Dreams don't put food on the table."

"Maybe so, but everybody's got one."

Embarrassment rolls up my neck. I tilt my face downward so he can't see the flush darkening my cheeks. "I really loved theater."

"Like, acting?"

My attention snaps up and locks on his shocked gaze. "Is that so hard to believe?"

"Just didn't expect it."

I cut another neat triangle from my pancakes. "I'll have you know that the school paper called my rendition of Sandy in *Grease*, 'more moving than Olivia Newton John herself.'"

A bubble of laughter riots within him.

"Aw, fuck you, man."

He slices the air between us. "No, no. It's just, I would have figured you to be more Rizzo than Sandy."

I narrow my gaze. "It's called *acting,* and I was good at it. I could have pursued it if I wanted to, but shit doesn't always work out the way you think it will."

"I'm sorry. You're right."

"I don't need your apology; I need your understanding. You got your head so far up your daddy's ass that you don't even bother to see the rest of us struggling to survive. You and your two probably equally blind siblings."

"One sibling. My brother died."

His admission is a punch in the chest. I subconsciously rest my hand on my chest to remind myself to breathe. "Oh, I'm so sorry. Was he sick?"

Dylan gets a faraway look in his eyes. "In a way, yeah. He had a drug problem. Wrapped a stolen car around a tree. He and the girl he was with died instantly."

"It wasn't Joy Ann Mulroney, was it?"

The blood drains from his face. "You knew her?"

"Only since kindergarten. We weren't friends, but I remember when it happened. The whole damn town was devastated."

"He was only fifteen. Didn't even have his license yet, but he and his girl stole a car to go get high. It nearly destroyed our family."

"That must have been hard."

He nods. No wonder he does everything his parents ask. He's trying to make up for his brother's mistakes. It's sad.

"So you can understand why I had to leave when I learned you were from Hell's Bend."

Ice forms over my bleeding heart. "What do I have to do with it?"

"Hell's Bend girls are trouble. Whether it's true or not, it's my family's belief, and I have to honor that."

My jaw drops. For the first time in my life, I'm actually speechless. Joy Ann was a nice, quiet girl. She got straight A's and ate peanut butter and jelly with milk for lunch every day. If anything, Dylan's brother is the one who corrupted her.

He swipes both hands down his face. "This isn't the way I saw this going in my head," he grumbles more to himself than to me.

"I can't believe you. Using your brother's death as an excuse to be a self-righteous, judgmental asshole is lowest of the low. And you knew callin' you an asshole after hearing your sad sob story would make me look like the bad guy." I pause to clap my hands. "Bravo, Dylan. You really know how to spin shit in your favor."

"I'm not spinning anything. I'm trying to make you understand why I had to duck out of our date."

"Oh, save it. I don't wanna hear your shit excuses. It's late and I gotta go home." I lift my arm to signal the server. "Check please."

"You don't get it."

"Get what? That my zip code makes me good enough to suck your dick but not good enough to date?"

He winces. "My parents would never accept you, and I liked you too much to put us through that. It was better to end it before it even started."

Heat pools in my gut. Of all the things I've ever been, ashamed was never one of them. Until now. "Well, that explains why you drove all the way out to God's country to take me to breakfast, huh? Go where no one knows who you are."

He doesn't reply, but he doesn't have to. The flush spreading across his cheeks says it all. Yet his sad expression makes me hesitate. This is a guy trying really hard to keep it together. There's a small shred of empathy living within me that wants to be there for him, but I can't spend another minute with someone who hates himself so much that *I* feel ashamed. He drops his gaze. "Darla, I don't even know what to say."

"You know what? I ain't even mad. I feel bad for you." The server wanders over and drops the check on the table with a friendly goodbye, but neither of us acknowledges it. "I'm gonna wait for you in the car. She's a good server. Leave her a good tip," I say before stomping away.

Cool morning wind blows across my bare arms. I cross them over my chest, hovering outside Dylan's car as I wait for him to come out. In hindsight, I should have insisted I take my own truck. I could call for a ride, but he drove us out to the middle of nowhere, and I'm not about to spend good money on a ride back to Hell's Bend.

Moments later, I see him emerge. He runs his hand through his hair, then shoves it into his pocket. In his other hand, a white bag dangles from his fingers. "Here." He lifts it between us. "I had her wrap your pancakes so you can eat them at home."

My stomach flips. That's out of left field. He's supposed to be a thoughtless dick. How can I keep the rage fire burning inside me when he does considerate shit like this? "Thanks."

He unlocks the door and lets me in before rounding the hood to the other side. The engine fires. It stirs up elicit feelings between my thighs. Feelings I don't want to have in his presence. I tell myself it's the car, but I know that isn't true. Dylan Masters is a piece of work. He acts as if he's above me. Hell, he thinks he's above my whole damned town, but in reality he's a little boy scared of his big bad father. At this stage in my life, I'm not looking for a little boy. I need a man. One who's confident in who he is and wants me for me, scars and all.

But sitting beside me with his long legs spread and his row of bracelets resting over the stick shift, I wonder if it's all an act. Sure, he's a dick in public, but when we're alone, that mask begins to slip, and underneath is the kind of guy who wraps my breakfast to make sure I'm fed.

It's a small gesture, but it thaws the slush moving through my veins, nonetheless.

My truck sits in the lonely parking lot. Darkness falls all around, but soon enough the sun will wake from its slumber, bringing on a brand-new day. He pulls up beside it and cuts the engine. "I know we got off on the wrong foot, but I want to see you again."

I side-eye him as if he's crazy. "Why? You said it yourself, your family would never accept me. Why bother?"

He shifts in his seat, slipping his hand behind my neck. "Maybe I'm continuing the rebellion."

Goose bumps rise on my skin. Something about the way his eyes sparkle in the dark, the shadows concealing half his face as if part of him no longer exists. It tries to pull me forward. I feel the tugging in my chest, but I'm resistant to give in. Dylan is the type of man who'll make me fall in love, then look the other way. I can't allow my heart to be dragged through the wringer again.

"I'm no one's dirty little secret," I say, then push open the door and step into the night, leaving him behind.

Chapter Nine

DYLAN

THOUGHTS OF DARLA STILL roll through my mind as I idle into my driveway. Her perfume lingers, enticing me with the sweet fragrance I can't seem to forget. I'm starting to think maybe I don't want to.

She drives me crazy—and not just physically. She's a bitch on wheels. A force to be reckoned with. A rattlesnake whose venom still courses through my veins after a single bite. I can't even talk to her without it turning into a fight. She's stubborn as a mule and so damn frustrating I want to shake her by her sexy shoulders just to shut her up for once.

It's her confidence that seals the deal. I envy her independence, her strong will. She may be a bitch, but she has to be. I want to be like that. I want to learn how to advocate for myself and speak my mind regardless of the fallout. Darla is strong, and that strength is what makes her sexy.

But why did I tell her all that personal stuff? My plan was simple. I would take her out, explain to her my family dynamic, and why I did what I did. Case closed. But before I realized it, I was going on about my dead brother like a raging lunatic. His drug use was a confidential matter that was swept under the rug, yet one look in her baby blues had me singing our secrets like a canary. I'm so stupid.

The sun peeks over the horizon as I wander up the front walk. Few lights are on inside the dark house. I go to slip my key in the door, but it opens like magic.

My heart jumps in my throat, but quickly subsides when I see Rick and his chick du jour on the other side. "Oh, hey man." I shoulder past them into the dim room to give them some privacy.

"You'll call me, right?" she asks.

"Absolutely," Rick replies, but we all know he's lying through his teeth. He gives her a kiss, then leads her out, closing the door behind him.

"Thought you were gonna meet us at the club?" he asks, turning toward me. "Where ya been?"

"Out." I shrug.

He stretches to the ceiling with a yawn. "You missed a wild night."

I consider his statement. Is hitting on women in a bar really that wild? Perhaps Aiden got up to his usual antics, and Xan laid on the old Masters charm. At almost thirty, Rick is the oldest of us all. He should be setting an example of how to act, not dragging us down Debauchery Drive every weekend. "Don't you ever get tired of it?"

"Of pussy? No."

"Of burning through girl after girl like you're collecting baseball cards. At some point, you must find it boring."

He lifts a brow. "Am I supposed to?"

Darla Fucking Burke, what did you do to me? "What makes you so scared of commitment?"

He brings his brows together with a laugh. "What?"

"It's a serious question. What makes you so afraid to settle down with just one?" I can hear the idiocy rolling off my tongue. It's not that I'm so invested in Rick's love life. I feel myself wavering. The game I once loved is starting to become drab and uneventful.

I was thirteen when I nailed Maxine Rivera who was sixteen at the time. She kissed me on the mouth at the harvest fair, then started laughing when I sprouted an erection. It was humiliating at first, but I'll never forget the way she gasped when she cupped her hand over it. Next thing I remember, I was lying in the back seat of her father's Mercedes as she rode my cock raw. Two firsts, back-to-back.

At the time, it was the most exhilarating experience of my life. But thinking about it now, I wonder if that moment set the stage for the man I'd become. She took something from me that I wasn't totally ready to give. I assumed that's what girls wanted, and from that moment on, I became the hunter, and they became my prey.

"Holy shit." Rick's low grumble pulls me from my thoughts. "You like someone."

I scowl. "No, I don't."

The laugh that rumbles from his throat makes my blood hot. "You dog. Who is she?"

"She's no one." I turn my back, hoping to hide the flush clawing up my neck.

He continues his brand of sarcastic ribbing, but I've already started moving toward the kitchen. The last thing I want is to confide in my cousin. Lord knows I love the guy, but he's about as deep as a puddle. If he knew I was pining away for the broad from the redneck bar, he would never let me live it down. That's the problem with having such a close-knit family. They tell you like it is, whether you want to hear it or not. He's like the annoying big brother I never wanted.

The kitchen is dark, save for the single light shining over the stove. The fridge illuminates the space as I pull open the door to grab a bottle of water. I fucked things up with Darla, now Rick. I've always felt so in control, but the past few weeks have found me floundering. With the election fast approaching it, I need to get my head back in the game. I cannot let my father down.

Speak of the devil.

The whisper of his slippers pads down the hall seconds before the chandelier blazes forth. I wince as my eyes adjust. "Oh. You're up early," my father says.

He must be leaving for Austin this morning. It's a reasonable explanation for why he'd be up at this ungodly hour. It's weird being the son of someone powerful. He dons his suit and goes out into the world to make important decisions that affect the lives of millions. People look up to him as if he's someone special, but at home he's an old man tightening his robe as he shuffles to the coffee maker. To me, he's simply Dad.

He checks me out from top to bottom before reaching into the cabinet. "Or are you just getting home?"

"That one."

He *tsks*. "When are you going to start acting like a grown up? Staying out all night doing God knows what with God knows who. There are eyes everywhere, Dylan. Any false move on your part could immediately affect the outcome of this election. Is that what you want?"

Instantly, I'm a child again getting reamed out for accidentally setting fire to the living room rug. I lower my gaze to the floor. "No, sir."

"You need to be a spick and span. Do not give them a reason to dig. Is this understood?"

"Yes, sir."

He waves his hand in my general direction. "Every time you leave this house—especially dressed in that get up—you run the risk of embarrassing this family. Get a haircut, tuck in your shirt, and for God's sake take off the ridiculous jewelry. It's not enough to look the part during the day. It's time to be a man and give up this childish behavior."

My chest tightens. When is he going to see me for who I am instead of who I represent? I try so hard to make him happy. I play the part and do what's right, but stuffed inside the real me is screaming for acceptance.

If Darla were in this situation, she'd open a can of crazy all over him, but I can't say a damn thing. Even if I tried, the words would lodge in my throat and refuse to come out. His campaign has just begun. Several Republican candidates have already fallen out. My father is a shoo-in to win the primary. I refuse to be the reason he loses.

"I was meeting a friend for breakfast." Regret sets in the second it falls from my lips. In my haste to absolve myself, all I've done is open myself up for further questioning.

"A female friend?"

"It's no one you know."

I take a strong drink of water, praying he doesn't see right through me. My father can always tell when I'm lying. In the public eye, he wears the typical nice guy politician mask. You know, shaking hands and kissing babies. But at home, he's shrewd. When the three of us were small, my brother, sister, and I used to stand for his examination before leaving the house. Not a hair out of place, not a wrinkle in our clothes. He demanded perfection from us at all times. "Gotta keep up appearances" he used to say. Looking like the average American family is a lot of work.

"What kind of work does she do that keeps her up this late?"

Think fast. "Um... She's a student. Going for her master's. She was up late studying."

He raises both brows. "Interesting. Is she from a good family?"

Another gut punch from dear old Dad. "It's too late for an inquisition. I'm tired."

He grins. "All right. Go off to bed. You can tell me all about her when I get back."

Wonderful. "Night, Dad."

I head for the stairs with a sigh of relief. Darla's words are still fresh in my mind. I'm a grown man. I should have the stones to tell my own father who I was with. It was nothing. Two people sharing a meal. But the old man's presence always fills me with the fear of disappointment. I couldn't stand to see that look in his eyes. The one that tells me I've failed him; I've ruined the vision he has of who he wants me to be.

Inside my room, I settle my guitar on my lap and start absent-mindedly plucking the strings. Music has a way of putting things into perspective. It speaks to the soul, calms the mind. When I'm up against a rock and a hard place, I strum my guitar until I know what to do.

But this isn't a rock and hard place.

I'm caught smack dab in the middle of a moral dilemma. What's more important: my family or my heart?

The light on my phone suddenly glows. I set the instrument aside and reach for it. My heart leaps into my throat when I see that I have a new message. I swipe my thumb across the screen, staring at the single statement as if it holds the meaning of life.

Darla: I never thanked you for breakfast.

I don't know what I'm doing. I've reached no answers, yet I still find myself thumbing a text to the girl I shouldn't be thinking about.

Me: YW. I didn't mean to offend you.

Darla: You think awfully high of yourself.

A wry grin tugs the corner of my mouth.

Me: Kinda, yeah.

I can't tell if the dots are jumping or if it's the exhaustion playing tricks on my eyes, but I sit on my bed with bated breath waiting for her response to come through.

Darla: Who even are you?

I stare at the message with my heart in my throat.

Me: ?

Darla: I've met three versions of you over the past several weeks. Which one is real?

Me: Being with you is the most real I've felt in a very long time.

My thumb hovers over the send button. I lost my head tonight telling her I wanted to see her again. Darla is a scandal I cannot risk. I already see it splashed across the page, "Presidential candidate George Masters' son seen slumming with local bartender." I don't want to lead her on, but I don't want to let her go. I'm the asshole here wanting what I can't have and refusing to admit defeat.

I tap the backspace button until the message is gone, then set my phone facedown on the bedside table. The best thing I can do for both of us is to make sure she keeps hating me.

At least until this election is over.

Chapter Ten

DARLA

THE INCESSANT CHIME ON my phone pulls me from my dirty dream. I lift my head, pushing the day-old curls from my damp face before plopping back onto my pillow. *Dammit.* Why are the good dreams always the ones cut short? The residual fantasy still runs through my head, albeit fuzzy. I can't see the guy's face, but I swear I could feel his lips on my body. Unfortunately for me, I'm lying here alone and wanting.

For a split second I consider yet another day of dry shampoo—I wear my hair in a bun for work anyway. If I continue to doze, maybe I can finish what I started, but as the sleep drains from my eyes, I realize how dumb that sounds.

Pushing myself up, I reach for the phone and check the incoming message.

We've been trying to reach you regarding your car's extended warranty...

I blow out a heavy sigh. *Fuck.* These robo-texts are merciless. Every time I block one, two more sprout up in its place like a fungus that won't go away.

Setting my phone facedown on my nightstand, I flop on my back and stare up at the ceiling. Water spots dapple the once white tiles. I close my eyes thinking back to the man in my dream. Need thumps between my legs. I slide my hand to the apex of my thighs, feeling my slick skin with tentative touches as he begins to come into view behind my lids.

A clipped moan stifles at the barrier of my gritted teeth. My knees fall open. I sink into my own wetness, my head pushing into the pillow while his imaginary hands work through mine.

"Yes," I breathe out in a shallow pant. Masturbation is a tricky thing. I can make myself come in a matter of minutes or build it up until I'm writhing in need, so hungry I can taste it.

But the guy in my head doesn't care what I want. He's in charge. I let him move me, allow him to control me. I give him permission to do what he wants with my body and take myself out of the equation.

His fingers trail along my chest and run down to my nipples, tracing small, torturous circles around my areolas. My back arches. A gasp puffs from my lungs as my fingers act out his movements in my head. They seek out my clit as he continues touching, exploring, tasting. Hard and fast, he brings me to the edge, then backs off slowly, leaving me wanting more.

The closer I get, the clearer he becomes. Blond hair swept off the nape of his neck, a storm brewing in his blue-gray gaze. I can see him above me.

Oh my God.

Oh my God.

Oh my God . . .

He doesn't just watch me come unglued; he stares as if he's looking into my soul. "You are so beautiful when you're vulnerable. Are you gonna be my good girl and come for me?" I hear Dylan whisper in my ear as he works his magic. Chills run down my spine, followed by a rush of wet heat. He knows what I like without being told. He praises me as he worships my body, and I can no longer hold back. "Oh, my sweet girl. That's it. Lose control for me. You're so good."

His name slips off my tongue as I do what I'm told. I lock my throat so the sound of my release falls quiet, but in my head, I'm screaming out. Just like that, Dylan disappears like smoke, and I'm alone. Dizzy in a wave of lust, I bat my lashes as I flutter down from the ultimate height.

What the fuck.

My masturbatory fantasies never include real people. They're mystery men, put there for the sole purpose of my own pleasure. I've never finger-fucked myself to a person I know, but I popped off hard the minute his face came into view.

Clearly, I'm disturbed.

I offered him an olive branch. I reached inside myself and pulled out the effort to contact him. We had a couple of texts, then he bailed. That was days ago, and I haven't heard from him since.

So much for wanting to see me again.

Now, I'm lying in a puddle of my own release, berating myself for being such an idiot. I let Cindy inside my head and let my guard down. I thought maybe he is a nice guy underneath it all, but it turns out my first instinct was the right one. He sucks.

Hopping out of bed, I reach for my robe. After a hot shower and a cup of joe, I'll feel a little more human. Sunlight shines through the window slats, casting shadows on the face-down lump on the couch. I pad through the space and kneel beside it. My mom's arm hangs off the threadbare cushions. I tuck it beside her and bring the old, crocheted blanket up over her shoulders.

"You okay, Ma?" I whisper.

She lets out a noise that tells me she's all right, but doesn't wake up.

It doesn't have to be like this. You could have done better. If not for yourself, then for me.

Emotion claws up my throat. I blink it away as I rise and sneak into the bathroom. There's no use crying for what could have been. Tears are never a solution to life's problems. They're a nuisance. Water leaking from our eyes serves no purpose. It's bullshit.

Instead, I duck under the steaming spray and let it wash away my moment of weakness. The fruity scent of my shampoo fills the tiny stall as I lather my hair.

A shadow of a figure moves across the curtain. I suck in a sharp breath and hold it there. Did I forget to lock the door? "Hello?" I cross my arms over my chest waiting for a response.

A grumble is the only reply I get, followed by the sound of the toilet seat hitting the tank. I peek through the opening to find Ray in his underwear taking a piss.

"Do you mind?"

He hocks up a wad in the back of this throat and spits it into the sink. "You ain't got nothin' I ain't seen before."

"Get out, you fuckin' perv!" I shriek.

He turns to face me, his dick still in his hand. My heart leaps into my throat. "How 'bout we shut that disrespectful lil' mouth a yers?"

Averting my gaze, I turn away. Chills take over the warmth washing over me. What is even happening right now? I'm naked in the shower while he's jerking his junk a foot away. I can't fight him off without clothes. My only line of defense is the curtain wrapped around my naked body. I pull behind it, praying he goes away. Ray has always been a sleaze ball, but I never thought he had the capacity to be a rapist until now. Ever since I turned eighteen, I feel his glare boring into me from across the room, picking me apart like a Sunday dinner. Uncomfortable, yes, but I assumed he was all bark and no bite.

The toilet flushes, and a rush of frigid water blasts on my skin. I gasp from the shock, but relief follows when I hear the door slam next. I stand stock-still waiting for my breath to regulate before peeking out to find myself alone.

I make quick work of toweling off, then run to the safety of my room. This time, I make sure I lock the door before doing anything else. My gaze wanders to the clock. It's too early for my shift, but if I stop for coffee on the way, that should kill a little time at least. Worst case, I hang out in the parking lot until it's time to go in. Anything's better than sitting in this damn tin can with the stepfather from hell.

Chapter Eleven

DYLAN

THE HOT SUN BEATS on my back. I lift my visor and smooth the sweat from my forehead before setting it back down.

For the past four hours, Rick and I have been hitting the links with Kevin McNamara. McNamara Oil is one of the biggest oil conglomerates in the south. They maintain substantial oil and gas operations, including exploration and production divisions, petroleum refineries, petrochemical plants, and retail service stations. They're the first name in oil, and a valued supporter of George Masters, Governor. Now we're back at the club with a round of IPAs between us, pretending we're here for a social call.

"Hot one today," Rick says, leaning back in his seat. The game is but a small part of the grand plan. We take the heavy hitters out, show them a good time, serve up some beers, and get them on our side. The trick is to gain their support without asking for it outright. You romance them a little. Let them feel like a big man on campus, then slowly insert the pitch after they've let their guard down. It's sales, plain and simple, and I'm great at it.

"Just wait until the dead of summer," McNamara says with a haughty laugh.

Lucky for me, McNamara is a family man. I've led some less than savory contributors into the bowels of hedonism. Strip clubs and brothels, places I would never see myself going if not for the need to

secure their backing. The world of the rich and powerful is self-indul-
gent. Some things done behind the scenes are questionable at best. I
don't like it, but it's part of the job. Secure the financing whatever it
takes.

"Shame your father couldn't join us."

"He wanted to be here, sir, but his duty to the country always comes
first."

In this case, Dad's duty included a day at White Tail Creek Spa. His
monthly massage and God knows what. I don't ask questions. I simply
do what I'm told.

A waiter who goes by the name of Angel stops at our table. A beautiful spring day, McNamara opted for a table on the veranda. The fans
spin lazily above, but it doesn't do much for the stagnant heat sitting
alongside us. The outer wall of the café opens for indoor/outdoor
seating. If I close my eyes, I can sort of feel the air-conditioning plume
from inside. "Another round?"

"Please. And bring out a plate of calamari," I say, fully aware that
McNamara loves the stuff. What can I say? I've done my research.
When the waiter wanders off, I zero in on my target. "You played a
good round, sir." I stifle a yawn building in my throat. I haven't been
sleeping. Every time I close my eyes, I'm bombarded with scenes from
the diner. I relive it, over and over, my foolish mind conjuring different
scenarios with different endings, until I begin yelling at myself inter-
nally to stop being a fucking chump.

"Thank you. But I know you didn't drag me across eighteen holes
to check out my long game. You got my attention. Lay it on me." He
sits back in his seat, resting his ankle over his knee.

Rick runs through the start of the pitch—my father's campaign and
what he stands for. I listen and wait for my turn to talk, but a vision
from inside the restaurant steals my attention. Darla meanders around

the open space, stopping at random tables with a smile.

Goddammit, she's beautiful. Weeks later, I can still taste her on my tongue. She floats around the dining room like the angel of death coming to steal what's left of my soul. I can't tear my eyes away. I'm a fucking stalker, drinking her in from across the room like a madman preparing to pounce.

"Dylan?"

I turn toward the sound of my name. A flush grows beneath my skin. I shake it off and try my best to get my head back where it belongs. The meeting. Mine and Rick's sales pitch for support. "That's right," I say, although I don't even know what I'm agreeing with.

McNamara replies in turn. "Your father and I go way back. He's always had my support, but this is a much larger scale than governing Texas . . ."

My pulse begins to come alive, but soon becomes a burning sensation in my veins when I see our waiter come up behind her. He touches her waist and ducks in the opposite direction when she turns around. She laughs, playfully jabbing his shoulder in return.

My breath beats faster. I clench my jaw watching him fix a lock of hair fallen from her messy bun. I grip my glass so tight I'm afraid it might shatter in my hand, but I can't look away. It's a car wreck waiting to unfold, and I'm powerless to stop it. All I can do is watch it happen. The only girl I can't have is the only girl I want.

"Yes, of course. I'm sure that can be arranged."

I have no idea what I'm agreeing to. Blind with jealousy, it takes all my willpower not to jump up from my chair and strangle the waiter when he returns with our food. The puny fuck is encroaching on my territory. Darla belongs to me, whether she knows it or not, and I'll be damned if I let some skinny twat get in the way of me having what's mine.

McNamara loads up his mini plate with greasy fried tentacles. "If that's agreed upon, then yes, you have my full support."

"Great." I offer a grin, but it falls flat. We continue with small talk, and by the time we've finished no sign of Darla remains. She's likely done with her shift and went off to another while I sit and stew in the Texas heat. My father will be thrilled we've secured McNamara Oil to our side, but I'm not exactly sure what the fallout will be when he learns the terms of the deal.

When all is said and done, Rick and I pile into the car to head home. He pushes me in the arm with his fist. "What's your problem, man? You almost blew it back there."

"But I didn't, did it?"

He puffs out a *pfft* sound. "Uncle George is gonna be pissed when he learns you granted McNamara an invisible seat at the table."

I wince. *Fuck.* I was so busy pining for the girl I can't have that I sold my own father's soul to the devil. If he wins, McNamara's going to be tugging at his ear any time he damn well pleases.

"You've been walking around with some fucking attitude for weeks."

My shoulders tense. She's affecting everything now—first my social life, then my family, now my job. I can't live like this. I have to get her out of my system so I can go back to the way they were before I saw her face. Before I felt her, touched her, tasted her.

I keep my eyes focused on the road hoping he drops the subject, but Rick's stare burns a hole into my profile. "Are you blushing, you fucking pussy?" He palms the side of my head like a basketball.

I swerve in the lane, shouldering him off. "I'm driving here, asshole. What the hell?"

A low rumble of laughter rattles his chest as he leans back in his seat. "You got it bad, man. You better pull your shit together before the next outing."

I play it cool, but he's not wrong. I'm a mess. I've never been this keyed up over a girl before. What is it about Darla that has me tied up in knots? One look at her with that other waiter and I was ready to take the guy's head off in a jealous rampage. It used to be bros before hoes. Now the only mantra I find myself chanting is her fucking name over and over. It solidifies my initial point. She doesn't fit in.

Silence sits between us as we pull into the driveway. Without looking back, I hop out and storm up the walk and through the door, slamming it behind me.

I duck into the bathroom, peeling the sweat-stained clothes from my body and turning the shower on cold. I need to calm down. The girl has me walking a tightrope between right and wrong, and it's starting to become a noticeable problem.

By the time I get out, my skin feels red and raw. I pull on a fresh pair of jeans and throw a T-shirt over my wet hair before heading down to plead with Rick to keep this incident to himself, but before I make it, Xan bursts through the front door. "How'd it go, guys?"

Rick gestures his chin in my direction. "Guy got it by the skin of his teeth."

"Losing your touch, huh?" Xan jokes.

My patience snaps like a slingshot. "Why is everybody on my goddamned case?"

Rick narrows his pointed gaze. "Jeez, calm down, dude. What is your problem?"

"You've been a drag ever since we snuck into that country club." Xan piles on. His head rotates slowly as he turns to look at me. A grin stretches his lips from ear to ear. "No way, man."

"Stop," I warn before he says something I regret.

"Are you seriously still lamenting over that chick who ditched you?"

"What happened?" Rick asks.

Xan swivels to face his brother. "He ate out some chick who duffed after she came."

White-knuckled fists ball at my sides. "It ain't about her."

Rick leans forward, glancing toward the kitchen before settling his gaze back on me. "Is that why you snuck in with the third-degree last week?"

"Let it go, man." I can't swallow the scowl pinching my face. This conversation is snowballing into territory I don't want to tread.

"This guy came in at four a.m. talking about settling down and shit," Rick explains. "Who is she?"

When I fail to respond, Xan speaks on my behalf. "Remember the WT bartender from that Podunk bar? I mean, she's a hot piece of snatch, but nothing to lose your head over."

Heat prickles my skin regardless of the A/C pumping through the vent. I pull a breath deep into my lungs and let it out slowly. My heart pumps to the point of dizziness. "You know, the reason Dad sends Rick on these outings instead of you is because you don't know when to shut your mouth."

That touched a nerve. Xan has been begging for more responsibility, but all he's been given as of yet is telemarketing and sign dropping. It's an idiot's job for which he's totally qualified. "You think Darla's gonna sit beside you as first lady? Nah. She's a fuck and forget kind of girl. I guarantee she's already forgotten about *you*."

I swallow hard, shaking my head. "You don't know shit."

He narrows his gaze, keeping his voice low.

"You're pathetic, you know that? She's a whore who doesn't give a shit about you. She'll be riding a new cock by sundown. There are plenty of cheap sluts just like her, so cut the shit, get out there, and fuck one of them until your head's back on straight."

Blind fury snaps my self-control like a rubber band pulled too tight. I grab him by the throat and slam him hard against the wall. He wraps his fingers around my wrist, his shocked gaze begging me to let go.

"D!" Rick's voice travels in from across the room. "What are you doing?"

I step back with a gasp, and Xan falls to the floor. I don't know *what* I'm doing anymore. My anger is directed at the wrong guy. This is all *her* fault. She got into my head, and I need to get her out.

Without a word, I step around Xan and storm out. Once inside my car, I crank up the stereo to clear my head. I weave around the residential roads hoping to gain a little perspective on my situation. No destination, no plans, I simply drive.

The sun slowly sets behind the horizon. When I come to a stop, I find myself staring up at the neon sign of The Great Notch Inn. How did I get here? It was almost as if the car took me here without asking permission. I reach for the stick shift to put it in reverse, but I can't let my foot off the brake. My heart tugs in the direction of the door, but I stay parked in my seat. Nothing good can happen by going in. I don't want to see her. On the contrary, I want to erase her from my memory. I want to pretend she never existed and do the last month over, but life doesn't work that way. I can't just lobotomize her off my brain. She's a barnacle that's attached herself to my mind. The only thing I can do is try to scrape her off.

Garth Brooks emanates from the old jukebox in the corner of the dimly lit bar. I blow a humorless laugh through my nose. If I had to choose the epicenter of "low places," The Great Notch Inn would be damn near the top of that list. Except I can't imagine a beer chasing these blues away. Naw, I need something stronger than that.

"What the hell do you want?"

I turn toward the question, my insides lighting up like a thousand torches when I see her standing there. Her shirt must be two sizes too small. It hugs every single curve of her luscious body from the top of her slim shoulders down to the strip of skin peeking out from above her jeans. If I look close enough, I can almost see the faint outline of her nipples poking through. This damn bar is the garden of good and evil, and Darla is the apple dangling just out of reach.

"Gimme a beer," I say, throwing my leg over a barstool in the far corner, away from everyone else.

"We're closed."

My gaze travels down the line of people at the bar and back. "You don't look closed."

She juts her hip out, crossing her arms over her chest. I try not to notice the way her tits rise from the V-neck of her plain white tank and focus instead on her kohl-rimmed eyes staring daggers through the fiber of my being.

"Okay. Well I reserve the right to deny service to anyone I want, so. Fuck off."

I look down. "I have on shoes and a shirt. What grounds do you have to deny me?"

"On the grounds of I don't like you."

Ignoring her jab, I peer around. "You got a break coming up?"

She leans on the back counter, crossing one cowgirl boot over the other. "I might. Why?"

My mouth goes dry. If she would give me the damn drink I ordered, I could wet my lips, but as usual she's a stubborn bitch who refuses to give me an inch. Eyeing her in her too tight clothes and her hair piled up in a Pebbles Flintstone ponytail, I hear Xan's words echoing in my mind. Darla is crude and uneducated, curses like a sailor, and acts like trailer folk. She isn't wife material, but that's not what I'm looking for. I don't need Miss Right, all I want is Miss Right Now, and she's perfect.

I lean in, keeping my voice low enough so only she hears. "Because whether you serve me or not, I'm going to sit here and wait until you have a free moment. Then I'm going to drag you into a quiet room and fuck you senseless."

A flush starts in her cleavage and rolls up her neck. Her lips part, then come together as she swallows. "I thought I was too low class for you."

"I can't promise you forever, but I want you tonight."

She rolls her eyes and pushes off the counter, turning away in a single stride. "Too little too late. You had your chance, and you blew it."

"If I remember correctly, you were the one doing the blowing."

Her back tenses. She swings around and comes in close enough for me to touch. "Do you mind not airing my dirty laundry all over my place of business?"

I push a lock of hair behind her ear, then trace her jaw with the tip of my finger. Her lids flutter closed. She leans into it just enough to make me think that maybe I'm getting to her. "Only if you promise to be a good girl and get me a beer."

She shivers the same way she did when I said it between her thighs, but she flips it off like a switch and reaches for a bottle of Bud. "You get *one*." With that, she turns around and saunters down the bar to help the other customers.

The crisp flavor pops on my dry tongue. I sip slowly and watch her work. She's different here than at the country club, comfortable in her skin. She smiles easy, laughs with abandon. I thought she was beautiful before, but the confidence she exudes in her own element makes her downright stunning.

Residual foam drips down the empty bottle in front of me. Darla and I make eye contact more than once, but she doesn't return to my side until Cindy emerges from the office. "Darla, you can go on break if you want, hun."

Darla's gaze snaps to mine. "If it's all the same to you, I'm fine to just keep on workin'."

"Suit yourself." Cindy stops in front of me. "You want another?"

"Yes, ma'am."

To Darla's chagrin, Cindy grabs another beer by its neck and sets it atop my coaster. This routine continues as the hours pass. One by one, the patrons begin leaving as closing time ticks near. It isn't long before only the three of us are left. Cindy takes what's left of my drink and chucks it in the bin. "We're closin' up, sugar. You don't have to go home, but you can't stay here."

"I'm waiting for Darla."

She lifts a brow. "She know that?"

I nod. "She does."

"Okay," she says, clicking her tongue on the roof of her mouth.

"If you wanna head out, Cin, I can close up."

Her dark gaze rolls in my direction, then back to Darla. "You sure about that?"

Darla grins. "Yeah. Go ahead."

"Okay." Cindy finishes counting the till and puts the stack of bills inside a small, zippered bag. On her way out, she hands Darla her accumulated tips. "If you need something, don't hesitate to call, okay?"

"See you tomorrow."

And then we're down to two. Darla wipes the bar as if polishing the statue of David. She's fucking with me now. Building the anticipation as if torturing me is a form of foreplay. She gets off on watching me stew.

When Darla goes for the mop next, I've lost the battle with my patience. "What else do you have to do?"

She grips the mop with both fists. "Well, I gotta run the dirty glassware through a wash cycle, lift the barstools, mop the floors . . ."

I kick my leg over the stool and hike it onto the bar.

"What are you doing?"

"Helping." I set the next stool right beside it and continue down the line.

"Don't bother."

"Less talking. More cleaning. Pretty girl."

She bites her bottom lip. "Do what you want, I'm still not gonna fuck you."

I link my arm around her waist and yank her against me. She gasps, but doesn't fight. "Still pretending you don't want this, huh?"

Her blue eyes darken to denim slits. "You think comin' in here actin' all macho and droppin' compliments is gonna get me to drop my pants for you, you're sorely mistaken. It's gonna take a lot more than that to win me over." She spins on the ball of her foot, wriggling from my grasp.

"What do you want me to do here, Darla?"

She chucks a glance over her shoulder as she pushes the mop across the floor. "Eat shit and die."

My restraint snaps like a thread. I'm done playing games. She's driven me to the brink of insanity, and I can't take it anymore. I wrap my hand around the nape of her neck, jerking her back to me. When I drop my mouth to hers, I brace myself for the fight, but instead she melts against me. A small moan leaks from her lungs, her kiss wanton and wet. I urge her further. My tongue glides past her teeth to tangle with hers. For a split second, she welcomes me in, but pulls away suddenly. "Fuck you."

"Fuck *you*."

Her chest rises and falls like the rushing tide, but her eyes burn with lust. "You're a scumbag."

"And you're a bitch."

Light shimmers on the shared saliva slicked across her swollen lips as she scowls. A low growl rumbles in her chest. "Goddammit." She lurches forward, her body molding to mine as her fingers tear at my scalp. "I hate arrogant men like you," she warbles, nibbling on my earlobe.

"And I hate mouthy broads like you."

Sweeping my arms under her ass, I hoist her off the floor and set her down on a wobbly table. She wraps her legs around my waist, pushing at my shirt to get it over my head. I snap back long enough to pull it off, then attack her mouth again.

I pull at her tank and expose her tits to my hungry mouth. Fuck, she's beautiful, and I want to hate her, I do. But I also want to make her scream, turn that smart mouth docile until she eats out of the palm of my hand. I need to hear her beg for mercy. She's a bitch, there's no lie in what I said. She openly admitted it, and welcomed the term. But the taste of her is a high I've never known.

I pull away for a second, just to see her lips part on a moan that makes my cock leak in my boxers. Can she feel me throbbing as she presses her needy cunt against me? My fingers tighten in her hair, the long blond locks taut against her skull. The venom in her eyes dances with the desire I see there.

She may want me to walk out and never look at her again, but she also knows I'm the only man who can make her come harder than anyone else has.

"Are you going to admit it?" I ask, my voice low and raspy as I tug at her bottom lip, catching it between my teeth. She replies with the undulation of her hips. The hardness of my zipper presses against her clit. The friction making her pussy warm the crotch in my jeans.

"Fuck. You." Her words are spat with poison as rage dances in those pretty blues. It's as if she's looking right through me, right into the soul of me. I don't like it, so I lower my head and capture one nipple in my mouth. Allowing my teeth to graze over the bud, I bite down until I hear her whimper.

Her hands tangle in my hair, and she pulls. Trying to get me to release her, but I don't. Her nails dig in, and I can't deny my cock enjoys the sting on my scalp. I allow her tit free and lick my lips. "Every fucking part of you is delicious."

"You're a bastard, you know that, Dylan?"

"Doesn't stop your cunt from dripping for me. Does it, Darla?" I throw back the forced vitriol as I reach between us and undo the zipper on her jeans. The moment my hand slips under the material and I press my fingers against her sodden panties, I want to growl like a fucking caveman. "This doesn't lie," I tell her as I run my fingers along the drenched material.

"The body is animalistic; it will react to stimulus." Darla is trying to deny it, but she can't hide her need behind words. I see it in her eyes, this tit-for-tat game of spite turns her on as much as it does me, but I play into her hand just the same.

"Oh?" I arch a brow, tipping my head to the side as I regard her. I take her hand and press it against my strained jeans. Her tongue darts across her lips, the wetness shimmering on the plumpness of her mouth.

I release her hand, and she unzips my jeans. For a split second, I fear I've misjudged the heat between us. She could hurt me if she wanted to, but doesn't. The moment her fingers wrap around the shaft, I hiss as pleasure zips down my spine.

"Men are easy," she tells me as she strokes me. "But you, Dylan, you're weak. Any girl, any time, you'll fuck her. Wouldn't you?"

We lock eyes, her challenging me. "I'm a hot-blooded man. Of course I'll fuck a good-looking woman. But I'm not easy. Not by a long fucking shot. You, however," I whisper, lowering my face to hers. "You're a needy bitch." My fingers dip under the material of her panties, which are now so wet there's no need for them anymore. I can't even imagine how good they'd taste if I were to rip them off and bring them to my mouth. I'd lick them clean, and then I'd bend this bitch over and show her how a real man fucks.

My fingers taunt and tease until she's clawing at my arm. When I pull my hand away, I bring my fingers to my nose and inhale her scent. The sweetness of her arousal makes my cock ache even more. I step back, and her hand releases me. Taking her wrist, I pull her to stand and tug at her jeans. When they reach her knees, I turn her around and press a palm to her back. She's bent over in front of me, her tits squashed against the tabletop.

"You think you can call me out?" My hand lands on her ass with a loud swat, causing her to yelp in surprise. But she doesn't stop me. I know she's dying to have me fuck her right now.

A pleasure-filled moan flies from her mouth. I spank her again and again. Each time harder than the last. The red mark on her creamy skin is almost enough to send me over the edge. "This pretty ass. God-fuckin'-dammit."

I yank at her panties, and the cheap material snaps against her skin. She gasps, but doesn't say another word. Shoving my jeans to my thighs next, I grip my dick with the other hand and run the tip over her wetness. Darla pushes back against me, but I hold her taut. Needy bitch. Her disgruntled mewl is a shot of desire right to my soul. Teasing her is quickly becoming my favorite pastime. Her cunt glistens, and I press my dick against her again. This time, sliding between those wet lips and her pert ass cheeks.

Her body trembles beneath me. It's a beautiful sight having her at my fucking mercy. I lean over, my body cocooning hers. With my mouth at her ear, I whisper, "Now beg me to fuck you."

"Never," she throws out, and I inch the tip into her before pulling out. "Fuck."

"Beg, pretty girl," I taunt her once more. "I know you want to. I can feel it dripping down your thighs, Darla." With my free hand, I grip her hair once more, turning her so she's facing me. Her one cheek flat on the table, her eyes straining to look up. "Your pretty, wet pussy is weeping for me to fill it up. You want me to stretch you out. Don't you?"

"You think you're special, Dylan? I can have any guy in your place right now." She throws the insult as if it's going to hurt. No one else can take my place inside her.

"Oh, darlin'," I say, using the lilted moniker with derision rather than affection. "Don't you for one second think I don't know that my dick will make you feel like you've touched heaven. And the moment I fuck you, I'll be the only man who can fill you, stretch you, and make you come."

She pushes back this time. Her ass right up against me, I release my dick and swat her once more. Her knees give out, but the table holds her up. My hand in her hair doesn't relent. I lean in and suck the soft, delicate flesh of her shoulder into my mouth. My teeth graze her, just enough to show her that I'm the one in charge.

"Now beg, beautiful," I say again seconds before I inch my cock into her wet heat. "Come on, sweetheart," I whisper, cooing in her ear. "Tell me how much you need me."

"Oh God, fuck, fuck you," Darla spits, and I don't wait. Instead,

I thrust all the way in, causing her to cry out my name so loud I'm pretty sure the whole fucking town heard her. I'm balls deep, and Darla tightens like a vise around me.

"Jesus," I hiss as I still my movements. Her arousal coats my dick. Her legs shake, and her hands claw at the table. "You feel good."

"Dylan," Darla mewls, and hearing my name on her lips, on her tongue, makes me pulse inside her. "Move. Please," she begs, and I can't stop the smile from curling my lips.

"What was that?" I taunt her once more.

"Fuck me like you hate me. Just keep telling me I'm pretty while you do it." Her anger at having broken down is clear in her words, but I'm not about to deny her request. I pull out and slam back in. This isn't making love. I'm ensuring she knows that I'm the best fuck she'll ever have. I want to ruin her for every imbecile who walks through her door and tries to make her love them.

I straighten and allow my gaze to trail over her. The bright red handprints on her ass cheeks are evidence that I've claimed her. With my free hand, I reach down and press my thumb against the tight ring of muscle and swirl it gently. The movement makes her cunt grip me, pulsing around my cock, and I must focus on not coming too soon.

"Is this more like it . . . *pretty* girl," I emphasize the *pretty* as I slip my thumb inside. "Is this what that bitch inside you needed?"

"Dylan, please," Darla begs breathlessly. "Just fuck me."

"That's good, beautiful. Beg," I tell her, and I pull back and thrust back in. I don't stop. I can't stop. She feels too fucking good. My hand tugs on her hair, causing an exquisite arch in her back, and I lean in to steal her lips. Her head twisted to the side, I'm able to kiss her. There's anger and desire, passion and rage, and it all swirls together as our tongues dance.

Darla bites down, and my dick thickens inside her. I release her hair and break the kiss before I swat her ass twice. "No teeth." It's a warning. I slip my thumb back into her ass. Her mumbling becomes incoherent. Her cunt tenses around my cock, and I know she's close. "Give that to me," I order. "Give me that fucking orgasm because it's mine. Come for me." I can't help emphasizing the word because it is for me. She's going to lose herself for me and me alone.

Her body shudders. The orgasm hits her hard. Darla cries out my name with a slew of curse words, soaking me in her release as I mumble in her ear how hot she is. My cock throbs one last time, and I thrust deep, making sure she can feel every inch of me.

Allowing the pleasure to course through my veins, I close my eyes. Stars burst behind my lids. I see fucking fireworks.

When I open my eyes again, I can finally see straight. I was so lost to the lust and anger that had overtaken me all I saw was Darla and how much I wanted her to admit she wants me.

I slip out of her and step back, bending down to adjust the pants still pooling at my ankles. Darla's back rises and falls. I press my hand to her spine, and she responds with a gasp. "Hey." When she pushes up on her palms, the deep V between her brows makes my chest ache. I didn't want to hurt her, I just wanted to make her mine.

"Don't move." I step toward the bar and steal a stack of napkins from the holder to clean the mess dripping down her legs. A mix of mine and hers, a concoction of hate and lust building at the apex of her thighs. When I'm finished, I lean forward on both arms, caging her in. "You really are beautiful, you know that?"

She rolls her eyes, trying to swat me away. "You don't need to say it anymore. We're done."

I cup her chin, forcing her to see the sincerity behind my words. "I didn't say it to make you come. I said it because it's the truth."

Her razor-sharp gaze softens, the brilliant blue turning pale. "Do you really hate me?"

"No," I answer honestly, but don't bother asking back. I don't care if she hates me. She's mine regardless.

"What happens tomorrow?"

Releasing my grip, I run my fingers through my hair, pushing it off my face. Tomorrow. I don't want to think about tomorrow when I'm not yet finished with today. I'm in too deep. This is not a one-and-done situation. I will want her again. It's not a matter of if, it's a matter of *when*.

By the time I turn back, she's fully dressed and staring me down with that gorgeous gaze in anticipation of my answer. "Maybe we fuck again. Maybe we don't."

She peers at me as if she can read my thoughts. If that were true, she'd know this was more for me than a simple hate fuck. It would be so much easier if she *could* read my mind. Then I wouldn't have to worry about sounding like a dick when I say it out loud. "You have no time for a relationship, and I've no interest in pursuing one. It's just your typical, hard-core casual sex."

"So you're gonna keep me in the dark and fuck me in the desolate hours of the night? No thanks." Her tone doesn't match her words. Her voice wavers, the jagged edge all wobbly and soft.

"C'mon. You have to admit it's a little hot."

She sucks her lips into her mouth as her eyes flutter closed. Her chest rises, then falls. "I think it's time for you to go. I have to finish cleaning up and get to bed."

"With your little waiter friend?" I bite my words through gritted teeth.

Her head flinches back. She tilts her head pulling her brows together. "Who?"

"I don't know his fuckin' name. I saw you at the club with his hands all over you. I have no right to be jealous, but—"

She cuts me off before I have a chance to finish. "Let's get somethin' straight here, Dylan. I ain't your property." She jams her finger into my heaving chest as I look down on her with a scowl. "So don't you dare come down here, hootin' and hollerin', thinking you're gonna piss a circle 'round me, markin' your territory. I'm my own person, and I'll do whatever and whoever I damn well please."

The anger rises in my throat like bile. "I can have anything I want in this world, and I want you."

She purses her lips. "Correction. You can *buy* anything you want, but I ain't for sale."

Her tone fuels my fire. I don't know if I want to smack her, fuck her, kiss her, or shove my cock in her sweet mouth to shut her up, but I can't move to do any of it. Instead I stand like a stone watching the Technicolor band of emotions swirl in her furious gaze.

"I'd rather pour salt in a wound before spending another second alone with you." She stomps to the door and tugs it open. A cool breeze floats in from the outside, but I'm boiling. "Get out."

I feel like a dick out of nowhere. I treated her like a whore, and I get the feeling that I'm not the first. She deserves better than that. "Darla, I—"

"I said out!" She yanks my arm and tries to pull me, but I easily outweigh her by fifty pounds. Her tug feels like the evening wind.

I got what I came for. I'm supposed to feel free. I'm meant to be light as air having fucked her away, but this little plan backfired in my face. Having her once is not enough. I'm still hungry. I need more of her to satisfy my insatiable need, but I think I've done enough damage for one night.

With nothing left to say, I slink away, giving her a chance to reclaim a small piece of her dignity.

Chapter Twelve

DARLA

"ORDER UP." REX HITS the bell as he slides a turkey burger under the heat lamps.

I swing around and set it next to the Cobb salad on my tray. "Where's my BLT?"

"It's coming, princess. Cool your jets."

Seconds later, the plate glides toward me. "Thank you!"

With my tray full, I back into the dining room and saunter down to table ten. The governor smiles as I set down his meal, his wife a blank canvas as usual. When I drop the plate in front of Dylan, I lock my shoulders, hiding the shudder that rolls down my spine. The memory of what we did haunts my every thought. I still feel the table threatening to give way beneath me as he slammed into me over and over. The cruel way he took control, the sweet ache building like a crescendo until he gave me permission to let it all go.

"Anything else I can get ya?"

Dylan shoves a fry in his mouth without looking up. I stuff down the feelings of inadequacy bubbling to the surface. I fucking hate him for making me feel this way. It was meant to be a one-time thing. I gave into the need that's been brewing inside since the moment we met. We got each other out of our systems and can move on with our lives, except . . . I'm not sure it did the trick. The risk of getting caught, the thrill of the forbidden . . . Giving in to him was a mistake that left me wanting more. Our coupling sparked like an electrical storm. Danger simmered low in my gut as I held on, preparing for the shock of my life. I never intended to go down in flames, yet here I am, bursting with fire and need while he sits there casually as if it never happened.

"I think we're fine, Darla. Thank you." The governor's voice is enough to pull me from the self-induced blaze. I offer a quick smile before slinking back to the kitchen where the poor folk belong.

"Why do you look like death warmed over?" Shyanne comes to my aid, but I can't tell her the truth. In my lust-filled haze, I allowed myself to become Dylan's shameful secret. Who even am I?

"Didn't sleep great."

"It's starting to quiet down a bit. Take a quick break. I'll keep an eye on your tables."

"Ima splash some water on my face. I'll be fine." I hug the perimeter of the dining room to the bathroom at the far end. The garish light does little to help my appearance. I turn on the faucet and let my hands fill before bringing them to my face. The quick jolt of cold makes me feel alive. I dab with a paper towel before heading out, but I'm caught in the vestibule like a fly in a web with Dylan as the spider.

"Hey."

"Hey yourself."

"I have not been able to stop thinking about you." His hands encircle my waist. He glides down my hip and trails his finger along my lower belly to the apex of my thighs.

His ministrations make my knees weak. I try to step away, but my wobbly legs won't let me. "News to me."

With small, controlled circles, he strokes my VCH with the tip of his pointer, his gray eyes half lidded. "You working at the bar tonight?"

I nod. The breath in my lungs becomes a shallow pant. I roll my hips as he increases the pressure on my piercing through the thin fabric of my uniform. If he keeps this up, I'm going to have to change my pants. "Dylan, I'm at work."

When his mouth drops to the base of my neck, I'm forced to clutch the wall for support. The bathrooms sit behind a single door. In the tiny space it's him and me, but someone could walk into the main door at any point. This knowledge heightens the arousal swirling at my tailbone.

"You have no idea how hard it is watching you run around this restaurant, bringing food to all these people, when all I want to do is bend you over the table and lick you like an ice cream cone."

"Dylan, please," I whisper in desperation.

"I'll be there before closing." He steps away, taking his heat along with him.

Chills ripple down my back. Jesus H. Christ, he's an asshole. How am I supposed to go back to work with my clit thrumming in my panties? Before he gets to the door, I snap, "I don't remember agreeing to that."

A wry grin splits his face. "You didn't agree the first time, but your body blossomed for me just the same."

It's hard to argue, but it doesn't stop me from trying. "Don't get a big head. It's biology, like I said."

His wry grin widens. "See you tonight, pretty girl," he whispers, walking off to rejoin his family.

I pull in a deep breath to calm my racing pulse. Dylan Masters has far too much control over my body. At this point, merely the smell of him gets me hot and bothered, and I loathe him for it, but I hate myself even more for wanting him again. The insecurities I keep hidden away show all over my face as he peels away the onion skin layers of strength I've wrapped around them. I seem tough on the exterior, but inside I'm soft as clay. Malleable in his hands.

Fuck, why am I letting him get to me like this?

With my self-control dwindling by a thread, I strut back out into the dining room to finish off what's left of the day. "Miss?" The sound of his voice lifts my shoulders. I turn toward his table, reaching into my apron to hide my trembling hands.

"Can I get you something else?" *I hate that you've seen me naked.*

"Just the check," the governor replies, but Dylan cuts him off.

"Actually, I'd like an order to go, please." His smug expression boils my blood. No doubt he called me over just to see the flush on my cheeks. The man is a sadist. He gets off on pulling my strings to watch me dance.

"Sure." I pull the pad from my pocket to find their receipt. "What would you like?"

He shrugs. "I dunno. What's your favorite thing on the menu?"

A nervous smile tugs at the edge of my mouth. *My* favorite thing on the menu? That's a joke. Why would I pay seventeen bucks for a sandwich I can get at the corner deli for eight? But I'm not about to say that out loud. Instead, I blurt out the first thing that comes to my mind. "People seem to like the country chicken sandwich."

"All right. Wrap it up."

With a curt nod, I walk away. "Rex. A country chicken to go," I call as I meander back into the kitchen. This is stupid. Dylan is nothing. He's a hot lay with a pretty face. He's not the first, and he sure as shit isn't the last. Yet I still find myself hiding in the back until the cook calls my number.

Armed with the sandwich and the check, I hold my head high and bring it back to the table. The Masters clear out, and before long, my shift is over. I rub the back of my neck as I reach for my phone to check the time. *If I skip dinner, I could possibly grab a disco nap before my shift at the bar.* My stomach grumbles in defiance. I press my fingers into my belly to calm the uproar. Okay, new plan: I grab a burger at the drive through, eat it on the way home, then nap.

But all my plans fade away when I see Dylan sitting on my tailgate.

Chills break over my skin. I stop short, cupping my hip. "Don't you have anything else to do besides annoy me?"

"Nope. Annoying you is the only thing I had on my calendar today," he says with a smirk.

I purse my lips to keep from smiling. "I thought you were coming tonight. Aren't you afraid someone may see you talking to the help in broad daylight?" Sidestepping around him, I wrench open the door of my truck.

He comes around and rests his arm along the top, keeping me from closing him out. "This is the employee entrance. No one important comes back here."

"Gee, thanks," I snap. His ego is starting to crowd the lot, and what's worse, I'm sure he doesn't even realize how offensive he is. He's blinded by his own privilege, and it's gross.

He rolls his eyes. "You know what I mean."

"I'm not sure I do." His Adam's apple bobs. Before I give him a chance to retort, I add, "Take your to-go order and go somewhere else. I don't have time for this."

He reaches around to the bed of the truck and snatches up the bag. "Let me at least keep you company while you eat."

I lift a brow as he drops it in my lap. "'Scuse me?"

"You run from shift to shift. When do you take time for self-care?"

A bubble of laughter bursts on my tongue. "Self-care is a term coined by rich white women who need an excuse for weekly spa treatments. It ain't a real thing."

His gray eyes darken. "I just wanted to bring you food. Why are you giving me such a hard time?"

I turn my head to stare out the windshield. The savory scent of fried chicken fills the tiny cab. My mouth waters, but I don't touch the bag on principle. I suppose on some small level it was a nice gesture. His heart's in the right place, but the execution was shitty. "That's the thing. *You* didn't bring it. *I* brought it. You merely carried it outside."

"What's the difference?"

I offer a sidelong glance. "There's a big difference."

Another hunger pang rumbles from deep inside me. I inwardly curse my traitorous stomach, hoping Dylan didn't hear it. He cocks his head. "Explain it to me."

"It's an insult veiled by a good deed. In the end, you still had me serve my own lunch to you, then expected a victory dance in your honor."

He frowns. "That's not how I meant it."

"That's the problem with you. Your intentions are irrelevant. It's all about how it's perceived by the receiver. This" — I hold up the bag — "says I'm nothing but your servant."

I see the thoughts turning in his light eyes as his gaze searches my face. Hunger begins to cancel out anger. I chuck the bag on the passenger seat and shove my key in the ignition with a sigh. "Follow me out."

He backs away so I can close the door. A few moments later, the low purr of a well-oiled engine echoes through the air before his car comes into view. The nearest rest stop sits a few miles down the road. The safety areas off the highway are meant for weary travelers to stretch their legs and have a snack, but they also offer a level of privacy from the prying eyes of small-town residents.

However, there's one in particular that I set my sights on—a 1950s road-trip-era gas station, the abandoned kind you see on old state highways left to rot due to the lack of traffic once the interstates were built. I pull into the lot with him on my bumper and find a secluded space beneath the trees, a welcome reprieve from the hot sun blazing above. He parks beside me and gets out, then hops into the passenger side of my truck.

He looks around the cab as he settles in. "Why do you have a bat behind the seats?"

Residual warmth rises from the sandwich as I set the tin on my lap and pull off the plastic lid. "Protection."

"From what?"

I offer a sidelong glance. "Anything that may arise."

Trying to pick this sandwich up without making a mess is no easy feat. Ranch drizzles out from underneath a layer of bacon. I bring it to my mouth and audibly moan as I chew. It isn't until I feel his eyes burning into me that I remember I'm not alone. I raise my free hand to my lips. "Sorry," I warble around the first bite. "I guess I was hungrier than I thought."

"It's okay." He chuckles.

Now I understand why these sandwiches are so dang expensive. Inside the thick breading, the chicken is juicy and soft. The in-house dressing adds a spicy peppercorn flavor. I can't help but lick it off my fingers in the most unladylike way. "If I knew this sandwich was for me, I'd have told you to get extra pickles."

"You're not shy about eating in front of people, are you?"

I pause to swallow. "Should I be?"

"Most girls I know have a complex about it."

"Why do guys get to sit around scratching their balls in their own filth, but we're expected to be prim and proper at all times?"

He bites at his bottom lip, then lets it go. "You don't have balls to scratch."

"It's a metaphor. I'm saying, toxic masculinity makes it okay for dudes to be pigs, but girls are held to a higher standard? It's bullshit."

"Don't go burning your bra on my account," he jokes.

I roll my eyes in his direction. "If I were wearing one."

"Really?" He reaches out and flicks my nipple with the pad of his finger.

I shift to slap him away, dropping the last of my sandwich into the tin. "Boundaries, dude. What the fuck?"

"Are you done eating?"

"Why? You want the rest?"

"No, I want you."

I sweep a napkin over my lips and throw it alongside my leftovers. "I knew this damn sandwich came with strings."

"No strings. Just telling you what I want. You have the right to say no." He bags up the trash and drops it on the floorboard. "Bluster and fight all you want." He slides his hand up my thigh. "But we both know where this is gonna end up."

"I ain't sure there's enough room in this truck for both you and your confidence. One of y'all is gonna have to go."

He leans over the console and nibbles at my neck, his fingers moving dangerously close to the hot zone. "Or we can finish what we started at the club."

Warmth pools in my belly. I shift in my seat, trying to smother the ache building within, but it only serves as an opportunity to open a space for him between my legs. My head hits the back of the seat. "Or I can bite your dick off."

"Considering the way you were screaming last night, I think you like my dick right where it is."

"You're a pig."

"Tell me to stop then."

My thin black leggings do nothing to dull the sensation of his finger gliding between my folds. They merely serve as a barrier to keep him from venturing inside. The flimsy material dampens under his touch. I feel it spreading down my thighs. If I do it because *I* want it, that's not the same as giving in, right? We're two sexual beings. Consenting adults who reserve the right to accept pleasure on our own terms.

My gaze pings around the empty lot. Not a soul in sight. I lick my lips and sit up, reaching between his legs to pull the seat bar. It glides back until it hits the window. "Let's get something straight. This" — I volley my finger between us — "doesn't mean I like you." I undulate my hips and force my pants down with my thumbs. With one leg free, I hop over the console and straddle his lap.

"Biology. Got it." He undoes his fly, letting his cock spring free. He takes it in his hand and guides it to my entrance as I lift myself to slide down the shaft. An instant moan tumbles in my chest. He sits high inside me, sitting back to allow me to lead, but he's the one in control. His hands slide up to circle my hips. They ripple in small, tight movements. My head tilts back as I adjust to the feeling of complete fullness.

"You get so fucking wet," he mumbles.

Last night was no-holds-barred. He had his way, but today it's mine. I grind on him hard, clutching the back of the seat for support. He shimmies up my torso and starts undoing the tiny closures on my blouse, but his patience wears thin. He tears it open. Buttons fly, but I'm too lost in the moment to care. He yanks my tank down to expose my breasts. I lean in closer to drop one in his mouth. Another whimper floats around us. He laps at my nipple before sucking it between his lips, then bites, eliciting a cry.

With both hands around my waist, he jerks upward. The hard length of him pushes deep. I slap my hand to the ceiling to keep my balance as I push back on his every stroke. "Yes, yes, fuck yes."

My hair falls in a curtain, shielding us from the world beyond the tinted windows. I tug at his ponytail. Blond tendrils wisp around his face. I secretly admit to liking him like this. Chaotic and wild. But when he groans about how hot my tits are, I swear I almost fall in love.

The muscles in my belly begin to tighten. His shaft rubs against the little ball in my clit, pushing me closer to the edge as I ride and buck, but his body stills. I try to move, but he holds me taut. A small puff of air blows from my lungs. He reaches up to smooth the hair off my face, then brings me in to taste my lips.

"God, Darla," he mumbles between kisses. "You're so fucking beautiful. You're so hot. You ride my cock like such a good girl."

"Then let me come," I beg.

I feel his smile take shape against my mouth. He lowers his head to circle my breast with his wicked tongue. Slow, slow, so goddamn slow I fall into madness. I move my hips to find the friction. My breath puffs in shallow pants, but he's holding back.

"Beg me like a good girl."

"I ain't your fucking girl."

His fingers tangle in my hair and yank. A gasp ricochets from my chest. "C'mon, pretty girl, tell me how much you love my cock, then maybe I'll let you come all over it."

Heat rolls up my face. The control he has on my body is maddening. I should have gone home to flick the bean, but instead, I find myself at the mercy of Dylan Masters. He gets off on building me up. He brings me to the height of pleasure, then takes it away, forcing me to my knees, pleading with him to give me what I need. "You feel so good."

He bucks up into me. "How good?"

"Fuck, so good."

He drives upward with a guttural groan. Three hard pumps that hit the back of my canal.

Lost in need, the words flit off my lips as a breathy chant. "Please, Dylan, I'm so close. Please."

"You're gorgeous when you beg."

Fingers biting into my thighs, he manually pushes me back and forth, my clit ring rubbing his shaft with each delicious pull.

"Play with your tits."

My hands spring to my chest. I yank and squeeze as he grinds me down on his crotch with a pace that nearly tears me in two. Pleasure tears through my middle. I tip my face to the sky, hollering out a string of curses as I plummet over the edge, my sanity slowly falling away. Satisfaction continues to ripple in waves. He pushes, he pulls, he bucks into my sopping pussy, grunting like a man possessed. With a raspy growl, he lets it go.

I fall to his chest as he pulses inside me. He sweeps the hair off my face and finds my lips again. This time, a slow, languid kiss. He teases my mouth, gliding his tongue lazily around mine. "How many napkins do you have left in the bag?"

Pushing on his chest, I sit up. "Is that a shot?"

"Not at all." He cups my face, his thumbs caressing my heated skin. "I love the way you come."

"Shut up." I shuck my busted shirt off my shoulders and hurl it at him. Slowly, I lift myself off his lap as he uses it to wipe us clean.

Why do guys gotta freak out over this shit? Females ejaculate, too. It's not that unusual. The first time it happened, the douchebag I was with told me I was gross. He was convinced I pissed on him, then went on to tell everyone else. For the longest time, I thought something was wrong with *me,* but in reality, that was their problem. I mean, what the fuck? They're allowed to expel fluid, but I can't? That being said, I can't help feeling a little sensitive when my partner comments on it.

"Holy shit," Dylan says, the corner of his mouth tugging upward.

"I embarrassed you."

I narrow my gaze. "Please. Embarrassment would indicate that I gave a fuck what you think, which I don't." I hop back onto my seat and try my best to adjust my pants.

"You don't have to be embarrassed."

A flush creeps up my cheeks, but it only makes me angrier. "Are you deaf? I just told you I ain't."

"Human beings are messy creatures."

My lids flutter closed. I'm way past embarrassment and veering dangerously close to humiliation. We both came. Party's over. "You can get out now."

He chuckles. "I don't believe you. You have a friggin' clit ring, but a little cum makes you uncomfortable?"

"It ain't a little." I stare out my window, watching the breeze blow through the trees.

Dylan's voice grows deep and serious. "Some asshole shamed you for it, didn't he?" When I don't answer, he piles on. "I'm sorry. You don't deserve to be shamed for something so beautiful."

"Biology," I whisper with trembling lips.

"Listen to me." His fingers catch under my chin and turn me to face him. "Everything about you is sexy. But if it bothers you, I'll never mention it again, okay?"

I nod.

"What time do you have to be in work?"

My stomach flips. I got so caught up I almost forgot. Snatching my phone from the console, I swipe the screen to check the time. "Shit. I have an hour. I gotta run home and shower before I head over."

"I'll see you later." He drops a chaste kiss to my forehead before hopping down from my truck and falling into his own car. I watch the dust fly behind him as he drives away.

That was awkward.

I throw the truck in reverse and back out of the space. The trailer park entrance isn't far. I weave through the rows of mobile homes, shaking my head when I see Christmas lights still hanging off a few. It's a living stereotype in my own backyard, and I hate it. Redneck roots run deep in these parts. Thinking of Dylan ever coming here makes my chest hurt. He'd realize instantly his family is right, then run back to his mansion on the hill.

The American flag waves in the wind as I park on the gravel pit beside my home. Relief washes over me when I see Ray's spot empty. I got lucky twice in one day.

"Mama?"

The rush of water echoes through the bathroom door. I head toward it, but the light glinting off the broken shards of glass on the floor catches my eye. I scowl, my gaze pinging around the room. Tiptoeing around the mess, I rap my knuckles on the thin wood. "Mama, you in there?"

"I'll be right out."

The pipes squeal before going silent. When the door opens, my mom slinks out, her gaze trained on the floor.

"You all right?"

"Ya, sugar bean. I'm fine."

But her tone says otherwise. I rest my hand on her slender shoulder as she reaches for the bottle on the counter. "What happened?" I slam open the cabinet under the sink and snatch the dustpan. I can't remember the exact moment when I slid into the parental role, but at some point in my childhood, I became the one taking care of her.

"Ray's in another one of his moods again."

I look up from the floor and catch sight of a yellow stain under her left eye. *That motherfucker.* After emptying the shards in the trash, I turn back to face her and take her by the chin. Badly applied makeup cakes over the fresh bruise. Nausea twists in my gut. Is she trying to hide this from me? "What happened to your face?"

She shirks from my grasp. "Nothing."

My heart begins to pound. Anger and guilt compound on my chest. I should have been here instead of fucking around with Dylan in the park. He's distracting me from being where I need to be. Here. I cross my arms over my chest to keep my hands from quivering. "Did that son of a bitch hit you?"

"You know how Ray is." She pauses to pull a swig from her cup. "He doesn't mean it."

I throw up my hands in frustration. "How can you still defend him? Look at your face!"

"Ray is my husband, and he takes care of us."

My jaw drops in wide-eyed shock. "*He* takes care of us? *I'm* the one working two jobs to keep us fed. What the fuck does Ray contribute?"

An agitated whimper lodges in her throat. "Don't sass me, Miss Darla. You know as well as I do that we wouldn't be able to live like this without Ray's pension."

When she lifts the cup to her lips again, I snatch it from her fingers. "Can you put the booze down for a fucking change?" I pull a calming breath into my lungs and blow it out hard. Emotion stings my eyes, but I refuse to allow a single tear to broach the dam. I am too damn strong for that. "We don't need Ray," I say on a more even keel. Twisting toward the freezer, I grab a bag of frozen peas, then gently rest it against her face. "We will manage without him."

She winces. "Then what? You go off and live your life, and I'm here all alone?"

A wedge drives the cracks in my already broken heart even wider. "That'll never happen, okay? What did you use to say when Daddy left? You and me, we're a team, remember?"

The beautiful woman she used to be peeks from beneath her crepe-paper skin. I remember thinking I had the best mom in the whole world. She'd let me do things no one else's parents would ever allow, like paint murals on the living room walls or have ice cream for dinner. It wasn't until I grew up that I realized it wasn't that she was an awesome fun mother. She was drunk and hiding it.

"It ain't your job to take care of me. You best go find yourself a man and start a family of your own."

I pull her in for a hug. "You're my family, Mama. I will always take care of you."

"My sugar bean." She pulls back and rests her hand on my cheek. "For all the mistakes I've made, I know I done somethin' right when I look at you."

"I gotta get ready for work. You gonna be okay?"

"I'm a survivor," she replies with a twisted grin.

Another quick hug before I add, "Call the bar if you need me, all right? I'll come right home."

"Don't you worry about me. Go do your thing." She takes her drink and flops on the couch. Seconds later, the comforting sound of the television blares aloud as I lock myself in the bathroom and cry.

Chapter Thirteen

DYLAN

Me: Hey, pretty girl. Whatcha up to?

Darla: Working, what else?

Me: Don't you ever rest?

Darla: resting is for the rich. What do you want?

Me: Feel like meeting up at the old creek after work?

Darla: What's there to do at the old creek?

Me: ...

Me: You.

Darla: *eye-roll emoji*

Me: I'll bring a pizza. We can have a tailgate picnic under the stars.

Darla: Why do I get the feeling you're trying to trade food for sex?

Me: I just want to spend time with you. If we happen to have sex during, so be it.

Darla: ...

Darla: ...

Darla: ...

Darla: Would it change your mind if I told you I'm on the rag?

Me: Your mouth still works, right?

Darla: ...

Me: I'm kidding! I'm not scared of a little blood.

Darla: I ain't driving out there alone. Meet me at the bar at 2.

Darla: FYI If there's no pizza, I'm gonna be pissed.

Me: yes ma'am. *pizza emoji* and *eggplant emoji*

Darla: you're disgusting

Me: And you like it. What's that say about you?

Darla: Can I get back to work now, please?

Me: Don't work yourself too hard. See ya later.

O FF THE BEATEN PATH, a gravel road turns to dirt. It winds through the trees and ends at a shallow body of running water. Any teenager growing up in these parts knows about the old creek. A private place in the middle of nowhere for kids to drink, it also serves as a secluded spot to steal away for a little privacy.

Stars shine over our heads, a half-eaten pizza by our feet as we lie side by side in the bed of her truck staring up at the sky. "I could fall asleep right here." Darla's light voice floats over the sound of the bubbling water. Texas days are hot as Hades, but the air cools as the sun goes down. She raises her arm over her head and slides it under the pillow. "This blanket is softer than my bed."

I chuckle. "My friends and I used to come down here to party all the time in high school."

"Us, too." She sits up and pulls her knees to her chest. "I beat up a girl right over there 'bout a year back."

My head lolls to the side. "Why?"

She shrugs. "I dunno. Didn't like her."

"You're a feral cat, aren't you?"

She turns to look over her shoulder. "She thought she was better than me. I showed her she ain't."

"I got into a fight once."

She twists and falls on her elbow. "Open-handed slaps don't count as fightin'."

I reply with a *har har har* of sarcastic laughter. "Some guy was picking on my sister. I knocked his ass out, and he never bothered her again."

"That was mighty chivalrous of you."

"That's what big brothers do." I shrug. "You have any siblings?"

"I might," she says with a giggle. "But none that I know of. My dad split when I was pretty young, so . . ."

"What's the story there?"

"That's a tale as old as time itself. Mom got pregnant young, got married out of obligation. They tried to make it work, but by the time I was five or so, their marriage was over. He stuck around for about a year after that. You know, one of them weekend dads, but weeks turned to months, months to years, and I eventually stopped seeing him altogether." She drops her head in her open hand, mirroring my position. "Guess bein' a dad wasn't much of a priority. What about your folks? I bet they're awesome."

I snort. "Far from it."

"They seem pretty nice at the restaurant."

"They don't understand me."

"Well, I mean, that's all parents, right?"

"It's more than that. It's like, everything I do isn't good enough. It doesn't matter how hard I try, my father will always find ways to be disappointed."

"Maybe you should stop trying so hard."

I chew the corner of my lip. Thinking about my family is enough to ruin the bubble of ease I feel whenever I'm in Darla's presence. With her this close, I'm able to carve out a secret sliver of happiness that's all my own. One that's just us — her and me — and no one else can enter. "Can we talk about something else?"

Her fingers graze my cheek, then sweep around to trace my jaw. A small gesture of support that loosens the tightness in my chest. "You should have brought your guitar."

I wince. "I don't actually play in front of people."

"Then why do it?" she asks with a lifted brow.

"I dunno." I shrug. "It's one thing I have that's just for me, I guess."

Sometimes I wonder what it would be like to get in her truck and drive away. Leave it all behind us and start a new life. A place where we don't have to hide who we are and be Dylan and Darla, full stop.

"If you could go anywhere in the world, where would you go?" I ask, changing the subject.

She purses her lips before replying. "I'd like to see the ocean."

My eyes widen. "You've never been to the beach?"

"Is that so surprising?" She lies to face me, our noses inches apart.

I bring my palm to her cheek. "I guess I never thought about it. I've never really . . ." I trail off for fear of saying something that ruins the moment.

"Hung out with the poor folk?" she continues my sentence.

"I suppose that makes me a bad person."

"No. It makes you blind to the world around you. There are a lot more of us than there are of you."

Guilt festers inside me. Darla's right in thinking I'm selfish. This is a woman who works herself half to death trying to survive while I sit atop my throne of family wealth holding my head too high to see the masses below. I've been given the world, and in turn, I've taken everything for granted. Including her.

"I'm sorry about the sandwich."

She pulls her brows together. "What sandwich?"

"The chicken sandwich from the club."

"That was weeks ago."

I sit up. "I know, but I've been thinking about what you said. How not everything is about me. You call me out on my shit, and I need that. You smack me right off my pedestal."

She lets out a quiet giggle. "Like you said to Ray that night at the bar. I deserve respect. Your money doesn't let you off the hook."

I roll onto my knees and use my body to push her back. She falls on her elbows as I hover over her. "Why does it always come down to money? Can't we just be *us* under the stars?"

"Under the stars, yes. But what about out in the sun?"

I lean in closer, inhaling her sweet scent into my lungs. "I'm here with you now. Isn't that enough?" I nip her lobe between my teeth and let it fall out slowly.

Warm breath fans across my cheek.

"I'm all yours." I latch on to her wild blue gaze, turned dark denim in the moonlight. "Use me however you want, Darla. I'm right here."

She bends her knee to rest her foot flat on the truck bed. In doing so, my thigh slips farther between hers. "Oh, so it's *me* using *you*, now? I was under the impression it was the other way around."

"Don't pretend you aren't getting just as much satisfaction from this arrangement as I am. Maybe even more. I can only have one orgasm at a time."

"Ohhh. Poor baby," she coos, circling her arms around my neck. My hair tumbles forward. She pushes it behind my ear, using my open palm as a backrest. "You're too good looking for your own good. It's given you a big head."

"You think I'm an egocentric dick."

A smile tugs at the edge of her lips. "Egocentric, big dick."

I lift a brow with a wry grin. "I'm gonna take that as a compliment."

Bending my leg, I glide it up under hers. I lay her back and press my palms on either side of her head to look down on her from above as I inch forward and push against her warmth. Her eyelids flutter. "I already told you. We can't do this right now."

"And I told you I'm not afraid of a little blood," I murmur, brushing our noses together. "You're too fucking hot. And you're smart and independent . . ." My fingers skate down her side and dance over her belly. "And so sexy."

She shivers under my ticklish touch. The moment I reach the apex of her thighs, a soft moan escapes her plump lips. They part on a sigh. She's fucking beautiful, lost in the pleasure I bring to her. Entwined with her, the bullshit from the past is no longer there. I can pretend she's mine, all mine for the world to see, but for now all we have are the stars overlooking the creek and this undying lust that tethers us together.

I work over her core, slow and steady, teasing her. Those blue eyes lock on mine, as a coy smile tugs at her mouth. I press harder against the tiny, hard ball I can feel through her clothing. She replies with a whimper, her lashes fluttering as she desperately tries to keep focused on me.

"You see." I sweep my lips along hers, but I struggle with the urge to kiss her. "You can't deny this is beneficial for you." I know I'm right.

"Perhaps," Darla whispers, her chin poised, but she doesn't stop me when I tug at the button of her jean shorts and slowly pull the zipper down. My hand slips beneath her panties to find her clit. The small metal piercing presses against my fingertip. A heavy breath escapes her lips. She arches her back, pushing against me. I can't stop myself from smiling. She fights me at every turn, but she can't deny the pleasure written all over her face. She's lost to it.

"That's it," I coax with my words and my fingers. Her body shivers under mine as her delicate hand grips my hard shaft through the thick material of my jeans. It makes me want to plunge into her pussy, deep and hard, until she's crying out my name, but I know she's uneasy because it's her time. I don't give a shit — I want her. I'll respect her wishes, but I won't be nice.

My fingers dive into her core, and her eyes shoot open. "Dylan, I—"

"Shhh."

With deft haste, she undoes my jeans and grasps my cock. The warmth of her touch has me biting my lip to keep from coming too soon. I didn't expect this to happen, but her scent, her smile, the way her eyes dance when she challenges me, turns me into a man possessed. I can't not have her. I lean in and capture her lips. Our tongues duel as I taste the sweetness to the usual bite that is Darla.

The electricity between us is stronger than ever. No woman has driven me as crazy as she does, but no other woman has made me want to be a better man. An intoxicating burn courses through me when I'm with her. I can't explain it. She's poison, leaching into my blood in tiny increments, a drug that makes me crave her more than I ever thought possible.

I push two fingers into her cunt, ignoring the tiny white string. Tightness pulses around both digits, and Darla's free hand grips my neck. She meets my gaze. I wait for her to tell me to stop, to ask me to cease my movements, but she opens wider, allowing me to delve deeper than I was before.

"God, you're so beautiful, spread out for me," I murmur along her lips. "Tell me how good it feels, pretty girl." Warm wetness builds. I fuck her with my fingers, flicking my thumb over the piercing in the hood of her clit. With each motion, she seems to unravel. That cold-hearted bitch is gone, and in her place is someone docile and eager to please.

"It feels so fucking good," she purrs, the honesty in her eyes shimmering, those blue orbs that turn dark when she's aroused. "I don't want to admit it." When she strokes my cock, I'm so close to losing control all over her delicate hand. Her touch is incredible. I allow myself to get lost in the euphoria.

"You don't have to admit anything. Just let go," I coax as I pull out and push back in, wishing it was my cock inside her. "When I'm alone, fisting my dick, I think about being inside this tight pussy." I shouldn't be telling her this. It's crossing the imaginary boundary I set for this relationship. I shouldn't allow her to see how much I want her, but I can't stop myself.

"When I'm in bed at night . . ." Darla starts, but then she stops as she slides her thumb over the tip. It sends a wave of lust racing down my spine, and a hiss escapes my clenched teeth. "I think about you inside me, and I think about tasting you, touching you, and . . ."

"And you come on your fingers the way you're about to come on mine," I finish the sentence because I know for a fact that I'm right. "Because you want me just as much as I want you."

"Fuck you, Dylan. Fuck you so, so much." But she says it with a smile as her cunt tightens.

"Come for me, pretty girl," I whisper over her cheek. My teeth graze over her sweet earlobe, and I bite gently before whispering, "Imagine my tongue flicking your clit. I want to make you soak me."

The corner of her mouth tilts playfully. She squeezes the base, her hands twisting as she slides up, over and over again, milking my fucking cock until I can no longer hold it in.

"I thought you were my good girl?" Arching a brow, I stare at her beautiful face. I can't deny she's gorgeous. It's why I can't get her out of my fantasies each time I jerk off.

"If I'm going to come, so are you," she fights back. That's the thing about Darla. She can never just submit. She has to be stronger than me, stronger than anyone.

"Fuck, Darla," I grunt as she cups my balls and squeezes them gently. The pleasure that jolts through me is insurmountable. My orgasm explodes over both her hands as I push deeper inside her, crooking my fingers until I find that spot that makes her muscles squeeze the life out of them. Her body trembles. "Fuck, yes." Her voice is melodic, her face the picture of perfect bliss. The way her lips part on a soft sigh as she slowly comes down from the high makes me feel like a fucking hero.

And deep down, I wonder if I can ever be that for her.

Chapter Fourteen

DARLA

MY MANAGER, EDDIE, POKES his head out of the office. "Darla. Clock out."

With an incensed eye roll, I rise from the break-room table and slide my timecard through the machine. "Heaven forbid I go a minute long on my shift," I grumble, falling beside Shyanne. "That whole eight cents is gonna break the bank."

Shy giggles.

"The past few days have kicked my ass. Thankfully, I ain't working tonight. You wanna get a drink or something later?"

She sighs. "I can't. I'm workin' second shift. I really need the money."

My brows shoot up. "You're a goddamn masochist is what you are."

"Ya, but a broke one," she says with a laugh. "It's not so bad. They're puttin' me behind the bar so all I gotta do is pour wines and bourbons and stuff."

The chime of her phone plays from her back pocket. She shifts in her seat to pull it out. "Hey, Summer, what's up?"

I peel myself off my chair and begin collecting my things from the cubby. From the corner of my eye, I see Shyanne lean forward on her elbows. "Oh my stars, that's terrible. I'm so sorry . . . yeah, lemme see what I can do. Thanks." She disconnects the call and puts her phone on the table.

"Everything okay?"

She blows out a hard breath. "That was my babysitter. Her gran died, and she can't stay with Savvy tonight."

"That sucks. Do you have a backup?"

"Summer's all I got. Not only does Savvy love her, but she works cheap. Other sitters want almost double what she charges. I may as well not even work, but I'm already committed. I can't back out now." She yanks the band from her hair and scratches at her scalp before gliding her fingers through her long red tendrils. "Dar . . ." She stands up, wringing her hands. "Think you can sit with Sav tonight? I know it's a lot to ask, but I'm stuck up shit creek, and you're my only paddle."

My shoulders slump. Spending my one night off with an energetic three-year-old is not high on my list of things to do. Savannah is sweet, but truth be told, I don't like kids. They're sticky and loud and never shut up. But I love Shyanne, and she needs my help. She'd do it for me without hesitation if the roles were reversed.

With a deep sigh, I nod. "Sure, hun. No problem."

She hooks her arms under mine to pull me in for a hug. "You're the best."

"Can I go home and change first?"

"Yes. I'll call Summer back and let her know you'll be relieving her soon. Thank you so much. I owe you one."

As she turns to make the call, I hike my purse on my shoulder and wave goodbye before heading to the door. The late-day sun shines at half-mast. I lift my arm to block the direct rays of light from burning my eyes. It heats my truck cab to a sweltering temp. I roll down the windows and crank the A/C. The truck may be old, but it cools like a champ.

Wind whips through my hair as I pull onto the main road and pick up speed. There's something about sitting behind the wheel of a 4x4 that makes my heart race. The freedom of the drive. Just me and the radio twisting down old country roads. I may never be flush with wealth, but in my truck, I feel like a queen.

Even if it's queen of the county fair.

The trailer's quiet as I let myself in. I walk through the compact space looking for a sign of life. A wisp of light hair carries on the breeze through the kitchen window. Mom's outside in a lawn chair, the smoke from her cigarette curling around her spindly fingers. I lean over the sink and yell out, "Hey, Ma. Whatcha doing out there?"

"Enjoyin' the sun before it gets too hot to go outside."

"Where's Ray?"

She shrugs and takes a deep drag from her Marlboro Red, the orange cherry glowing bright before dulling to ash. My mother worships the sun. Her legs stretch out from cut-off shorts, her pruney skin baking into leather. She twists in her seat, squinting to see me through the screen. "Why dontcha come sit with me, sugar bean? Take a load off."

"I can't. I gotta head back out."

A grin tugs at her lips. "Date?"

"Babysitting for Shy."

She stands from her throne and flicks her butt into the yard before coming round to the door. "Oh, that's sweet. I can't wait for you to make me a grandmother."

I cringe. "Maybe I should worry about finding a boyfriend first. Let's not put the cart before the horse."

She waves her hand. "Men don't stick around. Take what you can get while you're still young and pretty."

It's a wonder I've managed to grow up with any optimism at all. "Ima go change, then I gotta head out. I'll call to check in later."

She pours herself a big glass of vodka and heads back outside as I wander into my room. How the hell am I supposed to be a mother with a role model like that? She's talking about grandkids. Meanwhile, she barely managed to raise *me* without pickling herself into a stupor. That cycle ends now. I don't need a man to support me, and I don't need a pack of bratty little rug rats yanking at my skirt. I've been through too much hell to get myself knocked up and settle into this broken merry-go-round. I want more.

I step into shorts and a tank, then shove my feet into my boots before waving goodbye to my mom and climbing back into the truck. Shyanne got lucky. Right around the time Savannah was born, her number was picked for the low-income housing district. The only lottery people like us ever win. Her house isn't much larger than the trailer, but it's got a real foundation and a small backyard for the kid to play in.

Five small houses hug the bulbous end of a cul-de-sac, hers the one in the center. Signs boasting George Masters for president line the yards. I park in the driveway and jaunt up the walk to the screen door. "Hello?" I knock on the frame and wait for Shy's sitter to come into view. "I'm Darla."

"OH! Hi! I'm Summer." When she leans in to hold open the door, the sun picks up blue highlights in her light brown hair. When she lifts her glasses, then sets them back on her small nose, I notice the red hue in the whites of her eyes. It's almost as if she'd been crying. "Thank you for coming."

"Shy told me about your gran. I'm sorry for your loss."

A small smile works itself onto her lips. "It's okay. She was the face of pure evil, but my dad is devastated. I wouldn't have left Shyanne in the lurch otherwise."

I nod and follow her into the den. Toys litter the dirt-stained carpet. She pads to Savannah sitting on the floor beside the couch. A cartoon flickers on the television set, but she's too busy with her dolls to notice.

Summer sits cross-legged beside her. "It's almost time for me to go. Do you want to sing the cleanup song?"

Before I have the chance to ask what the fuck a cleanup song is, Summer starts clapping her hands. Savvy rolls forward, using her hands to push herself off the floor. She picks up her things and marches them to a wooden bin against the wall. She cleans her mess while Summer sings, then claps for herself when she's finished.

I have to admit, it's damn cute.

"Great job, Sav! Gimme five." Summer lifts her palm, and Savannah smacks it with delight. "Now gimme a hug." She folds the girl into her thick arms, drops a kiss on her part, then looks up. "She just ate dinner, but she'll want a snack in about an hour or so. She'll ask for juice but pour her milk instead. Bedtime is seven. Read her a story and turn on her ladybug light."

My stomach tightens. Shyanne should be the one reading bedtime stories and singing songs, but instead, she's working herself half to death to provide this meager existence. She's the kindest-hearted person I know, selfless to a fault. If anyone deserves better, it's Shy. Life shouldn't be this hard for someone so pure of heart.

I squat down to Savvy's level. "We got this," I say to Summer in a kid-friendly voice. I may not love children, but I can't deny that Savannah is cute. Two black tufts stick up from either side of her head held together by tiny pink rubber bands. With dark hair and green eyes, she's a perfect mix of Shy and Hunter.

She nods.

I fall backward on my ass and cross my legs like a pretzel as Summer tucks her bag under her arm. "Tell Shy don't worry about the pay for today. She can get me when she sees me next."

"Sure. Good luck with your dad."

"Thanks," she says before walking through the door.

Alone with Savannah, my heart begins to pound. She's a sweet kid, but I have no idea what to do with her. I babysat her once as a baby, but that was easy. She literally lay there and didn't move. Whenever she cried, I stuck a bottle in her mouth.

What the hell do I do with a three-year-old?

Savvy picks up her doll and offers it to me. "Who's this?" I ask in a light voice.

"Ariel," she replies, then points at her iridescent fins. "Mermaid."

"Yes, I can see that."

She puts it down, then grabs my hand in a tiny tugging motion. "You want to bring me somewhere?"

Her pigtails bob with her rigorous nod.

"Okay." I push to my feet and follow as Savannah leads me to her room. A tiny toddler bed sits in the center, white wood with an Ariel blanket and pillowcases. Off to the side, a small bookshelf sits against the wall.

She takes a book and walks it over to me. "Mermaid."

I look down at the book and feel my chest tighten. I can't help but wonder if her obsession with Ariel has less to do with mermaids and more to do with missing her own red-headed mother. Granted, Shyanne's hair isn't quite this color, and I know nothing about kids, but there's an innocent love in Savannah's eyes when she gazes upon the fictional princess. It's like she's longing for something.

"I'll read this at bedtime, okay?" My phone dings as I set the book on her bedside table. "You wanna watch some cartoons?" I ask, pulling it from my pocket. Dylan's name crosses the screen. The past several weeks have been a vulgar display of orgasms and ugly words. The man gets under my skin like no one else, yet still manages to get into my pants every single time we're together. It's maddening.

Dylan: Hey. What are you doing?

I urge Savvy into the den and reply.

Me: babysitting. Shyanne's still at work.

Dylan: Just you and the kid?

I scowl.

Me: Yes. That's usually how babysitting works.

Dylan: How many times have you cursed since you've been there?

Me: None. Asshole.

Dylan: That's once.

Me: Doesn't count if I don't say it out loud.

Dylan: It's a matter of time. I should come over to make sure you don't color that kid's vocabulary with f-bombs.

A bubble of laughter ripples up and pops on my tongue.

Me: No thanks. I think I can handle it.

Dylan: C'mon, I'm great with kids

My gaze shifts to Savannah smacking the television with her Dollar Store Barbie doll. "Savvy, don't do that." She turns to look at me, then goes right back to it.

Me: When have you ever been around kids?

Dylan: I'm almost five years older than my sister. I practically raised her.

When Savannah gives the doll another hard whack, the head pops off and rolls to the side. She looks at the neck peg, then at its remains. Tears well in her eyes. She lets out a wail that sends my hackles flying through the roof.

"Savvy, I told you to stop doing that!" I say a little louder than I meant to.

She slams the decapitated Barbie on the ground with an ear-piercing screech, stomping her feet.

Blood rushes my ears. "What can I do? Do you want me to fix it?"

I collect the pieces and try to fit the head back onto the neck, but I can't get it on. Savannah screams in my ear about her broken doll. Sweat breaks under my arms and leeches over my skin. I don't know how to shut her up, and I can't think over the sound of her howl. "You have other dolls. Look." I run to the toy box and pull out another naked Barbie-type doll, but she snatches it from my grip and hurls it to the ground.

What the fuck am I going to do?

My phone dings again over the sound of her screams. I steal it off the couch.

Dylan: Address?

Without a second thought, I type the address. Now I'm starting to see why they say it takes a village. Clearly, I'm not equipped to deal with the emotional outrage of a toddler by myself.

In my hour of desperation I blurt, "Do you want a cookie or something?"

She sucks in a stuttering breath and nods.

Lord fucking help me if Shy has no cookies in the house. I look through the cabinets until I find the one with food inside. I spy a box of Hydrox sitting on its side. Relief loosens the tension in my shoulders. I take one out and hand it to Savannah. Her tirade wanes to the occasional sniffle. I pick up the offending toy and stash it on top of the fridge for Shy to deal with when she gets home.

She's a menace in a dress.

She's cute but crazy.

She's the perfect advertisement for birth control.

The tornado that blew through the den now sits on the carpet and snacks on her cookie as if it never happened; meanwhile, my heart rate has barely had time to slow. Jesus, kids have a two second rebound rate. I plop on the couch praying for bedtime to get here in a hurry.

One cartoon rolls into the next. The gummy reminder of Savannah's snack clings to her lips and hands like corroded black goo, but the worst seems to be behind her. I wet a dishcloth and kneel beside her. "I'm going to clean you up, okay?"

She lifts her sticky palms in the air. I wipe each individual finger and sweep the cloth over her face. She wriggles but doesn't cry, thank God. I chuck the towel onto the counter and turn to join her back in the den when the sudden rap on the door makes me almost jump out of my skin. I turn to find Dylan standing on the porch.

Crap.

In desperate hours we do desperate things. Inviting him to babysit was one of mine, and I'd forgotten all about it until he showed up at the door. Craning my neck, I raise my hand in a two-finger wave.

He opens the screen and drops a quick peck on my mouth as he saunters inside. "Hey." The smell of fries wafts through the air. "I brought dinner." He sets the Burger King bag on the table.

Savvy stands in the center of the room staring at Dylan as if he's a ghost. I go to her side and crouch down. "This is my friend, Dylan. Do you want to say hi?"

She shakes her head, a vigorous no. It suddenly occurs to me that she hasn't been around many men in her short life. Shy doesn't make time to date, and her relationship with her folks is basically nonexistent. Between her mother and babysitters, Savannah lives in a female world.

Enter Dylan—towering over us both in height, with biceps straining the fabric of his tee and long hair framing his unshaven face—poor thing is probably scared to death.

"Do you like chicken nuggets?" he asks, the deep timbre of his voice raised an octave.

She spies the kids' meal and looks to me as if to make sure it's not a trap. "It's okay. You can have some." I rise to my feet and take her hand. Letting her lead, we take the few steps to the kitchen together. Settled in her booster seat, she waits as I set the mini fries and four-piece in front of her.

He grins. "I told you I'm great with kids."

He takes down half his burger in a single bite. I unwrap my food and lift the bun to check beneath. Warmth fills my chest. *Extra pickles.* I fight the emotion clawing up my neck. It was a stupid nothing mentioned in passing, but he remembered it. It's my experience that most people are out for their own selfish needs, Dylan included, but this infinitesimal gesture feels so huge. It shows he doesn't just hear me when I speak. He listens.

"You okay?"

The sound of his voice pulls me from my own head. I'm mooning over pickles like a goddamned lunatic. "This was sweet. Thank you."

My gaze pings around the table, Dylan, Savvy, and I sharing a meal like a regular family. I run my palm over the goose bumps that pop on my skin, hoping to rub them away. Most girls dream of getting married and starting a family, but not me. This was never something I wanted, and until this second, I believed that.

But deep inside the hollow shell of my heart, I think maybe I'd convinced myself because I knew I was undeserving. It's like Dylan said, I'm not the kind of girl you bring home to your parents. I'm the kind of girl you screw around with when no one's looking, then deny it later. I slept with half the guys in my high school, and the only one I actually liked wouldn't come close enough to touch me. He said it was because of our friendship, but I knew that was a lie. No one wants to claim used goods.

Now here I am again, opening myself up for another fall.

I don't want to care about him.

In the end, Savannah eats one and a half nuggets and maybe five fries. I wrap up the rest and put it into the fridge as Dylan throws the empty wrappers in the garbage. With her kids' meal toy lodged in her sweaty fist, she climbs off the chair and wanders into the den. "She's adorable," Dylan says on a low whisper.

"She's a good kid."

I turn to join her, but Dylan sweeps his arm around my middle and pulls me back. "You're adorable, too."

Butterflies flap in my stomach. This is too much intimacy for me. I almost liked it better when he was calling me a bitch. I'm ready to deal with Dylan the asshole, but this ooey gooey center is a little harder to get a handle on. "You're a pain in my butt."

"I'm gonna spank it raw, first chance I get, pretty girl," he growls low in my ear.

Heat floods between my thighs. I press my hands to his chest to push him away. "We can't do this here."

Fire flickers in his gaze, but he backs off. I step around him. "C'mon Sav. Time to get your jammies on." She looks up as I approach. "Show me which ones you want to wear."

She flips around and slowly lowers herself off the couch until her feet touch the floor. In her room, she yanks on a dresser drawer and pulls out a nightgown with some weird pig in a red dress. I help change her clothes, then bring her to the bathroom to do her business before getting into bed.

The book she chose still sits on the nightstand. I take it and sit on the corner of her bed. She curls under the covers as I hold it open so she can see the pictures while I read.

"Once upon a time there was a little mermaid who lived under the sea with all of her fishy friends . . ."

Savannah points at the colorful drawings. "That 'Bastian."

"Sebastian. Right! He's a crab, like this." I make a pincher motion with my hand and pretend to snap her cheek. She giggles with delight. I flip the page and continue, stopping every so often to let her show me the different characters. By the time the book is finished, her lids have drooped over her giant eyes. "Good night, Savannah," I whisper, pressing my lips to her temple.

Dylan's long legs sprawl on the threadbare cushions of Shyanne's couch. Sweat beads on my palms. He doesn't belong here. He's too beautiful for this hovel of a home. This is the world in which I live, but for him, it's a fascination. A chance to go slummin' with the second class before he returns to his silver spoon life. He'll always be better, richer, more educated.

He sits up as I come around. "Storytime and everything. I'm impressed."

I narrow my gaze. "Shut up. I'm doing my best."

But his expression remains neutral. "I'm not joking. You're fantastic with her."

"I have no idea what I'm doing," I say, pulling my brows together. "She started cryin' before, and I bribed her with cookies to stop."

"Whatever works." He shrugs.

I grab the remote and flick through the choices on Hulu. "What do you want to watch?"

"Netflix and chill?"

Something about his response puts a sour taste in my mouth. "You can go if you want."

He smooths back my hair and rests his hand between my shoulders. "Why would I want to go?"

"We're not gonna fool around on my friend's couch with her kid sleeping four feet away."

He lifts a brow. "I know."

"So . . . why . . ." I lick my lips. "I'm sure you'd rather be out raisin' cane with your cousins than streamin' shitty movies in section eight housing."

One corner his mouth tugs, then the other. A slow smile that makes my heart race. "Wherever you are is where I want to be."

Those damn butterflies come back with a vengeance. I curse their fluttering wings that make my insides feel light and airy, and I curse Dylan for putting them there. Inviting him here was a mistake. A lapse in judgment that I'm sorely regretting. Every fiber of being is screaming at me to cut this arrangement off at the knees before this goes any further, but I'd be lying if I didn't admit there was a small part of me that gets a thrill from sneaking around. He's so careful to ensure I don't encroach upon his territory, yet here he is all up in mine every chance he gets. It's not fair.

"Well, I think you should go."

"Why?"

I blow out a hard breath, trying to say what I want with as few words as possible. No reason to draw this out. "I'm willing to admit you're maybe not as bad as I originally thought, but spade's a spade, dude. You ain't my boyfriend, you're my secret fuck buddy. We don't need to pretend to be friends."

His gaze narrows to blue-gray slits. "That's a shitty attitude."

I snap back. "It's the truth. I'm a warm body to get your jollies with until someone less embarrassing comes along. I've accepted that. But when you play these games, it ain't nice."

"What the hell are you talking about, games?"

"This." I volley a finger between us. "You coming to hang out with me while I babysit, saying sweet things when I know it's all a lie." I jump to my feet and turn away to hide my quivering lips. I refuse to give him any more of my emotion. He doesn't deserve it. "You got something to say to me? Say it."

He stands without a word, then takes my arm and yanks me closer, fusing our mouths in heated passion. For a split second, I forget the ugly words slung back and forth. A momentary lapse. This is what he does. He scrambles my head and makes me crazy.

"No, no, no." The words come out as a breathless chant. I put some space between us to cool the ache that built inside me the second our lips touched. "This can't keep happening."

His chest rises, nostrils flare. "I can't help wanting you, Darla."

"Why?" A simple question. I stand at the foot of the couch, my heart exposed, waiting for an answer yet terrified to hear it at the same time.

A humorless laugh blows off his tongue. He runs his fingers through the loose tendrils breaking over his forehead. "I don't know. I tried to forget you. I wanted to. I went to bars and picked up other women, but it was useless. You're the one I want."

My chest burns at his admission. "Mama?" My gaze snaps to the door as Savannah's small voice floats through the crack.

"Shit," I whisper under my breath. "I can't talk about this right now. Just go home, Dylan."

I let myself into her room and lay on the edge of her bed. "It's okay, sweetie. Go back to sleep." She tuckers out almost immediately, but I make no move to get up. I stay beside her in the dark long after I hear the sound of the front door open and shut.

Chapter Fifteen

DYLAN

THERE ARE TIMES WHEN I look at Darla and feel as if I've discovered a secret gold mine. She's smart and sexy, someone who keeps me on my toes, and my dick hard.

Then there are moments like tonight when I realize the bitch is quicksand, and I'm sucked into her depths in a way that makes it impossible to get out. Her attitude turns on a dime. Sweet one minute, psychotic the next. Day by day, hour by hour, I have no idea which version of her I'm going to get.

Maybe Xander was right. I don't have time for this shit.

This is what I tell myself, but it doesn't stop me from checking my phone every ten minutes to see if she texted me back.

I chuck the device aside and leave the room looking for a distraction. "Dylan." My father's voice bounds from the bottom of the steps. "Just the man I was looking for."

"Well. You found me."

"Come." He beckons with two fingers and twists on the balls of his feet. A cold sweat breaks on my skin. I'm a grown man, yet my brain still counts down the multitude of things I could be chastised for. Insane how he still has the uncanny ability to make me feel like a disappointing child with the smallest amount of effort.

In the kitchen, he pulls a chair from the table and gestures for me to sit. I do, and he settles at the table beside me, tenting his fingers as he did when I was being reprimanded for bringing home a bad report card.

"I have an important job for you," he starts, and my stomach bottoms out. "Are you familiar with Ed Header?"

"The venture capitalist?"

He grins. "Yes. I've recently come to learn that he's aligned with Ideal America."

I quirk a brow. Ideal America is a political action committee that raises unlimited sums of money to influence elections. While this money can't go directly to the party, and they can't work directly with anyone employed by the campaign, they can use it to operate adjacent to the campaign, like, for example, spreading messages that the party doesn't want to be seen as coming directly from them. It's dirty business. Basically, they use this cash flow to put more power into the hands of the wealthy, leaving average voters with little-to-no influence. They're not illegal, but that fact in and of itself is super controversial.

"As you know, a PAC is prohibited from working directly with me as the candidate. I need a man inside to grease the wheels, get Ed Header on my side to gain their support."

"You want me to plan an outing or something?"

"No, it needs to happen more naturally than that. I don't want him to know he's being fished. I want you to start dating his daughter."

"What?" I jump to my feet, knocking my chair to the wooden floor. "No."

He points at the chair on its back and barks, "Sit."

My stomach in knots, I reach down and right it on all fours before reclaiming my seat. My voice falls to a harsh whisper. "Let's forget for a minute that you want to whore me out to some girl I don't even know in an effort to secure dubious funds for your campaign. This is unethical, Dad."

"Winners don't triumph from ethics. If you intend to take over my seat one day, this is a lesson you best learn quickly."

I feel the goose bumps travel down my body in a wave. "Then ask Xander or Rick to do it." Darla's name sits on the tip of my tongue. She's not my girlfriend, she told me this in no uncertain terms, but she is *something* to me. The thought of her being touched by someone else makes me blind with rage. The least I can do is offer her the same consideration. Darla would probably rip my balls off and shove them down my throat.

Dad shakes his head. "Too much possibility for denial."

I reply with a sidelong glance.

"You're a strong, handsome Texan from a wealthy family. No girl in her right mind will say no to a date with you."

"Xander gets more ass than a saddle," I shoot, my expression pinched.

He drops his hand over mine. "He's my brother's son, and Lord knows I love him, but shooting fish in a barrel is easy. I need you to hook the big whale."

I slide my hand out from under his and run it through my hair, holding it back behind my head as he continues.

"I'm not telling you to marry her. Take her out a few times, get to know the family. Once you've gotten in Header's ear, you can let her down gently."

"Assuming I agree to this—which I haven't—how would this even work?"

He pulls his phone from his pocket and sets it on the table. After a few quick taps, the Header family smiles up at me from the screen of his iPhone. "They are members of the Red Drum Country Club. How you bump into her is up to you."

Great. Another layer added to this shit parfait. This is more than a lose-lose situation, this is my job. If I say no, I'm not a team player. If I say yes, I'm potentially screwing up the one good thing I have in my life right now. Even if that good thing hates my guts most of the time.

I look into the eyes of the old man who raised me. Whether governor or president, he's still my father. I'd like to believe he wants me to be happy.

"You should know I'm sort of seeing someone." My heart pounds against my ribs as the words fall off my lips.

Wrinkles form on his forehead, his eyes wide with surprise. "The college girl you mentioned?"

I lick my dry lips. "She's actually a waitress. You know her from the club." Saying it out loud makes me wince. "Darla?"

He laughs, shaking his head. "No you're not."

"I am . . . actually."

His expression grows stern. "I can look the other way while you run about town sowing your oats with less than worthy women, so long as you're careful, but I raised you better than this."

"Better than what? It's an honest living." *More than I can say for you.*

He drops his head into his hand before meeting my stare. "I understand the appeal. She's a pretty girl, but come now. You cannot be serious about her."

In comes the guilt. It ripples through me, stealing my courage. "It's not a serious thing. But –"

He slices the air with his hand, cutting me off. "But nothing. Finish your business with her and do your job." He pushes back from the table with a screech. "I'm going to bed. I won't tell your mother about this."

Of course you won't. You barely even talk to her.

But I don't dare say it aloud. My family dynamic doesn't allow for spoken truth, only visual approval. I sulk back to my room and reach for my guitar, but its weight on my lap serves to add to the weight crushing my chest.

Finish your business with her.

My father's words roll through my head like a roulette wheel. I stare at my phone. Maybe he's right. Darla and I don't work outside of the bedroom. Our views on the world are too damn different. She sees life through a cynical lens. How can I ever make her happy?

Yet the thought of seeing her at the club and not being able to hold her, kiss her, touch her drives me insane. We can't go back to being strangers after all we've been through.

Reaching over, I grab my phone for the edge of the mattress and swipe the screen. My stomach flutters when I see an incoming message.

> **Darla:** I didn't mean to pick a fight. Sometimes arguing is easier than admitting what's bothering me.

> **Me:** What's bothering you?

The dots jump for an extraordinary length of time before her reply comes in.

> **Darla:** It's too late to talk about it now. Meet tomorrow after the bar?

Me: Yeah. I'll be there.

Chapter Sixteen

DARLA

"Hey, Cin, can I ask you something?"

Cindy flips the cap off a bottle of beer and sets it on the bar top. "Sure thing, sugar. What's on your mind?"

I rub my damp palms on the tops of my thighs. I don't know what I'm doing anymore. I've always considered myself to be strong, but Dylan has a way of breaking down all my defenses. "What would you have done if Jackson wanted to keep you a secret?"

A deep eleven forms between her brows. "Well, I suppose that depends on what you consider secret. Jackson, God rest his soul, wasn't real forthcomin' about his feelin's for me. We kinda snuck around a bit, but he never outright told me he was embarrassed by me, if that's what you mean."

I suck my bottom lip between my teeth, letting my gaze fall to the floor. Cindy dips her head to catch it.

"This about Mr. Blond?"

A quick laugh blows through my nostrils. "Dylan. And yeah, kinda." I move to the edge of the bar and start wiping a nonexistent spill to keep my hands busy. "He's so concerned about disappointing his stupid parents."

"So he's foolin' around with you in secret," she says as if reading my mind.

"I'm a jerk for letting him treat me like this, right?"

She seesaws her palm back and forth. "You're better than that. But I suppose it depends on what you're hoping to get out of this arrangement." She rests her hand on top of mine, stopping me from rubbing a spot in the finish. "If it's just about sex, then what's the problem? You're young and beautiful, may as well get all the dumb shit outta your system now. But if you think maybe you want somethin' more, welp, that's another conversation altogether."

"I don't know if I see myself married to the guy, if that's what you mean."

Cindy shrugs. "I guess you answered your own question. You deserve to have some fun."

I nod, but deep down I'm not sure I agree. I suddenly want to call and apologize to all those people I was mean to in high school. Back then I thought I was *the shit*, now I just *feel* like shit. This is karma coming back to bite me in the ass.

"Speak of the devil," she whispers, sauntering away.

I look at the door as Dylan comes through. My stomach tumbles with excitement I shouldn't be feeling. I'm no stranger to casual sex. In fact, I usually prefer it. Boyfriends require more attention than I'm ever willing to give, but Dylan brings the butterflies with him wherever he goes. All he does is smile and instantly I'm that girl doodling hearts on my notebook. Ugh. I'm becoming the kind of girl I used to mercilessly pick on.

Get a fuckin' grip, Darla.

He struts in and pulls up the closest barstool. "You almost ready to head out?"

"Still a half hour before closing." My pussy pounds with muscle memory, but tonight is different from all the others. That's not what I invited him for. I turn away from him and point at Garvin's empty bottle. "Last one for the road?" I ask.

Cindy bumps me away with her hip. "I'll get it, Garvin. Darla's off the clock."

My head whips at a full ninety-degree angle. "My shift isn't over until two."

"I'm the manager. Far as I'm concerned, it's over now."

I stand dumbfounded as she pops the top off Garvin's bottle and sets it down. "Are you sure?"

She glances over my shoulder, then brings her attention right back. "I don't know a single man who's gonna wait up until two o'clock for a fling, but that guy's been in here every night for weeks. Maybe this one's worth lookin' into." She taps my chin with her knuckle. "Go figure out what you want and report back tomorrow."

"Yes, ma'am."

I sidestep her and head to the back to grab my stuff. When I come out, Dylan's already standing by the door. He holds it open as I walk through, then falls in step as we walk into the lot. "You wanna grab some food before we head out?"

Dylan and I have fallen into a routine. He parks his car off to the side where it can't be seen from the street, then together in my truck we drive to the creek off the beaten path.

A smile tugs on the corners of my mouth. "What is it with you and feeding me?"

He shrugs. "I don't know. I'm sure there's some kind of psychobabble bullshit behind a lot of the stuff I do."

I stare up into the dim streetlamp light. "I don't wanna eat."

"You still mad?" He tucks a lock of hair behind my ear, but I shy away. Intimacy is meant for relationships, not fuck friends. He snaps his hand back and lets it fall to his side.

"You wanna do somethin' else tonight?" I ask.

He pulls his brows together. "Like what?"

"Just c'mon." I turn on my heel and head to my truck, but he doesn't follow.

"Where?"

Without breaking stride, I holler back, "I'll explain when we get there. Trust me."

The ride to our destination is short. We're both plunged into darkness as I veer off the road and pull onto an overgrown gravel path between the copse of trees hiding the moonlight. "Did you know Hell's Bend used to be called Sun Plains?"

"Really?"

"Yep." I slow the truck at an oncoming clearing split by a chain-link fence. "At the time, this was the most popular spot in town." I jump out of the truck and twist the gates to fit between them. Dylan stands on the other side. "You comin' or what?"

"Is this legal? I ain't up for spending a night in jail."

"Stop being a girl and get over here."

He rolls his eyes but ducks between the opening.

"No one today would consider any part of Hell's Bend to be a vacation spot, but for the first half of the twentieth century, that's what it was." I take his hand as I follow the trail up to our destination. "The town would almost quadruple in the summer to accommodate the tourists looking to escape the city and soak in a taste of small-town life."

"Who would want to vacation in this hellhole?"

An answer proves unnecessary as we broach the opening in the trees to a busted concrete slab with a waterless pool in the center. I close my eyes and try to picture it in its heyday. Crystal-blue water, the sound of laughter echoing through the trees, and music heard around the hill. It's been lost and forgotten since before I was born, but the remnants of pavilions, tattered shells of buildings, and pools filled with decades of neglect remain.

"It was a different place back in the sixties. Summers at Sun Plains were all the rage. So many bands on this very stage, unknowns who went on to make millions and forget about the cozy town where they got their start." I gesture to what was once a stage, now a broken wood platform with a tree growing up through the middle.

I look around, breathing in the nostalgia. Beyond the quiet road lies the ruins of a forgotten past. What was formerly a paradise is now rubble and memories degrading just a few hundred yards from the streets we live on. But those memories are nothing more than a tainted recollection of one night of horror.

A handful of overturned loungers still sit around the perimeter. Off to the side, the snack shack barely stands, yet finds the strength to keep from falling over. I don't have to bring him inside to know the remainder of Sun Valley's last visit still remains. Cups, plates, broken chairs, it all exists here to this day, left to rot like the rest of us. A shrine to my city's last breath.

"What happened?" Dylan asks.

Where I walk, he follows. I follow the path up to another clearing where a second pool sits, giving way to a view above the entire town. What used to be a slide sits off to the side covered in debris. "The seventies happened. All those shitty little homes we drove past on the way up here? Once upon a time, they were bungalows that sprung up to accommodate the vacationers. Eventually they were all purchased as private homes. I guess people loved it here so much they wanted to stay year-round and raise their families."

Dylan looks out into the city below. From way up here, it's hard to tell what lies at the bottom of the hill. It's all lights and shadows, sleepy homes blanketed in darkness. "How did you find this?"

I carefully climb the ladder that leads to the high dive. With my arms raised at their sides, I walk the plank to the end and sit. "Everyone in Hell's Bend knows the town's history."

Dylan stands at the other end, surveying the land. There's more to show, but here at the top is my favorite. "If it was so popular, why did it close?"

"By the time the eighties rolled around, tourism began dwindling. The owners hosted a festival hoping to boost profits. In the middle of the celebration, bullets rained into the crowd from a concession stand. A shoot-out ensued. A bunch of people died, and even more were hurt. I don't know if it was a gang shooting or the act of one unhinged guy. Either way, after that incident, the resort never welcomed another guest."

"Nah. I don't believe it. A shooting? That sounds made up."

I look over at Dylan. Highlighted by the moon behind him, his blond hair's ashen in the grayish light. "My mom was one of the wounded."

Dylan's expression grows serious. His lips part, but no sound emerges. I know it sounds like a tall tale that's been expanded over time, but every word is true.

"The place looks abandoned because it was. People ran for their lives and never came back. Everything that was here that day was left to rot. Property values plummeted. Anyone who had the means moved away. Sold their homes at a loss just to be able to put it behind them. The town lost everything. We're the riffraff left behind."

A shudder rolls down my spine. Thousands of people trampling over one another to escape through the only exit in an effort to avoid being shot. I can't even imagine what that must have been like.

"Is she okay now?"

I shrug. "She took a bullet to the back, but she was lucky. Sometimes I wonder if it's PTSD from that day that makes her drink the way she does."

He walks down the diving board and stops in the middle. "She drinks," he parrots in a whisper before moving down to sit beside me.

"You met my stepfather. Did ya think my mom was Carol Brady?"

He lets out a long whistle. I feel his fingers creep next to mine, then crawl over my hand and close around it. I rarely talk about my family. It's not that I'm ashamed. I love my mother very much, despite the demons living in her heart. I don't want people to think badly of her, and I don't want anyone's pity. It's strange how one piece of info leads to another and another until you're spilling your soul to a man you hardly know in the middle of an abandoned resort. I don't know why I'm revealing this much. Something about him makes me feel safe to be myself. I suppose it's because he can't think any less of me.

The low timbre of Dylan's voice floats into my ear. "I thought my family was fucked up."

I fall back against Dylan's back for support and drop my head onto his shoulder to look up at the stars. "We've all got our crosses to bear, I suppose."

He twists and sweeps his arm over my head to wrap around my back. He noses the shell of my ear, his hot breath fanning over my face. "I suppose that's true."

I tilt my head as he grazes my neck with small caresses, but for some reason I can't do this until he knows everything there is to know about me. I may be forced to hide from his world, but I don't want to hide from him. I need him to know what kind of person I am before I can let this go any further and give him a chance to run. "I'm not a good person, Dylan." The words eek from my throat as a hoarse whisper. He pulls away and thumbs my cheek, urging me to continue. "I'm a bully, a thief . . . a slut. I have an explosive temper, and I almost never apologize. I don't blame you for wanting to keep me a secret."

His hard exhale ruffles my hair. "You don't have to confess your sins to me. I'm not a priest."

Unable to look him in the face, I rest my head on his shoulder. "I want you to know what you're getting yourself into."

His fingers catch under my chin and lift. For a second, I fear he's pushing me off so he can get up and leave, but instead, he leans in and presses his lips to mine. A sweet flutter of a kiss, a promise in the dark. The breath hitches in my throat. He pulls back and touches my forehead with his. "I already knew what I was getting myself into. You're the most candid, sexy, beautiful, fucked-up girl I've ever met, and I can't stay away from you even if I wanted to."

I reply with a sigh.

He drops his hold and presses the palms of his hands into the board on either side of his hips. "So is this your seduction? Bring guys up here for a history lesson?"

A rock forms in my stomach. "You're the only person I've ever brought up here." I shove my fingers between my knees. "This is my safe spot. Whenever the world gets too loud or I start to find myself sliding into a funk, I come up here, and suddenly, my own bullshit doesn't seem so bad." He breathes out a quiet chuckle. I roll my eyes and turn toward the horizon. "Thank you for laughing at me. That makes me feel so much better."

"Hey," he says, resting his hand on my back. "I'm not laughing at you. I just . . . I . . . You seem so tough. I didn't think you had the ability to be this vulnerable."

My lip curls. "I ain't made of stone, jeez."

He brushes the hair off my shoulder and cups the nape of my neck. "Thank you for sharing it with me."

"It's a pretty spectacular place."

"It is. But I was talking about your soft side."

"Oh." I send a quick prayer out to thank God for the darkness so Dylan can't see the blush on my cheeks. With my walls down, my heart is open. I keep it impenetrable by design. If I'm not careful, he'll crawl in and nest like opossums under the porch, and I'll never get him out.

He drops his mouth to where my shoulder meets my neck, then leans on his opposite hand and pushes himself up with the heel of his shoe. "C'mon, let's climb back down."

I cock my head to look up to his towering height. "You scared?"

I slam the side of my butt on the edge, and the board bounces under his feet. He makes a t-pose to settle himself. "I'm not scared. Just a little concerned about the stability of this platform."

The sound of my giggle echoes into the night.

"Now who's laughing at who?"

"All right. I'm sorry." I pull myself off the ledge and push to a stand. "We can head back if you want."

The minute our feet touch the ground he wraps me in his arms. Another kiss on my hairline has me melting into him like butter on hot biscuits. I force myself out of his warm embrace and turn toward the exit, but his hand glides down to my forearm and stops my attempt to run from my feelings.

"Wait. My father wants me to ask out some girl to help further his career."

I shimmy my head as if trying to settle this information inside my brain. "I mean, if that's something you have to do—"

"I said no. I don't want to see anybody else." He swallows hard as I spin to face him. "You think you're a bully, a slut, and a bad person. I'm all those things, too, except I walk around as if I'm something special. When you asked me who I was, I never replied because I don't know the answer. I envy you for owning your place in this world. I've lived so long in my father's shadow that I don't even know where I belong."

His grip tightens as if he's a child clutching a balloon for fear it will float away. "The one thing I am sure of? I feel good when I'm with you. I can't explain what that means exactly, but I ask for you to be patient with me while I figure it out."

Lifting to my toes, I take both his hands and drop a chaste peck on his cheek. Tonight took a turn I hadn't anticipated. For all our bickering and petty revenge, we're both cut from similar molds — his made of gold, mine of dirt — yet our inner struggles have no monetary value. Up here, we're messed-up people finding our way, but our separate worlds get farther apart the closer we get to the road.

A blanket of numbness veils over me as I head back down to reality. I'm Cinderella running from the ball. The time's up on our evening tryst. Tomorrow morning, I go back to being a servant, while the handsome prince pretends he never met me.

Ray's belongings lie in a heap next to the trailer's front door. Inside, I walk into a crime scene of broken glass and upturned furniture. My gaze pings around the room. "Mama?" I call, stepping around the remnants of a fight gone horribly bad.

In the back bedroom, my mother's body sprawls on the bed. My heart pounds against my ribs. "Mama. You okay?" My voice wavers with concern. If he hurt her, he's a dead man.

"He's gone."

The weakness in her reply pulls me through the door. I sit on the edge of her mattress. "What do you mean he's gone?"

Hate and fear lodge in my throat. *Ray's dead.* My first thought as she sobs into the threadbare pillow. But the scene out front says something otherwise, something more sinister than death. It reeks of betrayal.

"Sit up."

I shove my arm under her chest and roll her over. She folds upward, bringing her knees to her face.

"He's been having an affair."

My jaw drops. Ew. It's bad enough that my mother sleeps with Ray, but another woman? It's disgusting. "You threw him out or he left?"

She sucks in a sniffling breath. "Does it matter?"

"Yes." It's the difference between him crawling back in and him being gone for good.

"I can take anything that man has to throw at me, but I won't stand for infidelity. I made him go." Her shoulders tremble. She hugs her legs as another round of gray tears flows from her black-rimmed eyes. "How could he do this to me?"

"Mama, you listen to me." I snatch a T-shirt from the floor and use it to wipe her sodden cheeks. "I know you don't see it now, but this is good news."

"No it ain't! I gave that man all the pretty years I had left, and look at me now! Cryin' on a broken marital bed, alone."

"You're not alone."

She lifts her head. "Who's gonna love me now?"

Shards of my heart break off in little pieces. Ray may have loved her once, but it's been a long time since he's touched her with a kind hand. I'd rather be alone than have to deal with that. "Someone out there will treat you the way you deserve, but you gotta get yourself better first."

She sniffles. "What do you mean, better?"

With both hands, I smooth her frizzled hair back from her face. She's not too far gone that she can't be saved. I believe it in my heart. "You dry out and start over."

Silent rivulets follow suit. One after another, they drip down her chin. "I don't think I can."

"Then I'll get you help."

"You're gonna lock me away?"

A sad smile sits on my lips, but it's a comforting lie. Something has to change. She can't live like this anymore. *We* can't live like this anymore. Ray being gone is the first step. I'm taking back control of our lives. "Rehab, Mama. There's a state-run facility not too far from here. I'll make a call first thing."

She shakes her head, lowering her gaze. "No. I-I don't wanna do that."

My fingers catch under her quivering chin. "I know you don't. But it's the best thing for you right now."

Terror clouds her vision, but she nods.

She lies back as I bring the sheet up over her lithe body. "Tomorrow is a brand-new day." I slide off her bed and bend at the waist to kiss her temple. "We're gonna get through it together."

As I turn to leave, she takes my hand. "Love you, sugar bean."

"Love you too, Mama."

With that, I flick off the light and wander back out into the hurricane that swept through our home.

"What a mess," I say with an audible sigh. I open the bathroom door, grab the broom that hangs on the back, and get to work.

Morning light crests the horizon. With the house returned to its normal order, I plop onto the kitchen chair and rest my head on the table. I'm not going to make it through work today. I'm blind with exhaustion, but more than that, I need to stay close to home. My mom needs me.

I yank my phone from my pocket and flip through my contacts to find my boss.

Me: Sorry for the short notice, but I had a family emergency and won't be able to make it in. Let me know if you have trouble covering my shift and I'll make some calls. Thanks.

After sending the text, I chuck the phone. It slides across the table as I drop my head onto my arms. Seconds later, it dings.

Dylan: What emergency? What happened? Are you alright?

I stare at the message in my hand, my tired brain unable to compute what's happening. Flipping back to my contacts, I realize my error. *Dylan* and *Eddie* sit side by side in my address book. In my haste to get out of my shift, I must have hit the wrong name.

Me: That was meant for someone else.

Dylan: But are you okay?

Emotion stings my eyes. For the first time in my life, I don't know the answer to that, but I put on a brave face. Fake it till you make it, right? If I act as if I'm strong enough to handle this, eventually I will be.

Me: I'll be fine, thanks. Mom and Ray broke up. It

was a rough night.

Dylan: Yikes. What now?

Me: Now, she has to get sober and be an adult.

Dylan: Good luck with that

Me: I can't tell if you're being sarcastic or sincere, but I'm too tired for another lesson in empathy.

Dylan: Sincere. I know how stressful it is to be the one parenting your parent. It sucks.

Me: ?

Dylan: Never mind. Grab some rest. Let me know if you need anything.

Me: Thanks.

Flipping back to my contacts again, I manage to text *Eddie* this time, before dropping to my bed.

Chapter Seventeen

DARLA

T HE LOBBY AT BEST Self Center for Rehabilitation reeks of antiseptic and rotten flowers. After the pre-admission interview, Mama put up a fight to come. In the end, we made a deal. If she can make a sober day on her own, I'll cancel the intake.

She failed.

Now she sits beside me worrying her hands raw as we wait for her to be admitted. Rocks sit in my stomach. The website made the facility look so clean and new. They boasted yoga classes and a beautiful fountain out front, but sitting on this wobbly chair, I have a feeling this place is nothing as promised. I hate the thought of leaving her here.

The sandy-beige paint may be soothing, but it does little to detract from the poorly constructed cinder block walls. I suppose real drywall wasn't in the government's budget.

Dylan immediately springs to mind. With his father in office, he could do a lot of good. Politicians have always favored the wealthy over the everyday masses. The rich stay rich so the poor stay poor. Nobody has ever made a difference. It's always empty promises with no follow through. But Dylan is different. I think he could be the one to make a real change in the system.

"Grace Bronson?"

"Mama, that's you," I whisper, touching her forearm with my fingertips.

She looks around as if she's surprised to be here. My heart aches thinking she hates me for making her do this, but it's the only way. Once she's working with a clear head, she'll realize it was for the best. A small blip in the course of a blacked-out life. She stumbled in a drunken mess, but soon enough she'll walk out of here a new woman ready to face the day.

As we rise, I hold her duffel bag in a white-knuckle grip. If I had the means, she'd be anywhere but here. A beautiful place with gorgeous furnishings and delicious meals. A real facility where she could get well the way she deserves. But that's not our reality.

Government-funded people end up in government-funded hospitals. Case closed.

The orderly grins. He pulls a pen from the pocket of his scrubs and jots some notes on a clipboard. "How are we feeling today?"

Mama snaps, "Like I been chewed up and spit back out."

With a full, fake smile, I hand over her bag and lean in for a hug. "You're gonna be fine, okay? Call me as soon as you're out of detox."

"Ima make you proud, sugar bean. Like you've always made me."

Blinking back tears, I watch her shuffle through the doors and disappear from sight. It's for the best, I tell myself, although I'm not convinced. I don't think I will be until I'm bringing her home again.

My eyes glaze over as I ride the miles down the highway. For a moment, I consider staying right to the end. A straight shot through Oklahoma and Kansas City, all the way up until I reach the Great Lakes. Leave it all behind and start over. A new place, a new life. I could be anyone I want to be.

But the dream is fleeting. Texas is the only place I've ever known. I was born here, and I will die here. Darla Burke, a girl who peaked in high school. I'll eventually settle down with a husband I hate, a couple of kids I hate, a life I hate. That's my fate no matter how hard I try to change it.

The truck idles outside the trailer, but I don't go in. Loneliness grips my throat in a vise. I don't have the energy to face it right now. I pick up my phone to make a call and find an unread text message waiting for me.

Dylan: Good luck today

Chills scurry down my spine. I hit reply and start typing out a message.

Me: I hated leaving her there. Tell me I did the right thing.

Dylan: You did the right thing. She's lucky to have you.

Me: Then why do I feel so damn hollow?

Dylan: Was it really that bad?

Me: Worse

Dylan: Anything I can do to help?

Me: Come take my mind off it?

Dylan: Boone's for lunch?

Me: I was thinking something more along the lines of getting hammered at The Great Notch.

Dylan: Day drinking? Isn't that a little ironic considering the circumstances?

Me: You can come with me or not, but I'm going regardless.

Dylan: I'm on my way

Darkness pulls me inside the quiet bar. During daytime hours, the place is dead, save for a few stragglers in the corner. Cindy's shift doesn't start for another two hours. I could probably coerce a few drinks out of her, but Pete is another story. I'm not sure the owner is willing to risk losing his liquor license to serve an underage girl, but I'm willing to take my chances.

He looks up as I enter. "Hey, Darla. You ain't on the schedule today."

"I know." I saunter all the way to the end of the bar and take the last stool next to the wall. "Any chance I can get a beer? Been a hell of a day."

He runs his hand down his chin and pulls his beard into a point. "You know the answer to that."

"C'mon, man. Can't you throw me a bone just this once?"

He presses his hairy knuckles on the bar and leans in. "Once is all it takes to shut me down."

I cock my head. "Get a lotta cops in here, do ya?"

He rolls his eyes.

"The place is basically empty. I look twenty-one anyway."

Deep laughter rumbles in his chest. "No you don't."

I lean back on the stool, crossing my arms in a huff. "I've had a string of very bad days, and all I need is a breath and a beer. Please, man, have a heart."

In the midst of my begging, Dylan blows in like the afternoon breeze. He's fresh from work, his pink polo pressed and perfect. I hate it. The refined Dylan Masters he shows the world is not the casual one reserved for me. He swaggers to the stool beside me and takes a seat. "You order yet?"

"No. And it ain't from lack of trying!" There's a clipped edge to the statement meant to sound sarcastic.

Ignoring me, Pete gestures his chin at Dylan. "Got ID?"

Dylan lifts half his ass off the seat to extract his wallet, then throws his ID on the counter. At least one of us gets to drink. If I'm lucky, maybe I'll be allowed to lick the foam from his lips. He looks up with a shit-eating grin. "Two Buds, please."

Pete lifts a brow. "You gonna drink both?"

"Yup," Dylan replies without missing a beat.

Pete pops the tops off two bottles and sets them both in front of Dylan. "Why don't you go drink 'em at the table in the far corner?"

"Will do." Dylan takes both bottles and moves to the bar while I mouth a silent, "Thank you," to Pete.

I choose a chair with my back to the bar. The cold brew pops on my tongue. I hold it in my mouth for a split second before letting it wash down my throat. A satisfied sigh follows.

"Do you want to talk about it?" Dylan rolls his untouched beer between his palms.

I pause to think before answering. "It was horrible. She just looked so damn terrified. Like I was throwing her to the dogs or something. And the place itself is a total dive. I tried to make the best of it, you know? Pointed out all its good features, but the truth is these state-run places are a joke. I'm not even sure putting her there was the right decision."

Emotion claws up my neck, but I swallow it down with another gulp. He reaches across the tabletop and threads our fingers. "I'm sure it's not that bad."

I scowl. "You didn't see it. I felt like I was leaving her in a prison. I know she hasn't been the best mom in the world, but she's all I have." I lower my gaze, forcing back tears that threaten to fall.

"That's not true," he says, cocking his head to catch my gaze. "You still have Shyanne and Savvy." The low timbre of his voice falls hoarse.

"Me."

"Do I, though?" I ask, peeking up through my lashes.

He takes a small sip. "As much as I can give."

My heart sinks. In the movies, this would be the moment he sweeps me in his arms and makes everything better, but real life is uglier than fiction. He's a star in the sky, beautiful and bright. He disappears with the sun, but for those brief, shimmering moments in the dark, he's all mine.

When I empty the bottle and set it in the center of the table, Dylan slides his in front of me. "You don't want it?" I ask.

"You seem like you need it more than I do."

"You know what we need?" Pausing, I take strong pull on my drink. "Music. Got a couple of bucks for the jukebox?"

He digs a few dollars from his pocket and hands it over. I wander to the old-fashioned juke in the corner, feed the cash into the slot, and make my choices. Lights brighten all around it as Cam's voice filters through the speakers.

With my hands on the top, I close my eyes and tip my head back. A beer and a half on an empty stomach made my head feel light. I warble along with the words under my breath. They seep into my heart, speak to my soul, allow me to forget myself for the smallest moment in time.

Dylan comes behind me. I smell his scent before feeling his hands wrap around my waist. Taking me in his arms, he twists me around, moving his hips to the slow, melodic beat. His heart thrashes close to mine. I wish we could stay like this forever. Locked in his gaze, whirling around the floor until the sun pushes out the night and we return to nothing but whispers in the morning air. I know this thing between us can never work, but we're together now, and that's all that matters.

He leans in and whispers in my hair, "Someday, we'll dance like this beside the ocean, the sand in our toes and the salty breeze blowing around us."

His sweet words wash over my heart. I close my eyes and imagine us there, the waves crashing against our bodies, bestowing us with all its power. A world where I can disappear into him and never say goodbye.

The thud of the door breaks my fantasy. I'm back in Hell's Bend, in this shittastic bar surrounded by the stink of my own reality.

"Darla?"

The sound of my name steals my gaze and brings it to the guys congregating near the bar. I step back from Dylan's embrace. This can't be happening.

"What are you doing here?"

"Summer break."

My stomach tightens. That means they'll all come crawling back like ants. Those who've bullied me, those I've bullied. Pieces of my past I'd prefer to keep hidden, a reminder of the girl I've tried to escape.

Casper gestures his chin toward us. "Who's your friend?"

"This is Dylan. Dylan, this is Casper and Wade. They graduated with Shyanne."

Wade's eyes widen. "Holy shit, Shyanne Delaney? How's she doin'?"

"She's all right. It was good seein' you guys." I take Dylan's hand and sulk back to our table like a lamb hiding from the slaughter. "I'm gonna need another beer."

"What was that about?" he asks, his voice a low rumble.

I rest my elbow on the table, using my hand to shield them from my peripheral. "That is a section of my past I'd rather not revisit."

When the door opens again, I wince. Dylan goes to get two more Buds. I sit like a stone pretending I don't hear the murmured voices floating in from behind me. I learned early on that you're either the aggressor or the victim. I could leave, slink out like a battered fawn, or hold my head high as if it don't bother me. Fake it till ya make it.

I choose the latter.

The second Dylan sets my drink in front of me, I bring it to my lips and suck down half in a single gulp. "I see you haven't lost your touch." Laughter surrounds Casper's shot.

I twist around and flip the finger. "Go fuck yourself."

"You can help me with that later." Another wave of chuckles rounds the table. Four of them now, making jokes at my expense.

"Should we go?" Dylan's voice, smooth as caramel.

"No. Forget those guys."

"Okay. You let me know."

Alcohol flows between us. Cindy relieves Pete like the changing of the guard. I lift my hand in a two-finger wave, and she calls me over. "Pete know you're in here drinkin'?"

A cotton coating covers my thick tongue. I run it over the roof of my mouth, hoping to file it flat but end up giggling instead. "Um. Hard to say?"

She blows a heavy breath over her face, making the fallen tendrils around her forehead dance. "I'm cuttin' you slack 'cause of your ma, but this can't be a regular thing."

"Yes, ma'am."

She gestures to the table of guys in the back. "That the kid Jace beat up in the eighth grade?"

"Casper Wiley, that's him." My teeth clench. Despite the two-year age difference, Jace caved in Casper's face when he blabbed to everyone at school what happened between us. A single punch that landed Jace a week's suspension.

Her pointed gaze narrows. "I never got the whole story, but I gleaned that it had somethin' to do with you."

I nod.

"Finish up with your friend and be on your way, ya hear? Place is gettin' busy. I can't have you in here drinkin' underage."

"Yes, ma'am."

I spin on my heel to return to my seat, scowling at the table as I pass. Wade yells, "C'mon, Amtrak, I thought we were friends?"

I throw up my hands. "Have y'all grown up one iota in the past several years?"

Casper erupts in a fit of laughter. "Oh my God, Amtrak! I forgot about that! Fuckin' brilliant!"

Rolling my eyes, I turn away and fall back onto my chair.

A flush creeps across Dylan's cheeks and forehead. He licks his lips, kneading his bottle between his palms again. He's not stupid. It's obvious how I've earned the nickname, and it involves half of the guys sitting at that table.

His stare moves over my shoulder, a veil of anger darkening his light eyes. "Excuse me a sec."

He gets up slowly, his chair sliding backward with the motion. I watch as he steps to Casper's table and leans in on both hands. "I think you owe Darla an apology."

"For what?" Casper's head lolls back as he looks up. "It's all in good fun. She knows that."

"Look, I don't know what happened between y'all back in the day, but I suggest you let it go."

Casper's amusement sobers. "Oh yeah, homo? You and your pink shirt gonna do somethin' about it?"

Dylan's reaction time is slow. He plays it off, making it seem as if he's backing away, then strikes like a cobra. In a lightning flash, Casper's out of his seat and up against the wall. His shirt tangled in Dylan's fists, he wriggles for freedom.

His friends jump to attention. Dylan clips Wade with his elbow as he comes around to pull him away. Wade stumbles into the table, knocking it onto its side with a crash. One friend goes to his aide, while the other jumps on Dylan's back.

Dylan grasps him by the collar and flips him forward. He flies into another table, but Dylan doesn't stop to watch the wreckage. He swings back around and takes Casper by the throat. Red rage darkens his face as he grits through his teeth. "You will stay away from Darla from this moment on. You got that?"

Sirens scream in the distance. My wild gaze pings around the room. It stops on Avery Decker—the guy who ran to Wade's side—holding his phone against his ear. Panic rages up my chest. "Did you call the cops?"

"Your boyfriend's a fuckin' psycho," he cries.

Uniformed officers burst through the doors. They wrench Dylan back by his arms. Casper falls, sucking in air as the color returns to his face, but I don't stick around for the aftermath. I run after them as they drag Dylan into the parking lot. The last thing I hear is Casper's ragged voice threatening to press charges.

Lights flash, red and blue. Everyone inside the bar oozes through the double doors to see Dylan shoved in the back of the car. "Wait!" I yell, bringing my fist down on the glass.

The car screeches to a stop and one of the cops lowers his window. "I suggest you clear the premises, miss. I don't want to have to haul you in, too."

"This isn't what you think it is!"

"Stand back, please." The car pulls away as I stand there stunned. If I run down to the station and they smell the beer on my breath, they'll know I've been served underage. As much as I want to go after him, I can't do that to Pete and Cindy. I'm stuck. There's nothing I can do but sit here and wait and hope he returns.

Chapter Eighteen

DYLAN

SITTING ON A FOLDING chair with the Hell's Bend PD was not my intention when I left the house today. Yet here I am, legs sprawled before me, my head resting against a concrete wall boasting fliers of missing children.

Do I regret what I did? Not even a little bit. We've all done shit we aren't proud of. Darla doesn't deserve to have it thrown up in her face by a bunch of redneck assholes like that.

I glance at my watch. It's 10 p.m. "Do I get to make a call or what?" My voice echoes across the quiet station. I lean in, waiting for an answer that doesn't come.

Footsteps clack along the floor. I sit up straight, hoping an officer has come to let me go, but my heart sinks into my stomach when I see my father's face coming toward me. "Get up," he growls under his breath.

My living nightmare unfolds as I push to my feet. In retrospect, I should have expected this. My father has been a large contributor to law enforcement for years, and these stupid cops aren't about to bite the hand that feeds them.

No, that's my job apparently.

He greets them all and shakes their hands, spouting generic non-sense like *keep up the good work* while I trail him like a frightened puppy with its tail between its legs. He doesn't say another word until we're in the front seat of his Cadillac.

"You disappoint me."

"What else is new?"

"Choose your words wisely, Dylan."

"Can I tell you what happened before you lose your mind?"

The dam breaks on his calm demeanor. "Lose my mind? You assaulted three men. What the hell were you even thinking? You should consider yourself lucky the police department worked as quickly as they did to assuage the situation before it got out of hand."

"I had it under control."

His head twists on his neck so fast I'm shocked it doesn't screw right off. "Under control? It shouldn't have happened in the first place! If this gets out to the media . . ." He takes a strong breath and blows it out hard, his placid tone returning. "How am I supposed to convince people I can run an entire country when I can't even manage my own son?"

"I'm a grown man, Dad. I make my own choices."

"Yes, and they're bad," he snaps through gritted teeth.

I press my lips together, watching the lights fly by like the thoughts in my head. When I was younger, I idolized my father. He was intelligent and strong, the kind of man who could make a change in the world. He wanted to help people, and I wanted to be just like him.

But I was brainwashed. I'm starting to see things the way they are. Money, power, status . . . He doesn't care about anyone. It's nothing more than the glitter of the almighty dollar. It doesn't matter how rich you are when your heart is black.

"Didn't I tell you to end things with this girl?"

His words are a punch in the gut that makes me wince. My hands ball into fists at my sides. I need to put some distance between the old man and me before I do something I'll regret. When he swings into the driveway, I fling the door open before he's come to a complete stop.

"Don't you walk away from me! I'm not finished."

"Well, I'm finished." The echo of my shout reverberates through the trees.

He slams the door and rounds the hood. I turn on my heel, but he catches up to me as I go inside. "I am still your father, and you will respect me."

"What about your respect for others?"

"I respect those who stay in their lane."

"You disgust me," I snarl.

Gray brows pull together. "Everything I do is for this family. Everything."

My jaw drops. "You don't give a shit about us. You never did. You only care about how we're perceived. You use us to get ahead in your career. We aren't a family, we're props."

"How dare you speak to me like that?"

My heart riots in my chest. It pounds against my ribs so hard I'm dizzy. I've never spoken to my father like this. I've always gone along with everything he said. I followed him blindly, convinced he would lead me in the right direction, but that was a stupid childhood fantasy. He's not special. He's a sad old man holding on to his status in a white-knuckle grasp. "If you really cared, you'd have taken care of your wife instead of pursuing a higher office and spending three-quarters of your life away from home."

Darkness seeps over his expression like a cloud of smoke. He steps closer, trying to intimidate me with his size the way he'd done throughout my childhood, but I'm not a little kid anymore. I'm as big and strong as he is, and I will no longer take a knee for fear of his wrath.

"Your mother is a good woman."

Emotion creeps its way in under the fire of my rage. I push my hair off my forehead and tuck it behind my ears, pushing it down from the surface. "She is, and you abandoned her when she needed you the most."

He lifts his chin, pinching his lips. "I don't know what you're talking about."

"She died alongside Caleb, and you left her to rot." The tears I'd been denying find their way to my eyes, but linger at my lash line. Men don't cry. Another rule I've been raised to obey. My father and I sat dry-eyed at Caleb's funeral. Even as they lowered his body into the ground, I kept them inside until the moment I was alone. Forced to grieve my brother in silence.

"You were just a boy. What do you know?" He waves me away as if I'm an annoyance.

"I was!" I pound at my chest to drive my point. "I was a scared, sad little boy dealing with death and making sure his mother and sister were fed while you were off playing golf. We needed you. *I* needed you, and all you thought about was yourself."

His nostrils flare. "Caleb was—"

I slice the air between us, my tone softening. "Caleb was a kid trying to break free from the suffocating bubble you forced us to live in. If you stopped for two seconds and looked, you'd have seen that."

My words knock him down a peg. "Your brother's death wasn't my fault."

"Maybe not." I shake my head. "But a son in the ground is less embarrassing than a son in rehab, isn't it? And now you have the nerve to stand on your grand platform preaching about drug prevention and reigniting the values of the American family when you've done nothing to acknowledge your own."

"Caleb fell into the wrong crowd. What's so wrong about using his death to prevent it from happening to others?"

I throw my hands up. "Wrong crowd. Do you hear yourself? Caleb *was* the wrong crowd. That girl he was with wasn't the catalyst, she was collateral damage. Maybe before judging people, you should make an effort to immerse yourself in their situation and see how the other half lives."

An evil laugh bubbles from deep inside his belly. "Is that what you're doing? Rolling around in the mud to see what it's like down in the hollow?"

"Watch it."

"I am watching it. I'm watching you crash and burn just like your brother, running after skirts in the dirt. I've given you everything. I've worked my ass off to pave the road for you, and what do I get in return? Disrespect. Political leaders don't rumble with poor white trash."

A sharp breath hits my lungs. "Don't talk about her like that."

"I will continue to say it until you get it through your thick head. You don't make a relationship with a girl who's only worthy of a one-night stand."

I shove my hands in my pockets to keep from lashing out. I've done enough fighting for one day. It's a waste of breath. If he wasn't such an elitist scumbag, he would see what I see whenever I look at her. Yeah, she's beautiful with a body that would turn any man's head, but Darla is so much more than how she looks. She's remarkable, unstoppable in her pursuit to gain some footing despite people like us constantly trying to kick her down. She is a pure soul trying to live her life as honestly as possible. No motives, no agenda. Being with her has changed me. She's shown me the world from a whole new perspective, a chance to see it through her eyes, and I can't go back to the way things used to be. Darla made me want to be a better man.

"You will have nothing to do with any of these people ever again."

This is pointless. I can't make him understand what he's unwilling to comprehend. I step around him as I head for the door.

"Where do you think you're going?" he asks.

Standing at the threshold of the house, I pause to reply. "First, I'm going to get my car. Then I'm going to find Darla and make sure she's okay."

"You're throwing your life away."

"That's where you're wrong. I'm finally starting to live it."

The Uber driver slows to a stop outside The Great Notch Inn. Darla's truck still sits in the lot, lonely under the single streetlight. My Mustang's on the other end, hiding in the dark. I poke my head between the front seats. "Can you wait a sec?"

"Yeah," the driver says with a curt nod.

I let myself out and stop at my car. In the glovebox, a small parcel sits in the corner. I shove it in my pocket, then canvas the lot, yank the heavy door, and peer inside. Cindy chucks a thumb over her shoulder. "She's in the back," she offers without being asked.

Twisting around, I wave to the driver to leave, then enter the space. The usual crowd sits around the bar. No sign of the college boys or my fight remains. Guilt stews in my belly. Those guys had it coming, but Darla doesn't need me to go all alpha male and fight for her honor. She is capable of handling herself. That's one of the things I love about her most. Her strength.

My shoes pad across the worn wooden floors to the office in the back. I knock on the door and wait. "Yeah?" Her voice filters through and wraps itself around my heart. I turn the knob and push it open. She scrambles from her seat and wraps her arms around me, the sweet scent of her hair pulling me farther into her embrace. "I'm sorry," she whispers.

I take her by the shoulders and gently push back. "You have nothing to be sorry about."

Her mouth turns down. "I should have left when they came in instead of trying to make it seem like it didn't bother me." Her gaze drops to her feet as she falls back on the edge of the desk. "When I was younger, I got a little drunk at a high school party and ended up screwing half the Hell's Bend football team. One by one. That's how I earned the nickname Amtrak. Everyone gets a ride." She crosses her arms over her chest as if shielding herself from the cold. "I ain't proud of it, but I did it, and I know that's the kind of shit that makes me a liability in your career, so if you wanna leave, that's fine."

I take her face in my hands. "I'm not going to shame you for having a past. We've all done things we aren't proud of." A wry grin tugs at my lips. "I once beat up three guys in a bar for picking on my girlfriend."

Her expression grows soft around the edges, her liquid blue gaze latching onto mine. "Your girlfriend?"

I feel the box pulse against my leg. I reach into my pocket and pull it out. "I got this for you when you first told me about your mom, but there was never the right time to give it to you."

The jewelry store insignia is lasered into the fuzzy surface. She stares at it in my open palm. "What is it?"

"Open it and find out."

Her gaze pings to me, then comes right back to the box. She pauses for a beat before reaching out with tentative fingers, as if she's disarming a bomb instead of opening a gift. She flips the lid and gasps.

The small diamond-studded pendant glitters in the fluorescent light, a platinum eye with a sapphire iris on a delicate chain. I pluck it from the insert and let it dangle from my fingers. "In ancient times, the evil eye was said to ward off curses and bring blessings and positive energy at the same time. It's kind of a lucky charm, protection against the negativity surrounding whoever wears it." Working the tiny clasp with my thumbnail, I manage to open the lobster claw and separate the chain. "It will watch over you."

She stares at it, draped over my fingers, the eye swinging back and forth as brilliant and blue as hers. It's nothing fancy, but when I saw it, I thought of her. Simple, yet beautiful all the same. Her throat moves. "How much did that cost you?"

"It doesn't matter."

She touches my wrists with her warm fingertips. "It does. You have all the money in the world. You could use it to help people, but instead you waste it in a jewelry store. For someone like me, it's food, rent, gas . . . A real rehab for my mother." She lifts her hand to the eye to hold it steady in her palm. "It's beautiful. And I know your heart is in the right place. I appreciate it more than you'll ever understand, but it's a symbol of everything that keeps us from being together."

Chills shudder down my arms. "That wasn't my int—" I stop myself and rephrase my words in a way that comes off less abrasive. "I'm sorry if my intentions impacted you poorly. I didn't mean for it to upset you." I latch onto her liquid gaze and speak with my heart instead of my head. "All you do is work and worry about everyone else. You deserve something that's just for you."

Her lips quiver. She runs her fingers through her long hair and lifts it off her shoulders as she turns around. Baby hairs curl around the nape of her creamy neck. Her smooth skin beckons to me. I have to physically restrain myself from pressing my mouth against it as I slide the delicate chain around her neck and fasten it closed. "I just want you to be happy."

I look at Darla, and those shimmering blue eyes hold me hostage. I can't bring myself to look away from her. It's like this all the fucking time I'm around her.

"Good," I say, unsure of what I can tell her after that. The necklace was a small token of . . . What? I don't know. My feelings. Maybe.

The pendant glitters at the hollow of her throat, her mouth pressed a tight-lipped grin. "I'm happy." I half expect her to say she's going to give it to charity or sell it. But instead, she pushes up onto her tiptoes and kisses me again, her body leaning into mine. This isn't a thanks for the necklace kind of kiss. Her tongue dances along mine, and my thoughts of anything innocent fly out the window.

I wanted to talk to her, but this right here I did not expect. My hands trail down her arms, and when I grip her hips, I pull her toward me. My thumbs hook into the loops of her denim shorts, and I know she can feel how hard I am for her. I'm in constant need of this woman.

"We can't," Darla murmurs against my mouth, and I pull away and look at her.

"Lean back," I order without a second thought.

"Dylan—"

"Darla," I throw back before dropping to my knees. My fingers move to the zipper of her shorts, and I tug it down, then undo the button. Sliding them down her supple legs, along with her panties, I smile when I inhale her scent. She's so fucking gorgeous, every part of her.

"You know that there are customers out there," she warns as I discard her bottoms on the floor beside me. Then I help her onto the desk before I spread her thighs and once again kneel before her. I'm going to enjoy this. My hands land on the inside of her thighs, and I lean in to taste her. "Fuck," Darla hisses when I run my tongue over her pussy, her arousal coating it in the most delicious taste. She's an oasis to me, and I've been lost in the desert for far too fucking long.

"You're delicious, pretty girl." I dip two fingers into her tight, wet cunt. My cock throbs. I'm dying to thrust into her, deep and hard, but I need to savor her, savor this moment between us, and enjoy the sweet flavor of her pleasure. It's always been about her. Making her happy, making her feel as good as I feel whenever I'm with her. I want to drown in her soft sighs and throaty moans, relishing in the knowledge that it's me that makes them happen.

With my fingers fucking her, I flick my tongue over the piercing, causing her hips to undulate. Her one hand grabs my head, her fingers tangling in my hair as she pulls me closer.

"Fuck, Dylan, yes," Darla murmurs. Her voice low and hoarse as she takes her pleasure from me. I allow her to move. Looking up, I can't help but enjoy the look of bliss on her face. Her eyes closed, her head tilted, a pink hue spreading across her creamy skin.

When she opens her eyes, those blues land on me. "You're going to . . ." Her words fail her when I add a third finger, dipping deep inside her wetness. The sounds of her moans, and the wetness dripping from her body make my cock weep with need. I have to be inside her, but this is about her. I want to make her come first.

I graze my teeth over her clit, suckling it into my mouth as I finger-fuck her harder, faster, and then I crook my fingers to massage that spot inside her that has her thighs trembling on either side of my head.

With a harsh vise-like grip on my hair, she twists until the sting burns my scalp, but I don't stop until she's shuddering and calling my name. I'm pretty sure everyone who's in the bar can hear her, but I don't give a shit; she's mine, and I want the world to know it. Her flavor is like a drug to me. I'll never get tired of tasting her.

A soft knock rattles the door. "Everything all right in there?"

Cindy's quiet voice makes her body still. "Yeah." She pauses, gulping a breath into her lungs. "We'll be out in a minute."

Cindy's footsteps move across the outside floor, then grow quiet as she walks off. Darla giggles. "Maybe this is a bad idea."

My solid cock throbs with need to be inside her. This love-hate relationship isn't good for either of us. If I were a better man, I would walk away from her, give her her life back. We didn't expect this to go on for as long as it has, but now I'm not walking away. I can't deny my feelings for her.

I push to my feet and cup her face in my hands. Holding her steady, I lean in and kiss her. She laps at the flavor of her juices on my tongue, on my lips. Knowing she can enjoy the deliciousness of her arousal the way I did causes a groan to rumble in my chest.

"You like the taste of yourself on me?"

She nods.

"I'm going to fuck you, Darla. When I walk out of this office, everyone will know the beautiful bartender is mine."

Those deep, intense orbs of blue look up at me. "I didn't expect this," she whispers, a soft smile curling her lips. Darla isn't a meek girl. She's strong and fiery, and she fights for herself. She doesn't need a hero, but I need to be one. She has to accept that I will protect her with all I have.

"I'll always take care of you," I tell her as I swipe my thumb over her lips. "I'm not going anywhere."

I step back and undo my jeans. Darla reaches for me and strokes the shaft. I moan her name.

"I like the power I have over your pleasure."

I can't help but smirk at her. "Of course, you do." I didn't expect anything less. She pulls me closer by my needy fucking cock, and I watch in awe as she spreads her thighs for me to fit between.

And then euphoria. Her warmth, her wetness, it pulls me into her, and I can't let go. I grip her hips and pull her closer to the edge of the desk. My cock already snug inside her, and I thrust all the way in.

"Jesus," I hiss through my teeth as I fill her cunt all the way. "You feel good."

A satisfied little smile plays on her lips, but her body heats like a furnace. "If you're not going anywhere," she says as she looks up at me, her body accepting me fully. "Then I'm not either." I pull out gently, then slam back in. Gripping her hips, I don't stop because I can't. Moving back before fucking her deep. "Even if you did." I annunciate each word slowly and methodically as I fuck her. "I would find you because, pretty girl, you're mine now. And I don't take kindly to losing."

The sound of the desk scraping over the floor echoes along with her moans of pleasure. Our bodies move in sync. She clutches the lip with one hand while her other arm hooks around my neck. She pulls me closer. I lean in to kiss her. Our tongues intertwine as I feel her body clench and quiver.

My orgasm swirls, but I hold it back. "Fuck, Darla," I growl, trying to keep from letting go and ending too soon. She belongs in a bed, with white cotton linens and the ocean breeze blowing in from an open balcony. Not being loved on this filthy desk in this filthy bar in this filthy town. I want to give her everything, all she desires, but until that day comes, we have to work with what we have. And all we have is each other and this constant need humming between us.

I reach between our bodies and pinch that hardened little nub, and she cries out. Her body tightens around my dick and pulls me deep, and I can't hold back any longer.

My release pumps through me, and I can't stop the groan that vibrates in my chest. I fill Darla with my arousal, and she smiles up at me. Happiness beaming on her face as she regards me with more affection than I ever anticipated.

This will work.

It has to.

I want the world to know that Darla Burke is mine.

She falls back on her palm as I carefully extract myself from her between her trembling legs. Her glassy eyes search my face. A flush still colors her cheeks and chest. She's the picture of tattered innocence, my angel with dirty wings. The only thing I've ever wanted bad enough to fight for.

"I didn't plan that," I say.

"I know." A wry grin tugs her lips. "I did."

Resting my forehead against hers, I smile. "I think you were made for me."

"I think you're punch drunk." She pokes her finger into my belly, and I curl into a chuckle. With my pants still around my ankles, I lean in to snatch one of the several rolls of paper towels lining the rack against the wall. She spreads her thighs and lets me wipe her clean.

I've never been with a woman this intimately before. I've always been a hit-and-run. Never stuck around long enough to open myself up to another person. But Darla changed me the way opening a curtain changes a dark room. She's the light I never knew existed, and I don't want to go back to living in the shade.

Chapter Nineteen

DARLA

"DARLA, CAN YOU COME into my office, please?"

Speeding past Eddie's office, I stop short. "What's up?" I lean backward to see in the open doorway. He never closes it, insistent that we keep an "open-door policy." He's one of those managers who refers to us all as a family. You know the type. The kind that will shell out for donuts in the morning, but won't dare to pay you more money. It's such a joke. Eddie would drop any one of us in a heartbeat if there was something in it for him.

He beckons me over with a two-finger wave. "Come in. Have a seat."

A nauseous feeling stews in my stomach. If he fires me right now, I'm going to reach across this desk and smash my fist into his fat face. "Everything all right?"

He swats the air in front of him. "Yeah, yeah. Everything's great. I think you're ready to start serving at events. There's one next week I can put you on if you're interested."

"Events?" I ask, lifting a brow.

"Yeah, like weddings, parties, fundraisers. It's an extra five dollars an hour in your check, plus eighteen percent gratuity shared among the other servers."

"Are you serious?" My eyes go wide.

He leans back in his chair, steepling his hands over the mound of his stomach. "You've done good work here these past few months."

Goose bumps dapple my skin. "Thank you."

"No need to thank me. You've earned it."

Pride swells in my chest. It's a good feeling when your work gets acknowledged. It happens too infrequently in today's society. Do something wrong, however, and heads will roll. It's like that old saying, *the beatings shall continue until morale improves.*

"Put you down for next Thursday night, then?"

"Yes."

He scrawls something in the open datebook on his desk. "Great. Come in a little early. I'll have Angel give you a quick rundown on what to expect."

"Sounds great. Thank you, again." I rise from my seat and leave his office as if I'm floating on air. Fourteen an hour plus tips won't make me rich, but it certainly comes in handy. Ray's insurance should cover most of my mom's rehab stay, but I'm expecting a cost-share bill in the mail any day.

Wandering into the main part of the kitchen, I absentmindedly touch the pendant at my throat. My fingertips graze over the tiny bumps and divots, tracing the outline of the almond-shaped eye. I didn't know what to say when he gave it to me. As usual, my mouth got in the way. It moves faster than my brain sometimes, and I don't know how to turn it off. I've spent a lifetime hiding behind a barricade of curse words and snide remarks. It's always protected me from getting hurt.

Though lately, I'm starting to wonder if by deflecting the bad, I'm also keeping out the good. Things with Dylan are complicated. My head constantly reminds me that the last thing I need in my life is another hurdle, but my heart keeps telling me it's worth it. *He's* worth it. Dylan Masters might be the best thing that ever happened to me.

He broke through my carefully constructed barricade and touched me in a place I've kept well hidden. He cracked my foundation, and as a result, I'm finally letting the good trickle in.

Evenings at home are eerily quiet. On nights that I work, it's not so bad. I sneak inside in the wee hours and crawl to my bed the way I've always done. It's easy to imagine the place is still full. But times like tonight, when the sun trades places with the moon outside my single window, the emptiness cries aloud.

Legs pretzeled, I sit in the center of my bed, scrolling through the vast wasteland of social media. Sometimes I wonder why I bother. I give zero fucks about what anyone is up to, and I never post anything myself, rather silently watch as a twisted voyeur. This girl's new dance, that guy's gourmet dinner, video after video after video . . . *Flick. Flick. Flick.*

It's a mind-numbing pastime that sucks you into the void. You want to stop, but your brain craves the quick shot of dopamine, so you quietly suck up each fifteen-second gratification, mainlining the lives of idiots like a content junkie.

This generation is doomed.

I flip to my text messages and hover over Dylan's contact. His folks have been in the restaurant twice this week without him. Intrusive thoughts weasel inside my reticent mind. Is he avoiding me? Has our thing run its inevitable course? Getting thrown in jail can be quite the eye-opener. I wouldn't blame him for backing off. The skeletons in my closet are piled up to the damn ceiling. I should have known they'd all come spilling out eventually.

The sound of footsteps pulls me from my strain of sudden self-doubt. My hackles raised, I tuck my phone into my back pocket and slowly inch off the bed. I search the room for a weapon but come up short. The bat I keep handy stays in my truck. I curse myself for letting my guard down. I was sure I'd locked the door.

My false sense of safety hangs by a thread. The way I see it, I have two options. I can hide—there's nothing in this trailer worth stealing anyway — or I can fight. The latter has always been my immediate go to. This is *my* house. I don't give a shit that it's full of secondhand garbage.

But when the door to my room flies open, I stumble back with a gasp. I raise my hands as Ray stomps toward me. "The fuck are you doing here?"

Sweat stains his yellowing tee in a V that inches toward his round belly. In his fist, he crushes a letter. Holding it up, he sneers. "What the hell is this?"

I roll my eyes, but my heart thuds in my chest. "How the fuck should I know? It's in *your* hand."

He balls up the letter and hurls it in my direction. "First your bitch mother throws me out of *my* house, now she thinks I'm gonna pay for her to hang out in the lap of luxury, she can forget it!"

A curse flies under my breath. I knew I should have stopped at the mailboxes before coming in. That bill was supposed to come addressed to *me, not* Ray. I bend to pick up the envelope. With my attention elsewhere, Ray charges. Lightning cracks beneath my lids. I fly onto the bed, bouncing on the soft mattress, but a heavy weight keeps me from getting up.

A fist lands in my side. I jackknife from the pain. My forehead smacks against something hard, and I grunt. Fear grips my throat. The stink of cigarettes and stale booze wafts into my nostrils as the truth settles heavy on my limbs. I've physically fought Ray a hundred times, but I was always on my feet. With him on top of me, pinning me down with all his weight, I'm useless to defend myself.

"Get off me!" I struggle to break free, but his hold is unyielding.

"You're one of them wild horses, ain't ya? Need a good breakin' in."

Of course. The second mom leaves the house, Ray goes full psycho. The panic is all consuming. I flail blindly hoping to make contact with something. And I do.

A heavy grunt flies from his throat. He rolls over clutching his crotch. I scramble off the bed, but a yank on my hair tugs me back. My necklace pulls taut against my throat. The thick part of my skull smashes his face. I hear the sickening crack of bones, but they aren't mine. Pain flashes in my head. I roll to the floor and scramble to my feet. Without looking back, I run.

Gravel bites my bare feet, and my lungs burn. The adrenaline slows as I come to the opening of the trailer park. I fall back on the stone pillar and slowly slide until I'm sitting in the mix of dirt and weeds. My phone pushes against my ass cheek. I tilt to slip it out of my pocket. Dylan's contact still highlights the screen. Normally, I'd rather eat mud than ask for help, but I'm stuck. I have no shoes, no money. I don't even have the keys to my truck. The only thing I have is my phone and a maybe boyfriend who hasn't let me down yet.

I hit the icon, and the numbers flash. "Hey. What's up?"

The sound of his voice wraps me in comfort like a blanket just out the dryer. I reach for the pendant that hasn't left my neck since Dylan put it on and find it missing. *That fuck.* With the phone to my ear, I drop my head to my knees and sob. This is karma getting me back for all the wrongs I've done in my life. If I could go back and change them, I would, but you can't change the past. You can only work to be better going forward. I thought that's what I was doing, making up for being a shithead teenager, but we always get what's coming to us in the end.

"Darla? What happened? Where are you?"

"Can you come get me?"

Through the earpiece, I hear his engine roar in the background. "Tell me where you are."

"Come to the end of Sycamore Street?"

"I'm on my way. Hold tight."

I disconnect the call and wipe my face with the butt of my palm. Sycamore Street is off the main road, a short walk from where I live. I've always had people pick me up there instead of coming down to the park. It's easier that way.

Blood rushes my ears as I start up the road. I enable the flashlight on my phone to see where I'm going but quickly turn it off. In this neck of the woods, it's more of a calling card than anything else. I'm better off in the dark.

My heart pounds with each passing pair of headlights. I raise my arm to shield the light as the final set comes right toward me. Dylan jumps from the driver's side and envelopes me in his warmth. "What the . . .?" The low timbre of his voice cracks. He wrenches away, staring at his hands in the headlights. "You're covered in blood."

"Am I?" I reach behind and touch the spot. Slimy and warm. I run my fingers through, then bring them to the front. "Oh fuck."

He springs to action. "Are you hurt?" he asks, picking through my hair like a gorilla in the wild.

I touch my head to check for damage. Another band of emotion snaps inside me. The sound of cracking bones rings in my ears. "No. It's not mine."

"Whose is it then?"

"It's Ray's. He broke in and attacked me."

"I'll fucking kill him." He starts to move down the road, but I jump in his way. "No. Just get me out of here."

"Get in." He ushers me to the passenger side and helps me in before closing the door. As soon as he's beside me, my lungs open to allow the breath to trickle in. I close my eyes, melting into the buttery leather, the smell of his interior mixed with the masculine fragrance of him wrapping around me.

Silence swims between us. I stare out the window as he pulls off the main road and down the winding dirt to the old creek. This time of night, it's crawling with high school kids. Bonfires blaze, sending wisps of orange dancing toward the trees. It gives the lake an ethereal glow as he pulls into a quiet spot beside it.

I watch the kids on the other side, their trucks parked in a row with their tailgates down. It seems like just the other day that was me. Things felt simpler then. The family I lacked didn't matter because the family I'd chosen were all around me. A band of misfits seeking solace in each other. Misery loves company.

The entire story tumbles from my lips starting with the letter from the rehab center. Emotions roll across his expression, but he doesn't interrupt. As soon as I'm finished, he takes me in his arms again. "I'm so glad you got away." The relief in his voice settles into my chest.

"He took my necklace. I'm sorry."

Resting his palms on each side of my face, he holds me firm. "I don't care about the necklace. He can have it. I care about you."

He covers me in tiny kisses as if he can love away the pain brewing in my heart. It hurts more than any smack or kick. Anger is a feeling I'm used to. I'm comfortable with it. Love is alien. I never knew what it felt like until now, and it scares the bejesus out of me.

A piece of a conversation from weeks ago bubbles to the surface. Why it chooses now to rear its ugly head, I can't be certain, but I need to know the answer to a question burning in my brain. "A while back, at the dead pools, you told me your dad wanted to fix you up with someone and you said no. Were you telling the truth?"

His gaze grows soft. "I don't want anybody else but you."

"Is *that* the truth?"

A lazy grin rolls over his lips. Butterflies kick up in my stomach. "I'd never dreamed that I'd meet somebody like you." He drops one hand, letting the other linger. "Before you came into my life, I had it all planned out. I was going to use my connections and ride my father's coattails up the political ladder. Probably marry a groomed and proper woman, have a few kids, and end up bored to tears until I eventually die. You ruined all that. Now all my dreams consist of you."

I scowl. "Are you saying I ruined your life?"

"No," he says with a small chuckle. "I'm saying you made it worth living. I don't want that life. I want whatever life has with you beside me."

"I don't want to be the one who steals your future."

Another tear falls from my eye. He catches it as he thumbs across my cheek, my lips. "You won't steal it; you could only make it better. My entire life was wasted doing what I was told, what was expected. I don't want to waste another second."

He flings the car door open and steps out. "I don't want someone to stand behind and silently watch me succeed." Gripping the hem of his polo, he yanks it over his head and drops it on the dirt. "I want someone who'll light the match and stand beside me as we watch it all burn together." He digs a matchbook from his pocket and holds it out for me to take.

I meet his gaze before taking his offer. With the matchbook tucked into my palm, I kick open the door and step out. The yellow heap of fabric sits at his feet, the moon shining on his bare skin as I come around to his side. "This is fuckin' nuts," I say, lighting the match and letting it fall. The cotton fibers catch. A small flame flares, the smell of burning fabric rising around us. He grabs me in the shadow of the pyre and kisses me as his future turns to ash. He tips his head, stretching his arms to the sky as if worshipping his own demise.

"Torch it all," he murmurs, resting his forehead on mine.

My breath hitches as I take in what he's trying to say. It's a grand gesture with a simple meaning. He finally sees me as his equal.

I run my fingertips down his stomach, feeling the way his muscles contract under my touch. "Now you have no shirt."

"You have no shoes. I think that makes us even." His words rain warmth down upon me. That's all I ever wanted to hear. He stands tall, tucking me against his bare chest. I melt into his embrace, ready to accept his love. All the good, bad, ugly, and sweet it brings. "You know, I don't even like politics? I never did."

A small giggle escapes. "What are you gonna do instead?"

"I don't know." He trails his fingers down my spine, tracing every peak and valley with the tips. "Maybe I'll teach music."

"Poverty doesn't suit you."

I try to burrow in closer, but he holds me out to look at me. One arm still crooked around my back, he slides the hair off my temple with his free hand. "I can do anything I want to do, pretty girl. As long as you're beside me."

I envy his optimism. He's out of his mind, but my grin is uncontrollable. "You're crazy."

"Crazy about you."

I pull away, keeping my gaze trained on the dirt and soot. Looking into his gorgeous face, I find my confidence crushing to dust. "But I'm still a secret, aren't I?"

His fingers slide over the crook of my neck and under my hair, a possessive hold that turns my knees to jelly. I want to be his—completely and utterly—but underlying forces still keep us apart. "I'm stuck between a rock and a hard place here, Darla. With my father, it's complicated."

I glance up to see the shadows darken his stern expression. "What about the rest of the world? You say you're crazy about me, but I still won't be attending any dinners at the governor's table, will I?"

His grip tightens. He pulls me in again, holding me as if he's afraid to let me go. His heart pounds against my cheek. I close my eyes to the sound, the rhythmic *thump, thump, thump* matching the wild cadence of my own. The truth weighs heavy on our tender moment. Dylan is a dreamer, and I'm a realist. He may think this is what he wants, but his actions speak louder than words. I'll always be his dirty little secret.

We stay locked in each other's arms until the small blaze settles to soot. He kicks it apart to fan the smolder. "I don't think you should go back to your house tonight."

"I'll be fine."

"What are you gonna do if Ray comes back?"

A lopsided grin tugs at the corner of my mouth. "His fist is big, but my shotgun's bigger. He comes near me again, ima kill the son of a bitch."

His face falls in a *be serious* look.

"Ain't no sugar and spice up in these parts. Little girls 'round here are made of gunpowder and lead."

He chuckles. "Okay. Let's put murder on the back burner for a second."

I shrug. "Believe me, Ray took that necklace and ran. He's not coming back. I'll be okay at home."

He shakes his head. "No. Absolutely not. I'll get you a room somewhere."

A deep breath fills my lungs. "I don't need a room—"

"Non-negotiable, Darla. You're not going back there by yourself with that lunatic roaming around. I should have called the cops and had him arrested for assault."

I lift my hand with a sigh. "No cops. I'll take the room."

"Thank you." He grins. "Let's go get your stuff."

He turns and falls back into the car as my stomach hits rock bottom. Rounding the hood, I climb in beside him. He drives back to where he picked me up. "Where do I go from here?" he asks as we near Sycamore Road.

"Um . . ." I chew my lip. "Wait here. I'll go and come back."

He lifts a brow. "No. I'm not letting you go back alone. What if he's still there?"

I lift my hands. "I'll be ready for him this time."

He runs a hard hand down his face. "I know you're tough, all right? But if you think I'm letting you go in there by yourself, you're nuts."

"It's fi—"

"Darla," he barks, cutting me off. "What is wrong with you?"

I pull my quivering lips between my teeth. Emotion rushes through my chest and claws up my throat. Dylan Masters is crazy about me. He's willing to throw everything away to be with me, but all those sweet words will surely smolder like the fibers of his shirt the second he sees firsthand where I come from. "I don't want you to see where I live, okay?"

He cocks his head, his hard expression growing soft. "I know you don't live in a palace."

"No, you don't understand. You can't."

"There's a lot I didn't understand until you taught me." He sweeps his knuckle down my cheek. "Where you live is just geography. It won't change the way I feel."

A moment of silence passes as we idle in the road. I can't hide from him forever. I may as well rip off the Band-Aid and pray the wound doesn't start to bleed.

"Take a right."

My body trembles from deep inside the closer he gets to the entrance. When he passes the stone column, I instruct him through the maze of trailers until we get to mine.

"This is it," I say, my voice small and meek. Shame sits on my chest as I stare at the only place I've ever called home. I never cared about what anybody thought. I never worried about being judged. But sitting in Dylan's flashy sports car surrounded by the dregs of society, I feel unworthy of him.

He elbows the door open, then jogs around to help me out. I start to walk up, but he steps in front of me. "Hello?" he calls, but no response follows. I stay at his back as he moves through the space, his size making it feel more suffocating than it already is. A small bloodstain is the only remnant of Ray that remains.

"It looks clear. You get your stuff together. I'm gonna wait outside in case he comes back."

I nod. The second I hear the screen door slam, I plop down on the corner of my bed. It's best that he knows everything about me now. At least, that's what I tell myself, but it doesn't stop my heart from hammering against my ribs as I start to shove my clothes in a backpack.

Armed with the things I need for a single night, I meet him in the lot. "I made you a reservation at the Lone Star Motel."

Stop feeling sorry for yourself, Darla. This isn't who you are. I chastise myself for allowing self-pity to enter my heart. And just like that, the pathetic switch flips back to stone-cold bitch.

I jut my hip out, hiking the pack higher on my shoulder. "Couldn't shell out for a place without hobos out front, cheapskate? I mean . . ." I lift my arms, gesturing to the rows of trailers around us. "Clearly,

I'm used to luxury."

A wry grin tugs the corner of his mouth. "I asked ahead. They promised me a hobo-free room. You wanna follow me in your truck?"

"Yeah."

I don't bother telling him I know where the Lone Star is. Not only is it the only motel in town but it rents without a credit card or a license. It's the perfect place for underage kids to party. Suffice it to say, I've been to this dive motel more times than I can count. I could probably get there with my eyes closed, but I follow him anyway, allowing him to lead.

A few cars scatter across the open lot. Dylan and I park side by side in front of the office. Behind the desk, a person with the most impressive mullet watches a small television set up in the corner. The looks-like-a-man-but-I-think-is-a-woman barely looks up as we enter. Dylan leans both elbows on the counter. "I made a reservation on-line."

The garish light shines on the nametag over her low-hanging breasts. *Lois.* Definitely a woman. She grunts, tapping on the keyboard of the computer. "Name." She finally looks up but either doesn't register that Dylan's shirtless or doesn't care. Judging by the state of the place, I'm going with the latter. Working at a roadside motel, I'm sure ole Lois has seen a thing or two. A few abs are not going to have much of an effect.

"Masters. Dylan."

"Room twelve." She twists to swipe a key off the wall and drops it on the counter. A *real* key on a keychain boasting the motel's insignia. No flashy cards around here. That's how you know the place is old. "Fresh towels and linens are already in the room. Ice machine is on the fritz."

"Thanks," he replies. "Do you have room service here?"

Lois stares at him as if he's speaking another language.

"I assume that's a no." He lifts the key and turns back toward the door.

"You really are clueless, aren't you?" I ask once we're outside.

A wrinkle forms between his brows. "What?"

"Do you have room service?" I mock the deep timbre of his voice. "We're lucky we got clean towels." I stop outside the number twelve room and wait as Dylan unlocks the door. The room looks exactly as it always did. Brown carpet and crappy art permanently attached to the walls. Instantly, I'm transported back in time, lying on top of the shitty floral duvet while some random boy pounds away with no regard for anyone's pleasure but his own.

"Is there a problem?" he asks.

My mouth goes dry. "I have been here before, you know."

The expression on his face is unreadable. He hovers in the doorway, his icy gaze moving from me to the bed. I won't elaborate on my sudden confession, but having said it aloud tears a tiny chink in my armor. I can't possibly gauge what he's thinking right now, but the set of his jaw and his raised shoulders say everything I need to know.

"You can come in if you want." The mattress springs as I plop on the edge, hoping to make a new memory, one that's wholesome and pure. Something that serves as a reminder that I deserve to feel wanted instead of used. "Might be nice to be in a real bed for a change."

His gaze searches the room before landing on me. "I have an early day tomorrow."

I sit up. "Doing what?"

"Um." His Adam's apple bobs. He runs his hand through his hair, avoiding my stare. "My dad has a big event happening. I'm kind of the one hosting it, so . . ." He takes a single step in and drops the keys on the dresser. "I still work for him, you know?"

My chest burns. I knew this would happen. He caught a glimpse of the real me, and it's too much of a reality check. Dinner dates and truck bed hookups are one thing, but *this* isn't what he signed up for. *This* is me. A girl who comes from nothing is comfortable with nothing, but Dylan is soft. He's been pampered and protected, while I've been left to fend for myself. I've been doing it my whole life. I don't know why I assumed now would be different. "Yeah. I mean, if you have to go. I understand."

He bends at the waist and drops a chaste kiss on my mouth. "Call me if you need anything, okay? I can send over food or whatever."

Rejection stings like a swarm of wasps. He's fucked me all over town—the bar, the creek, my truck, the stables, behind the diner—but faced with an actual hotel room, he hightails it out as fast as he can. The least he can do is throw me a bone before leaving me high and dry.

I nod, unable to speak over the lump in my throat. If I talk, I'll cry, and that ain't gonna happen in front of him. I'm better than that.

He moves toward the door and then stops. My heart skips a beat. Maybe he changed his mind. Maybe he won't leave me. Maybe he'll stay and worship my skin the way he does until I'm washed of my sins and feel brand new. I know it sounds weak, but after this fucking nightmare of an evening, all I want is some reassurance that he's all in. Actions speak louder than words, and no matter how much I despise the fact, Dylan Masters makes me feel safe.

The bed dips under his weight. He cups my face and bestows me with a kiss as soft as cotton. "Are you going to be okay?"

I want to say no. I want to admit that I'm not strong enough to deal with the recent blows of my pathetic life and beg him to stay, but it's so hard to find the words lodged in my throat. Not when I've been forced to roll with adversity, to smile in the face of any hardship that comes my way. My strength is both a gift and a downfall. When push comes to shove, it doesn't allow me to be true to my feelings. "Yeah, of course."

"I don't want to leave you here."

"I'm a big girl. I'll be fine," I say it as if it's a hard truth. My entire life I hoped if I said it enough, it would become fact, but it's always been a bold-faced lie. I'm not okay. I never was.

He touches his forehead to mine. "I'll call you tomorrow."

"Okay."

"See ya." His usual goodbye.

My heart breaks as he walks out the door. I lie back, staring up at the brown spot in the ceiling tile. I want to believe him. He wouldn't have brought me out to the creek and said all those beautiful things if he didn't mean them. Right? He wouldn't have come to my rescue and taken great care to ensure that I'm safe if he didn't feel for me at least a little.

I don't know what to think, but my heart wants to give him the benefit of the doubt. Rolling over, I slide to my knees and slip off the bed. It does me no good to sit here stewing. I grab my phone and type out a quick *thank you* text, then head to the bathroom to wash away what remains of this dreadful night, but it can't hide the tears that well in my eyes or soothe the bone-crushing ache that started the second he walked out the door.

I hate him for giving me hope, for showing me love, for making me feel. But I hate myself for giving him permission.

Chapter Twenty

DARLA

Dylan: Checking in. Everything alright?

Me: Yeah. Thanks.

Dylan: I'm glad. You working tonight?

Me: Yeah, but I should be done early. You wanna get together?

Dylan: I have some family obligations tonight, but I could meet up later. I have a surprise for you.

Me: What kind of surprise?

Dylan: Well if I told you that, pretty girl, it wouldn't be a surprise anymore. I'll text you later.

Me: Sounds good.

Dylan: see ya

THE RESTAURANT WHERE I'VE worked for the past few months has been transformed. Colorful throws grace the tops of the heavy white tablecloths, expertly crafted floral centerpieces reaching toward the ceiling. American flags drape over the walls like tapestries. Patriotism rings true in the red, white, and blue.

In the corner opposite the kitchen, a DJ begins setting up his booth, and beside it, a podium set up sits under a giant banner that reads, "George Masters, Republican for the People."

"Darla, you got that?" Angel's question filters over the sound of my spinning thoughts. He and I walked the same stage at graduation, but I'm not sure I've said two words to him since grade school. That is, until we started working together.

Never thought I'd be friends with Angel Ramirez.

"What type of event is this?"

He twists his lips. It's a quirk I've seen him do a thousand times. He'll chuck me a twisted glance from across the room, and I can't help but smile every damn time. I call it his *fuck-this-shit* face. "Fundraiser."

"Oh." My body droops so low it wants to hit the floor. A chill slithers down my arms. In less than an hour, this entire place is going to be crawling with wealthy political figures . . . and Dylan. This must be the *family obligation* he mentioned. Why didn't he tell me about this? I could have been upfront and chosen to deny the job. I can't walk around this place as a domestic servant when all I want to do is run into his arms.

"So you think you got it? The menu is already set, so it shouldn't be too hard."

"Yeah, yeah. Chicken or steak, got it," I mumble, still thinking about the look in Dylan's eyes right before he walked away. A look that cried we've reached the beginning of the end.

"Tally up the orders per table. Everyone gets the same salads, appetizer, and intermezzo, then you bring out the entrée."

I let out a frustrated sigh. "Angel, I got it. It's not rocket science, okay?"

He raises his palms in defeat. "All right, all right."

I instantly feel guilty for snapping at him. He was told to train me, and that's what he's doing. My personal life is not his problem. It's best if I wipe it from my head and concentrate on work. I'll deal with it later. "Why weren't we friends in high school?" I reach into my tidy updo to adjust a bobby pin digging into my scalp.

A deep chuckle rattles in his throat. "Because you were scary in high school."

I land a playful jab on his shoulder. "I was not."

"Easy for you to say. You didn't have to share the halls with *you*."

My face falls. "Was I really that awful?"

He lifts his thumb and forefinger an inch or so apart. "But I know you now, and you're a lot nicer than I gave you credit for."

"Thank you."

He absentmindedly searches his apron pockets to double-check their contents. "High school was a different experience for me than it was for you. It's easy when you're pretty and popular. Not so much when you're a gay Mexican kid in the middle of beer country. I found it best not to engage."

My blood turns cold. No one should have to live a lie, but it's better than living in fear. The guys in our school would have brutalized him, and I likely would have piled on just for fun. I'm not proud of it, but I learned a long time ago that you're either the bully or victim. Having been on both sides of that coin, the former seemed the less painful choice.

"When did you stop faking?"

His devious smile sucks tiny divots in both cheeks. "Who says I have?"

"Thank you for trusting me with it."

He shrugs. "There's a big world out there. Once I've enough savings, I'm leaving this redneck hellhole and never coming back."

"Good plan." I fall back on the break-room counter and curl my fingers over the side. "So I gotta ask. You hooked up with a guy yet?"

Another dimpled grin lights up his face. He leans in, dipping his head as if telling state secrets. "You'd be amazed at some of the people I hooked up with."

My eyes widen. "Who?"

"I'm in no position to out anyone else. Suffice it to say, it is *dark* in some people's closets."

"We're gonna have to go out for drinks, you and I."

"Someday." His gaze rolls to the clock on the wall. "People are gonna start showing up soon. Any last-minute questions that don't involve my sex life?"

"I think I got it."

"All right. Well, call me if you need me."

"Thanks, Angel."

I run to the ladies' room one last time before the mayhem starts. Stepping from the stall, I check my reflection in the mirror as I wash my hands. If only Angel knew how alike we were. Both of us live secret lives, with love in the shadows and contempt in the light. I've gotten myself into an impossible position. I can't let Dylan give up everything he's worked for. I am quicksand. I'll inevitably bring him down, and he'll end up resenting me for it. The motel was just another screaming example of how different we are. He turns his nose up at filth; I was raised in it.

I rush back to the kitchen before the crowd begins flooding in. Boring music fills the main room. Old person music, like Kenny G. and Michael Bublé. It's the soundtrack to Eddie's constant pacing. Maître d' for the night, he's stuffed himself into a tuxedo that makes him look more like a limo driver than the guy in charge of a giant banquet consisting of the Texas elite. He lines us up and gives us a pep talk that isn't worth repeating. Bullshit about fading into the background and letting the richies do their thing. I got it. Everyone wants to enjoy the food on their plate, but no one wants to see the trashy broad who brings it.

When he claps his hands, we all scatter. The room was split between servers, each assigned a set of tables that will be solely ours for the night. I breathe a sigh of relief knowing I won't be serving the Masters' table. I'm far too new for Eddie to take that risk. With any luck, he's put me at a set of tables occupied by no one important.

Then again . . . I'm pretty sure everyone here is important. Angel told me people pay top dollar for a seat at the governor's table. It seems insane. Imagine having so much money that throwing it away to sit with some boring old coot for a couple of hours is nothing. I've been serving the guy lunch twice a week for months now, and I can tell you he isn't that interesting.

They drink and dance and socialize, a horde of big shots in black suits and sequined gowns invited for the sole purpose of writing a check. Big-haired old ladies and vapid trophy wives clinging to their husbands' arms. I hate it. I hate *them*. As the jealousy festers in my gut, another feeling begins to take hold. The familiar flight of butterflies brought on by Dylan Masters.

Dylan Masters in a *suit*, no less.

The tailored jacket pulls his narrow waist into a perfect V, showcasing the broad width of his shoulders. His hair pulled into a tight knot at the crown of his head, he shakes hands with another man, then gestures to a woman coming up beside him.

My heart leaps into my throat. Her light blond hair is twisted off her elegant neck. She wears a simple black gown, strapless, no doubt to show off her diamond-cut shoulders and yoga-toned arms. He touches the small of her back making introductions. Her smile makes my chest ache.

Beads of sweat dapple my forehead. Tell me he didn't bring a fucking date. The sound of blood rushing through my ears almost makes me miss my cue. Armed with a salad tray, I file into the room along with the others. I take a deep breath to calm my nerves. We're thirty minutes into a four-hour event, and I'm already perspiring through my blouse.

It could be nothing, I tell myself as I make quick work of setting down the plates. He didn't have to tell me about the girl his father wanted to set him up with, but he did. He even went so far as to assure me he didn't want anyone but me. Was any of it true? I can't help but wonder if that's her. The beautiful girl who floats on air while I barrel through just to be seen.

With my tray empty, I move back to the kitchen, averting my gaze. As soon as the DJ announces the first course, we'll go back out and collect the dinner orders. I have to calm down before that happens. I remind myself he was never my boyfriend. It was casual sex. A fling. I had no business letting him into my heart, but I did it anyway. I'm the fool. I let him in when I knew I shouldn't have.

Out in the main room, I try not to stare, but I can't look away. There's a comfort between them, a coziness. This isn't someone new. This is someone he's known for a very long time.

The realization rolls down my back like the goose bumps on my skin. Is *this* why he kept me a secret? He didn't want to get caught screwing around with the help? I believed him when he said he cared. I fell for his charms. *Twice.* How could I be so stupid? I may be easy, but I'm nobody's mistress. I'm not going to let him get to me. Eventually, he'll see me here, and he'll have to come clean. And when that happens, I'm gonna punch him square in his gorgeous fucking face.

I slowly canvas my tables, jotting down the entrée orders as people stuff their faces with overpriced greens. As soon as this event is over, I'm giving my notice. I can't risk running into Dylan and his too pretty girlfriend once everything's out in the open. A clean break, a chance to move on. I just have to manage getting through the night.

My gaze sweeps across his side of the room as I turn to head back toward the kitchen. Our eyes lock. The blood drains from his face, but he doesn't make a move.

Why would he pursue me with such fervor if he had someone else at home? He wouldn't take no for an answer. He chased me until I caved. He made me love him. God-fucking-dammit, I tried not to, but it came on too strong. It hit me like a storm. Slow at first, then all at once. I was powerless against it.

"Darla, second course. Go!" Eddie's voice booms in the kitchen. I bring myself back to reality and start piling the plates onto my tray. The weight of my anguish makes it hard to hold. I saunter into the room with it teetering on my palm, praying my strength doesn't give out. I keep my eyes forward. I can't look at him. I can't risk letting those gray orbs pull me into their depths yet again, but my gaze moves with a mind of its own. A quick glance that kills me faster than a bullet.

The two of them locked in conversation. She lifts her fingers over her mouth and giggles, his hand on the bare skin of her upper back. I tear my gaze away, but it's too late. I collide with a suit and drop my tray. In the slow motion of my panic, the ceramic plates crash to the floor. I cover my mouth with a gasp.

"You stupid idiot!" the old man sneers. "Don't you watch where you're going?"

When the tears start to rise, there's nothing I can do to stop them. Born of anger, they burn my throat. My jaw falls open, but my brain all but stopped. I can't think beyond the thousands of eyes poised at the stupid server who ruined this important event. The man continues his gunfire of insults. I stand like a stone, my armor open, my chest exposed. I look at Dylan, silently begging him to come to my aid, but find him turned away.

He can't even look at me.

I'm an embarrassment.

I'm nothing.

I can't do this anymore.

I step around the mess and fly through the open doors. The evening air is thick with humidity. I try to pull in a heavy breath, but it feels too much like breathing through water. Fury builds inside my chest, its hairpin trigger set to blow. No one makes a fool of me. *No one.*

The blood heats under the surface of my skin. I clench and unclench my fists, trying to work through the adrenaline infused twitch that pops up out of nowhere. I never wanted any of this. I was fine before Dylan Masters slid into my DMs, but now I'm second-guessing everything I thought I knew. It could have been me on his arm in the elegant black gown, but I'm not good enough, am I? No. I'm only good enough to fuck when no one's around.

And that asshole who thinks he could berate me in a room full of onlookers. Where does he get off thinking he can treat me like that? I'm a person, too, goddammit. I may not be as educated and well mannered, but I have a soul. I bleed when cut like anyone else.

The valet attendant sneaks around the side of the building for a smoke. I jog to the stand and pull open the door. Keys hang in neat little rows. I snatch the one with the Mustang emblem and run through the lot jamming my thumb on the fob.

The Shelby chirps. Once located, I jog to my truck, then run right back. His smell surrounds me as I slide into the driver's seat. Tires squeal on the pavement. I back it out and bring it to the front. I want it to be the first thing he sees when he comes out. A beloved car that matches the current state of my heart. A heart he ripped from my chest and stomped on in front of me.

I leave the keys in the ignition and grab my bat. A single swing takes out a headlight. Glass shatters in the pale moonlight. Adrenaline whips through my veins. I bring it round a second time. *Smash!* Webs spread across his windshield.

"You're a fuckin' liar!"

Hair falls from the secured pins. I sweep it away with my bicep before slamming my weapon into his passenger window.

"How do you like that, you piece of shit?"

Smash! His taillights explode into red crumbles.

"Crazy about me? I'll show you crazy, you son of a bitch!"

Bam! A bat-sized dent caves in his quarter panel.

"What are you doing?" The valet's wild voice carries on the breeze.

I point my bat in his direction. "You stay out of this, Ramone!" But a crowd begins to grow. Love makes a person do crazy things, and I've lost all control of my sanity. I bring my weapon down hard on his rear window, grunting like an animal and cursing his name.

"Darla! What the fuck?"

A sharp gasp hits my lungs. I whip toward the sound of my name seconds after removing his side mirror. "I should ask you the same thing, asshole!"

Smash!

I raise my arms again, but he wraps his around my middle, fighting the bat from my hands. It clatters to the ground with a heavy thud.

"What is wrong with you?" The deep timbre of his yell echoes through the night.

Whispers rush through the crowd. *What's happening? How does he know her? Who is that?*

"Go ahead, tell them who I am!" I pound my fist on his chest. "And while you're at it, tell them who *you* are! Lying, cheating, piece of human garbage!"

His grip tightens around my arms. "Have you lost your goddamn mind?" he seethes.

Worse. I've lost all semblance of myself. People pour through the doors wanting to watch the insanity unfold, but I don't give a shit. I've already been humiliated by father gray hair. I don't care who sees me now. It's time everyone knows who Dylan Masters really is. "Is she the reason you didn't stay with me last night?"

Wild eyed, he runs his hands through his hair. "Who?"

I point at the pretty blonde standing at the edge of the crowd. "Her." I slam my palms into his chest. "Did you tell your little girl-friend about me? Huh? I bet you didn't."

He stumbles back but recovers, his eyes rolling to the sky. "That's my sister. Tara. She's home from college."

She wriggles her fingers in a petite wave. "Hi. Dylan's told me so much about you."

The irate high buzzing in my head evaporates like smoke. I look around the group of judgmental faces wishing I could crawl into a hole. What have I done?

"Do you honestly think I would cheat on you after everything we've been through?" His expression falls when I don't answer. "Show's over," he calls. "Everyone go back inside." The band breaks apart and starts to filter back in.

"Then why didn't you stay with me?"

His nostrils flare, his chest puffed in smug arrogance. "I didn't stay with you because I couldn't bring myself to be another asshole fucking you in that shithole motel. You deserve better than that."

Rage turns to tears on a dime. They rush down my cheeks and blur my vision until everything swims in front of me. He takes a step but doesn't reach out to touch me. Instead, he digs in his pocket and pulls out a card.

"I booked us a real room at the Hilton in White Tail Creek for tonight. That was my big surprise."

My gaze pings from him, to the card, to the girl who suddenly looks just like him. The blond hair, the gray eyes, the plump little lips. *Fuck.* How did I not see it before?

Emotion rushes my head so fast I feel dizzy. He's not the asshole. I am. The second an opportunity presented itself, I lost all faith in him. He doesn't deserve this. And I don't deserve him. Guilt steeps low in my gut. He's done so much for me. He put his trust in my hands. He fought his family on my behalf, and all I've done in return is prove everybody right. I'm nothing but the low-class troublemaker they say I am.

"I can't do this anymore." I press my palms against my eyes to stanch the flow, but it keeps coming. An unstoppable flood that will surely drown us all. "Look what you've done to me!"

"What *I've* done to *you*? You humiliated me in front of my entire family. You destroyed my car on a fucking whim."

Heat creeps up my neck like a roiling cloud of lethal fumes. I dig my nails into my palms, hoping to dull the ache radiating in my chest. "This is who I am." I suck in a pathetic snivel. "I thought I could be someone else. Someone special, someone worthy. But I ain't. I'm a white-trash fuckup down to my core. A fact that never bothered me until I met you. My confidence was the one luxury I had, and you took it. I don't like the way I feel when I'm with you." I turn away, unable to look at him any longer for fear of running back into the safety of his arms, but I feel his searing gaze seeping into my soul. "Go back to your family and your fancy party and leave me be."

"Darla, stop."

I stomp my foot on the pavement. "No, you stop. I was fine until you came along."

"*You* were fine?" he shouts with an air of pride. "My entire fucking life was planned, and I was willing to blow it all up. For you. But none of that matters, does it? You'll forever see me as the privileged rich guy lording his wealth over your head."

I turn back with a scowl. "That's always been your biggest problem, Dylan. You think you're better than everyone else."

Darkness falls over his light eyes. It rages in bold swirls of denim and ash that rake over me as I stand on the sidewalk with my heart in my hands. "I *am* better than everyone else. We both are."

My lips tremble. Why does he have to look at me with that intense gaze that slices me open? I don't want him to see me while I'm shattering into shards. Every second I'm with him is another tear in the fabric of my being. Soon, I'll be nothing but an untethered ball of twine, an unwound pile of my former self laid out on the concrete. "I wish I never met you. I wish I never accepted that stupid date in the first place."

He rolls his eyes, throwing his hands in a huff. "You don't think my life would be easier without you in it? All the shit you put me through . . . But I'm willing to work on it because, fuck, I can't stay away."

"Well, I'll make it real easy for you."

My shoes clack on the ground as I walk away, but his voice pulls me back. "You're a fuckin' tornado, you know that? You fly in, destroy everything in your path, and then blow away on the breeze."

Pain radiates in his darkened gaze. I hate that I hurt him. All I want to do is lie at his feet and say I'm sorry for being a complete and utter lunatic, but my pride won't allow it. I take a deep breath, trying to control the traitorous hormones that rage through me every time he comes too close. "Goodbye, Dylan. Enjoy your life. I hope it's every bit as miserable as you hoped." My voice trembles, but my stance remains strong, although my knees are ready to give at a moment's notice.

When I turn my back, he calls out, "Sure, Darla, run. You think you're so tough, but you're a coward. For the first time in your life, you feel something real, and it terrifies you."

My heart somersaults in my chest. There's nothing left for me to say. I am a coward. He offered me the world, but I'm too much of a realist to take it. We've reached our inevitable end. It's better to do it now and save ourselves the heartache down the line when we realize we aren't right for each other.

I know all that is true; I know it. Then why do I have this empty hole inside my stomach? I'm hollow like a pumpkin who's had its guts ripped out. I'll smile through the pain, but the ache is constant. Everyone worried that being with me would ruin Dylan Masters, but when push comes to shove, *he's* the one who ruined *me*.

Chapter Twenty-One

DYLAN

A SOFT KNOCK RAPS on my door. "Yeah?" I call out.

"It's Tara."

I slide off the corner chair and twist the lock. "What's up?" I ask, pulling it open.

She shrugs. "Nothing. Just wanted to hang out." Pulling the door open wider, I gesture for her to enter. "I haven't seen much of you since I've been home."

I fall back into the leather armchair and let my foot dangle off the ottoman while Tara sits on the edge of my bed, her legs crossed at the ankles like a proper lady. Between the siblings, she's the one most like me. Four years my junior, she followed me everywhere. I hated it, but I put up with it because she idolized me. Caleb always did his own thing. He'd be out in the fields shooting birds from the sky with a slingshot or raising cain out by the creek while Tara sat quietly on the floor with her Barbie dolls listening to me horribly teach myself how to play the guitar. Seen but not heard. The trait of every good woman.

"Well, you're seeing me now."

She offers a polite grin, but I can tell that it's fake. I know everything about her—how she calls everyone sweetie in an attempt to soften the blow after a thinly veiled insult or the fact that she prefers coffee yet orders tea when we're out because it feels more appropriate. It seems we're more alike than I thought. Two big liars.

I reach for my guitar and set it on my lap. "What do you really want?"

"Can't I want to spend time with my brother without an agenda?"

"Not since you started high school."

When she smiles this time, it's genuine. "You heard from Darla?"

The name is a razor. Hearing it filets my chest wide open. "If you came here to talk about that, you can see yourself out." I strum the strings, playing nothing in particular. It's a crutch. A way to keep my hands from picking up the phone and dialing her number.

Tara purses her lips. "Why are you being like this?"

"Like what? A guy?"

"The world is full of guys, Dylan. There are three of them filling the guest rooms already. Be a man."

I press hard on the fretboard, and the instrument lets out a muted whine. "What do you want me to say? She broke up with me. That's it. It's over." I look back down at the strings, plucking my fingertips from low to high E. "That shit was never gonna work out anyway," I mumble more to myself than to her.

My pulse takes off like a race car. It pumps my blood faster, and my hands pick up speed. After the dust cleared, I realized how stupid I was being. I was willing to walk away from everything I worked for. What the fuck was I thinking? It was that unicorn pussy. It had me out of my mind. You know the kind . . . so perfect and magical it will make you feel like you've fallen in love for no real reason.

"So is this what you've been doing the last couple of weeks? Sitting here alone in your room feeling sorry for yourself?"

I lift my gaze to hers, gray like mine and our mother's. Caleb's eyes were hazel like our dad's. "I'm not feeling sorry for myself. I'm spending time with me."

She lifts her feet and scoots backward until she hits the headboard, then crosses her legs out in front of her. "I heard Dad fixed you up on a date."

My stomach clenches. There have been a handful of occasions when I've seen my father lose his cool, but after that night, I thought the flesh was going to melt off his face. I had no argument. My only option was to sit there and take it as his red-faced *I told you so* rant went on and on. In the end, I had no choice but to agree to date Katherine Header. Darla knew exactly what she was doing. She chose a major public event to make a scene at my expense, and now I'm paying the price.

"You're really gonna put Dad in charge of your love life."

"What do you want from me, Tara?"

"I want you to stop acting like a spoiled brat and go after her."

With a heavy sigh, I lift the instrument off my lap and set it back into the open case beside my chair. Yet another thing Darla ruined. "I don't want to go after her. I want to go on with the life I had before I even knew her."

"You're so tough, aren't you, sweetie?" She lifts her dainty fists, lowering the timbre of her voice to a mocking tone. "I'm Dylan Masters, king of the world. I don't need anyone."

I scowl. "When are you going back to school?"

"Dylan . . ." Her expression softens. She pulls her legs in and folds them like a pretzel. "I don't know what you two were like together because I wasn't here, but I can tell you with full certainty that I've never seen you as happy as you were over the past few months. She was good for you."

I lean forward with my elbows on my knees. "She's a waitress who destroyed my car in a fit of rage." I'll never forget the look on her face as she turned away. She was so . . . broken. The fire in her eyes smoldered to a minuscule flare before going out completely. I did that, and it haunts my dreams.

"The term is *server* you misogynistic ass, and she isn't one anymore, is she?"

My chin falls to my chest. That little stunt got her fired, a lesson I learned the hard way when I went back to the club hoping to find her. I begged Eddie to give her a second chance, and he told me he'd think about it. I don't want to be the reason she lost her job. Mistakes were made. Yeah, she lost her goddamn mind, but I'd be remiss if I didn't take a little sliver of the blame. I came on way too strong, then left her flat when she needed me most.

"It doesn't matter, you know how Dad is . . ."

She rolls her eyes. "Who cares what Dad wants? This is your life, not his. What do *you* want?"

"I don't know." I push to my feet and stalk the floor in a tight circle.

"You have to stop caring what everyone else thinks and do what makes *you* happy."

"That's easy for you to say. No matter what I do, I'm going to let someone down. It's inevitable."

She glides off the bed and comes toward me, her gentle touch stilling my raging blood. "Your big heart has always been your downfall."

I tuck my little sister into my arms and drop a kiss to her head. "When did you become such a grown-up?"

"Finishing school," she jokes, detangling from my embrace. "You stink. When's the last time you took a shower?"

"That's not very ladylike of you," I reply with a superior grin.

She turns back toward the door and pulls it open, then chucks a final glance over her shoulder. "Do whatever you have to do, Dylan. But don't let love walk out of your life because you're too proud to chase after it," she insists before leaving me alone with my thoughts once again.

When I kick the open guitar case closed with my toe, something stirs inside me. A plan hatches like a baby chick. Slow at first. A tiny crack in the shell before the top opens, and it all fumbles out.

I snap the case closed and collect my things. Matters of the heart are not my specialty, but there is one thing I know like the back of my hand—nothing sets a tortured soul free quite like the right song.

The smell of barbecue wafts through the open space of the Sycamore Acres Trailer Park. My stomach roils from the smell and the nerves rattling my bones. I settle on the roof of my rental car, hoping the hot metal doesn't burn my skin through my jeans. My conversation with Tara still rings fresh in my head. I thought I could have my girl and eat her, too. I'm a selfish fuck. A spoiled brat like my sister said. I should have treated her better. I just hope it's not too late.

I crisscross my legs and fit the slim waist of my guitar on my thigh. I think I remember that her bedroom was in the back. I parked outside the window. I clear my throat and slowly start to play.

My trembling fingers move across the frets, my pick hand plucking the strings. The melody bursts through the tiny speaker, the first song we listened to together in my car. I'm not a songwriter, nor a real musician by any stretch of the imagination. I play for myself. It's the only thing I've ever had that was mine and mine alone, and now I'm sharing it with her.

I open my mouth to warble the words. My heart leaps from my chest and floats through the screen. I hope she can hear it, feel it. I never knew how to love before. I tried my best, but my best wasn't good enough. I need to work harder. I should have made her feel as though she was my entire world and not a secret swept under the rug. I loved her on *my* terms. I fucked with her feelings because I wasn't sure about my own. It's always been about me, never about her, about us. I've done so many things wrong, and now I want to make them right.

A flash moves past the open window. I cry out the lyrics, a plea, a promise. They call to her, pull her out. For the first time, I look up and realize I have an audience. People who heard my song came out to listen, but the only one I care about is standing in front of me, wild blue eyes brightened by the sun. "What are you doing here?"

My tongue slides across my dry lips. Face-to-face with the girl who stole my heart, I'm at a loss for words. "Free concert in the park?"

She looks down at the dirt as she toes it with the tip of her boot. "You don't belong here."

"You wouldn't take my calls. You wouldn't reply to my texts. What else was I supposed to do to get your attention?"

When she looks up again, her eyes are ringed in pink, a vast ocean swimming before me. "We said all we needed to say, Dylan. It's over. Go back to your mansion and your fast cars, your fancy life, and your big future. Leave us alone." The pitch of her voice goes up an octave but cracks as her attempt to be stern falls flat. Her friends rally round, onlookers watching an accident unfold.

"We can work this out."

Darla's expression remains hard, but I know she's pretending. She's thrown up her wall to try to act tough. I set the guitar down and slide off the car. "You still don't get it, do you?" The tears she was holding back breach the dam of her lashes. My fingers ache to wipe them away, but I keep them at my sides for fear if I touch her, I'll never let go. She wrenches open her truck door, turning away. "Too little, too late, Dylan. I want more."

Before I have a chance to reply she revs the engine and throws it in reverse. Dust flies from her tires as she speeds away.

Chapter Twenty-Two

DYLAN

KATHERINE HEADER HAS ZERO personality. I watch her from across the table, slicing a piece of dry, grilled chicken into perfect quadrants before sliding a small cube into her mouth. When I asked her out, she practically jumped up and down, just as my father said she would. Now I sit in this bullshit restaurant, my tie choking the life out of me, as I try to come up with something to talk about. Katherine and I have everything in common and nothing to say.

"So have you finished college?"

"I just graduated."

"And what's your next plan?"

Another long pause. With her raven hair and deep-set eyes, she isn't necessarily unattractive, but nothing about her is memorable either. She's just void. She's like the princess from *Coming to America*. I guarantee if I asked her to bark like a dog, she would yelp on command.

With Darla, the conversation flowed like water. She'd hit me with a snide remark, and I'd reply with an immediate comeback, her snark igniting my arousal like a fire in a drought. By the time I sank my dick inside her, I was so keyed up I could hardly hold it back. I doubt Miss Header even does it with the lights on.

"The usual. You know."

Yeah, I know. Spend four years earning a degree so you can get married and never work a day in your life. Why bother? It's a pointless waste of time. Like this entire date.

"Tell me something about yourself. What do you like to do for fun?" She sets her fork and knife on either side of the plate, contemplating the question as if I asked her the quadratic equation of two rational roots. I thought I'd start with the easy questions, but getting a simple answer out of her is like pulling teeth. "Do you like music?" *For the love of all that is holy.*

"It's okay. I really love Tom Holland."

I lift a brow. Pretty sure Tom Holland is not a musician, but for the sake of conversation, I let it go. It's the most I've gotten out of her all night. "That's cool. I'm into rock myself, but I've been getting into some country, too, lately."

When she replies with a smile, I know I've lost her. I should save us both the trouble and whip out an engagement ring and my bank statement, but I stuff a forkful of filet mignon in my mouth and think about how the hell I'm supposed to engage with a woman who has nothing to offer but status.

This is the type of woman I'm supposed to end up with. Rich, submissive, reserved, classy. She wouldn't dare use the f-word and would never consider throwing back tequila shooters. She'd do anything I asked. We'd redefine the term power couple. She'd be the doting wife to my rise in success. We'd have it all. A mansion on the hill and a vacation home in Aspen. Our children would attend the best schools. We'd make everyone jealous.

We'd have the perfect life. Perfect for anyone else except for me.

I lean in, resting my forearms on the table. "You wanna get out of here?"

She pauses mid cut to look up. "Where would you like to go?"

"I dunno." I waggle my brows. "Let's get a little crazy."

She stares at me as if I've lost my mind.

"Skinny-dippin' in the creek? Make out at the movies? I can bend you over the table right here, but I don't know if we'll be allowed back."

Her mouth falls open, but she forces it closed. "This is not appropriate dinner conversation," she seethes on a sharp whisper. Looks like I finally figured out how to get a rise out of her. Let's see how far I can push this baby without getting slapped.

"So let's get inappropriate. Whatcha got on under that dress?"

Her horrified gaze pings around the surrounding tables, but I don't care who hears me. "I bet you like to shower first, don't you? Make sure everything is squeaky clean before getting sloppy?" She pulls her lips between her teeth, her cheeks burning red. "You ever been fucked so hard that when you're done, your hands are full of the guy's hair, but you don't remember pulling it out?"

She shakes her head ever so slightly.

"If it's something you're interested in, it can be arranged."

She shakes her head again, this time more vigorously. I hold in a laugh. Kathrine gawks at me as if I'm some kind of a sex criminal, but if Darla were here, she'd already be grabbing at my belt. My body aches at the thought of never seeing her again.

What am I doing here? Darla walked into my heart like she always belonged there. She took down my walls and set my soul on fire, and I stood back and watched her walk away without a fight. Twice. I may have taken the hardest route to find her, but our paths crossed when they were meant to. Being with her is worth every conflict and heartbreak. She's not a stop on life's path. She's my final destination. I have to get her back.

"This was a mistake." I ball the napkin on my lap and drop it in my half-eaten plate before standing. "I have to go."

Her eyes go wide. "Sit back down," she grits through her teeth.

I pull a couple hundred-dollar bills from my wallet and throw them on the table. "I'm sorry. I don't belong here. I'm in love with someone else."

She tilts her chin. "What does love have to do with anything?"

"I hope that you someday learn the answer to that question." Mine is out there waiting, and I hope it's not too late.

When her voice filters through the low din of dinner chatter, I swear I'm hallucinating. Far as I know, she's been fired from the restaurant, but the unmistakable sound of her laugh pulls me closer to the kitchen door.

Through the porthole window, I see her standing with members of the waitstaff. My heart leaps into my throat. The door is the only thing separating us physically, but we may as well be worlds apart. I thought I could keep us flying under the radar until the election's over, but I see now how selfish I was. How selfish I *am*. I've reached a crossroad. It's time to choose between my family and my heart. Looking at her now, I don't understand why the choice was so hard in the first place. It was always her.

Turning back toward the dining room, my mind races. She deserves more than I was ever willing to give. I wasted my life worrying about what other people thought. I'm a coward, too afraid of being judged to live a life that's true to myself. It stops now.

"Hi. Can I borrow this?" I say, stealing the drink from a woman sitting at a nearby table. I tap the glass. It pings throughout the space, a hundred eyes lifting toward the sound. From the corner of my eye, I see the staff beyond the door look out. I step on a chair, then onto the table. People whisper as they watch, but I don't care. Let he who is without sin cast the first stone. With my audience engaged and my heart on my sleeve, I let out the words I should have said months ago.

"My name is Dylan Masters. My father is George Masters, Republican candidate for president. But that's not why I'm up here interrupting your dinner . . ."

Staff pools from the double doors, Darla included. The blood drains from her face when she sees me up here, but I swear she's never looked so beautiful.

"I want to admit to everyone, here and now, that I am desperately, madly in love with this woman. Her name is Darla Burke" — I point at my pretty girl as she stands slack-jawed — "and I treated her badly. I took her for granted. I'm an asshole. But she is the most incredible, sexy, amazing woman I've ever met in my entire life, and I will spend the rest of my life making it up to her if she'll let me."

I offer my hand, but she stands like a stone. Adrenaline whips through my veins, panic seeping into every pore. I understand now that my first attempt to win her back was wrong. Yes, it was "in the daylight," but that isn't what she was trying to say. Once again, my heart was in the right place, but my thinking was off. She doesn't want to be wooed on her own turf. She wants to stand proud on *mine*. I think I have it right this time. This is what she deserves. An overt display, a public offering. I'll tear the entire place to shreds if that's what it takes. I don't give a damn about anything else but her.

"I see you. Not the face you show to the world but the real you. The one who helps everyone and wants so badly to make the world a better place. I see your heart, and I want to be a part of it. I know you love me, too."

The whites of her eyes turn pink and glassy. She crosses her arms over her chest, pressing her trembling lips in a thin pink line. "I do love you. But I'm done fighting for your attention."

She turns on her heel and storms back into the kitchen, leaving me standing there cold and alone. A jagged pain slices through my heart. I bring my hand up to dull the ache, but it doesn't soothe the burn lingering in my chest. She loves me. We could have had the most excellent happily ever after, but I blew it. I took her for granted. I kept her at arm's length for so long that she was too far out by the time I was ready to pull her close.

A hundred eyes bore into my back. I crumple into myself, a puddle of self-loathing and disgust. Another painful ball of regret bounces in my gut. I've done everything I could think of to make her stay, but in the end, it was all for nothing. She doesn't want me. But I can't help being in love with her, and I will always take care of her, even if it's from afar.

Chapter Twenty-Three

DARLA

I SIT CROSS-LEGGED ON Shyanne's floor watching Savannah teeter around me. Her homemade princess dress juts out at the waist in a hand-tied tutu the same color as the headband holding back her wisps of hair.

"Lunch, Sav." Shyanne sets a bowl of mac and cheese on the table. Savannah looks up, the strands of tulle bouncing around her chubby legs as she jaunts over. "So let me get this straight. He actually sang to you? Like out in the open?" she asks, helping her daughter into her booster seat.

"I wish you were there to see it. It was mortifying."

She shrugs. "I dunno. It sounds kind of sweet."

"Comin' down to my trailer and serenading me with someone else's words is the illusion of sweet. It's the least amount of effort."

"What about what he did at the restaurant?"

"What about it?"

"He stood on a table for you. He admitted to the entire room that he loves you. I can't imagine that was easy for him."

"You read too many damn romance novels. This is real life, Shy. Shit like this doesn't happen to people like us."

"Sure it does."

"Really?" I hold my arms wide, gesturing around the space. "I don't see Hunter anywhere around here. Do you?" She winces as if being slapped, and I immediately feel like shit. "I'm sorry. That wasn't cool."

"It's okay," she says with a sigh. "But that's exactly why you should give him another chance. There aren't a lot of men beggin' for those, and he's done it twice."

I narrow my gaze. "The guy got me fired."

"You got yourself fired." She cocks her head with that mother hen look that drives me crazy. Is that something that you just learn after giving birth? Or is it something they teach during Lamaze classes? Either way, Shy's ready for Savvy's teen years. "He kept your relationship a secret, and that wasn't ideal, but honestly, he did nothing wrong that night. He showed up at a family obligation, just like he told you. You're the one who went all *Darla Smash* and made a big scene."

I roll my eyes. "Once again, your logic irritates me." I'm still too angry to admit she's right. Dylan hasn't left my head since the moment I walked away. His presence still lingers. When I close my eyes, I feel his hands on my skin and the rumbling vibration of his voice calling me his pretty girl. Nights alone in that empty trailer, I miss him so much it hurts. He uncovered parts of me I didn't know existed, and in him I found a love I never believed was real.

But it doesn't change anything. Dylan and I are still doomed to end in failure. I convinced myself that his arrogance was merely a product of family scars, but I can't continue pretending I can breathe underwater. If I took him back now, we'd devolve back to the same old pattern. He'd gain, and I'd lose. I have to protect myself.

Pushing to my feet, I pad over to the kitchen. "You have any of that mac and cheese left?"

"Yeah, help yourself." She moves through the small space picking up toys. "So have you heard from him since?"

"Of course not. I didn't bend to his will, and he moved on." I reach for a bowl, but my phone chimes in my back pocket. An unknown number floats across the screen. I intend to ignore it, but for some reason my thumb hits the green instead of the red, as if it knows something I don't. "Hello?"

"Hi. This is Paramita from the Serenity Wellness Center calling for Darla Burke?"

"This is her."

"Good afternoon, Ms. Burke. We received your transfer notice from New Day, but we need you to come down and sign the paperwork before we can proceed."

My lips twist in a scowl. "I'm sorry. Proceed with what?"

"The treatment of Grace Bronson."

Slush forms in my veins. My brain snaps to the last conversation I had with my mom. She was crying again. She cries every time we speak, but the last time was different. As with most state-run facilities, the patients outnumber the counselors at an alarming rate. They can't possibly offer the right kind of care, and she doesn't feel safe. "Is my mother okay?"

"Yes, of course. We have her bed ready, a private room as requested. All we need now is a signature."

"I'm confused."

"Can I put you on hold for a moment?"

"Sure." A gamut of emotions rolls through me. Catching Shy's nervous stare from across the room, I cover the mouthpiece and whisper, "Look up Serenity Wellness Center."

Her thumbs fly across the screen. She wanders over, her attention glued to the device in her hand. "It looks like some kind of posh rehab center in Dallas."

Before I have time to question, a man's voice comes on the line. "Ms. Burke?"

"Look, whoever you are, I didn't put in for any transfer. Far as I'm concerned, my mother is still working through her recovery at New Day, so I suggest you save your scams for someone else. I don't have any money."

"This is not a scam, miss. Her stay is already paid for. We simply need a signature."

"Who paid for it then?"

Papers rustle. I wait on pins and needles, half expecting him to vomit Ray's name, but the one he gives me knocks me off my feet. "George Masters."

My heart stops. I'm dreaming. That's the only explanation I can think of for why Governor Masters would pay an arm and a leg for a private rehab center in Dallas, but when I pinch my arm, I'm still standing in Shyanne's kitchen.

"When did this happen?"

"Looks like . . . a week ago."

My lips part, but no sound emerges. *Dylan*. He did this days before professing his love in a room full of his peers. He had nothing to gain from this and did it anyway. Why would he do this for me after everything I've done to him? It makes no sense.

"I can come by tomorrow if that's okay."

"Sure. We'll see you then."

The call disconnects in my ear, but I continue holding it in a white-knuckle grip.

"What was that about?" Shyanne asks.

"Dylan had my mom transferred." Saying it aloud sounds strange. My voice is hollow like me, a pretty shell wrapped around nothingness.

She curls her lip. "Are you serious?"

The room spins in a circle. I clutch the edge of the counter to keep from falling. This unexpected news stopped my brain from firing at full capacity, lobotomized by one simple phone call. "I don't know what to do."

Petite fingers wrap around my biceps. "You stop playing it safe and follow your heart."

I hear her voice, but I'm trapped in my own head. No one has ever done anything like this for me before. Anyone who ever claimed they loved me took. This is the first time in my life someone gave without expecting anything in return. I don't know how to accept it.

"Darla." The stern way Shy says my name brings me back to the present. When my eyes focus, she's staring hard with her orange brows pulled together. "Did you hear me?"

My tongue darts over my dry lips. I was hoping to continue my blissful state of ignorance, pretending what we had couldn't possibly be the love story I secretly hoped for. It was supposed to be a fling. A mutual attraction that kept us tangled up, skin to skin, yet when it turned to more, I got scared and ran.

I will my heart to slow down, I command it, but it doesn't listen. "I have to find him."

"Go."

I don't know which moves quicker, my legs or my pulse. I climb into the truck and back from the drive, tires chirping as I switch gears. I don't know where he'd be this time of day, but I have to look for him. I won't be able to sleep until I've gotten this squared away.

A quick phone call goes straight to voicemail. I prepare to send a text when the phone rings again in my hand. Cindy.

"Hey, Cin. What's up?"

"You might wanna get your cute little hind down to the bar."

"Everything okay?"

"Welp, your guy friend came in here rip-roarin' drunk and refuses to leave until he talks to you. I told him you ain't workin' but ..." She pauses to sigh. "I don't wanna have to call the cops."

"No, don't do that. I'll be right there."

I cut the wheel, doing a full one-eighty in the middle of the road. The bar comes up fast at seventy miles an hour. I swing into the lot and slam the truck in park. Darkness pulls me in like a magnet. "In the corner," is Cindy's only greeting.

Blond hair cascades over the dingy brown table. My boots clack on the wooden floor, competing with the never-ending slam in my chest. I squat beside him and rest my hand on his back. It slides into the short tendrils at the nape of his neck. My fingers tighten to a fist and pull until his head lifts from the cradle of his arms. "What the fuck are you doing here?"

"Huh?"

"Ugg." I drop my hold, and his head falls back onto the tabletop before popping back up. Wincing, he smacks his palm against his forehead. "What are you thinking coming in here hammered?"

His eyes look right through me at first, then focus on the *me* in the middle. "Darla," he slurs. "I needed to see you." He tries to stand but falls back down, the chair sliding out from under him.

I look at him on the floor, his head in hands. I should leave him here. Let Cindy get him thrown in the drunk tank to sober up and realize his mistake, but I'm not the same callous bitch I was when I met him. He's softened my rough edges smooth, and I can't go back to the way I was.

"C'mon, get up." I throw his arm over my shoulder and help him to his feet. "One foot in front of the other." We shuffle slowly to the door, his weight heavy on my back. Cindy runs beside him and offers herself as another crutch. Together we get him inside the truck, and I find myself back on the road en route to my house.

By the time we get there, he's able to get himself out. I unlock the door and take him by the waist, leading him to my bedroom. With a simple push, he falls on the mattress stomach down. I push his hair behind his ear, looking at his face as he burrows into my pillows. Long lashes cast shadows on his cheeks. I dreamed of this moment so many times. He and I in an actual bed, midnight snuggles and morning coffee. But in none of those fantasies was he too drunk to remember.

I yank the curtains closed to blot out the sun before curling in behind him. How did we get here? We went from hate to love and back to hate so fast I have whiplash from the ride. I read a quote once that said, *sometimes the best moments in life are the ones you can't tell anyone about.* That's what Dylan is for me. My beautiful secret.

Chapter Twenty-Four

DARLA

"PRETTY GIRL." A TICKLE runs from my temple to my jaw. I shake it off, but it moves to the shell of my ear and circles my lobe.

When my lids flutter open, I'm certain it's another dream, but it's not. Dylan's fingers sink into my hair as I begin to come to. The small amount of skin-to-skin contact sparks like a flint. The intimacy of the morning after is far too great. I slide onto my elbow to hold myself up, and his hand falls to the mattress. "What time is it?"

"It's early."

"Did you puke yet?"

The deep sound of his laughter rumbles in my chest. "Yes. And I used your mouthwash. I hope that's not a problem."

I flop onto my back and look up at the ceiling. "I appreciate you going the extra mile."

He sits up and kicks his legs over the side. "I'm sorry about yesterday. Thank you for putting me to bed."

"Yeah. What was up with that? You never get drunk."

"I'd just lost the best thing that ever happened to me." His spine curls as he leans his elbows on his knees. I watch the way his shirt stretches over the muscles in his back. He's the picture of perfection, but beneath that chiseled jaw and sculpted chest is a man who's as flawed as the rest of us.

I push up, resting my back against the pillows. "Can I ask you something?"

"Yeah."

"Why did you help my mother?"

He pauses for a beat. "I dunno."

An exasperated breath vibrates off my lips. I push myself higher on the bed. "I'm not your whore. I'm not going to sleep with you for footing the rehab bill."

He turns to face me, his palm sinking into the soft bedding. "That was not my intention. If you don't want to see me anymore, that's fine. I just wanted to know that you were taken care of for once in your life."

"I don't need you to take care of me."

"I know you don't. But someone special once told me I should use my money to help people instead of throwing it away."

Warmth pools in my belly. He listened. I downplayed what we had as nothing more than a physical connection, but it was more than that. My feelings for him terrified me. I pushed him out of my life because I couldn't fathom why someone like him would want to be with someone like me. Used goods. That's all I've been my entire life. Used and abused, and thrown away like trash. When people treat you like you're nothing, sooner or later you start to believe it.

"Thank you." I want to be strong, but the words crack in my throat. "I don't know where we go from here."

He reaches out and glides his knuckle down my cheek. "We can start over."

Tears reach the dam of my lashes. I've cried more in the past few weeks than I have in years. I have to get off this boat before I drown. I shake my head, pulling away from his gentle touch. "It's still gonna end up the same. I'll never forget what you did for me, but I'd rather walk away from the sweet than be buried by the sour."

He rears back, his lashes fluttering over his blue-gray eyes. "You're afraid to get hurt."

"It's just I—"

His mouth crashes onto mine, stealing every negative thought from my head. His full lips, strong as I remember, coax mine open, giving him access to the cavern of my mouth. My hands find their way behind his neck, slipping through the silken hair that falls to his shoulders.

Memories grab me, reminding me how perfect it feels in his arms. How right. I lose myself in him again and again no matter how hard I struggle to admit the truth. A growl escapes his chest, followed by a soft moan of my own. He takes hold of my bottom lip, letting it slide between his teeth before letting it go.

Our chests heave with ragged breaths. He grabs my hand and rests on top of my wildly beating heart, his larger hand holding it firm against the violent thump. "This tells me everything I need to know."

His heat clouds my brain with lust too thick to think clearly. He tastes like mint and trouble, and the desire for more is so strong it's crushing. "What does it say to you?"

He lifts my free hand to his chest next, our hearts beating in unison. "We're connected. It doesn't matter where we come from. All that matters is that you're here. You'll always be here, no matter what."

"That's easy for you to say behind a closed door."

Our hands touch. He lifts mine to his mouth, letting it graze across my skin before sliding off the bed and bringing me with him. "I'll shout it off the rooftops if that's what you want. I love you. I think I loved you the moment I saw you sitting in that bar alone, waiting for me. I was just too stupid to see it until it was too late."

"Well, you are kind of the worst."

He grins. "You think there's hope for me?"

"Maybe." I shrug.

Falling against his chest, I allow my eyes to flutter closed. No more what-ifs, no more worries. I allow myself to fall into the moment and be happy with the here and now. I breathe him into my lungs and hold him in until I feel that familiar burn in my chest and I have no choice but to let it out.

"Get dressed," he says out of nowhere.

"Where're we going?"

He palms my cheeks, tipping my head back. "First, I want you to meet my parents. Then I'm gonna take you out to eat, anywhere you want. And after that, we'll come back here and christen every room in this trailer."

I stare up at him as if he's too good to be true. Maybe he is. No one knows what the future will hold. Maybe we'll end up together, or maybe we're destined to fall apart, but he loves me now, and maybe that's enough.

But before we do anything, I have to attend to something. "I need you to come somewhere with me first."

Guilt festers inside me as I ride shotgun in Dylan's rental car. How he still wants me after that debacle, I'll never understand. The guy must be a masochist. Either that, or I'm the luckiest girl in the world, and we all know that's a load of horse shit.

Yet sitting beside him, that's how I feel. So damn lucky my heart hurts. I don't know what I did to deserve it, but I'm not going to take it for granted. Trailer trash and the politician. Sounds like a crappy Hallmark romance I'd blow right past. Little did I realize I'd be the main character.

He pulls into the parking lot at New Day Rehab Center, and we both get out. A nauseating mix of flowers and antiseptic greets us in the lobby. I walk up to the counter and wait for the woman behind the glass to notice me. "I'm here to pick up Grace Bronson."

She replies with a curt nod and instructs me to have a seat. A slow churn starts in my belly. I absentmindedly tap my feet, but the feel of Dylan's hand sliding into mine offers a sense of comfort I'd never known.

I don't have to do this alone.

"Don't be nervous." He touches his lips to my temple, a sliver of intimacy that acts as a blanket warming my heart.

"You're the first guy I've ever brought home."

His fingers squeeze around mine. "And the last."

I drop my head on his shoulder. "I never pictured my boyfriend's first meeting with my mom being at rehab."

A smile stretches from ear to ear. "That's the first time you've called me your boyfriend."

Goose bumps break out on my skin. "Yeah, I guess it is."

"I liked it," he whispers against my hair.

Me, too. When the fear bubbles up in my chest, I push it down before it boils over. Someday, the word will roll off my tongue without the panic getting lodged in my throat, but today isn't that day. He's the only man I've ever wanted like this, yet slapping a label on it makes it seem so serious. It's new and scary, yet wonderful at the same time.

Mom's slender frame comes into view. I stand, emotion stinging my eyes as I go to her. "Hey, Mama."

"Ain't you a sight for sore eyes, sugar bean?" She wraps me in a tight embrace. Under her thin skin, she's nothing but bones. I don't want to break down. This is the time for me to be strong. So I reach inside myself and muster the courage to put on a grin. Dallas is more than an hour's drive, but I know it's for the best. A new life on the right foot.

"You look good."

"Well, I feel like somethin' the cat dragged in."

Dylan's presence comes up behind me. "I want you to meet someone, Mama." I slide my arm around his waist and rest my free hand on his chest. "This is Dylan. He's the reason you're moving facilities."

Her eyes sparkle with renewed life. "Hi, Dylan. It's nice to meet you."

"Likewise, ma'am." He bends and takes her bag. "Are you ready to see your new temporary home?"

"Long as it gets me the hell outta here."

After signing her out, we all climb back into the car and head out to the highway. In true Dylan fashion, he insists on feeding us. At first, I couldn't figure out the fascination with watching me eat, but I think I'm starting to get it now. Sharing food is his love language. He's a closet nurturer. He may act tough on the surface, but deep inside his arrogant shell is the need to protect and care for those he loves.

He and I are more similar than I thought. We both love with an intensity that's forged in fire. It's not something given lightly. I love him today, and I will continue to do so until I take my final breath, regardless of whatever happens in our future. It's the reason people like us remain closed off. When we finally open, it's forever.

Epilogue

DYLAN

STEAM FILLS THE BATHROOM. I wipe the mirror with my fist to catch my reflection, but I see an unrecognizable man. Sure, the details I'm used to remain—the hair, the mouth, the nose—but the change isn't in the features; it's what is hiding beneath. It's the gleam in my eyes, the smile permanently fixed on my lips, the trace of pink highlighting my cheeks. It's the way I feel bubbling to the surface, the physical traits found on the face of a happy man.

Water drips from my hair. I dry it with a towel, then finish my morning routine before stepping out. A breeze greets me in the doorway. I pad through the room to the open balcony where Darla sits with a coffee and her cell phone. "Yeah, Mama. That's great." I sit in the seat beside her, listening to the sound of seagulls in the distance as she finishes up her call. "I'll see you when I get back, okay? I love you. I'm so proud of you." She takes the phone away from her ear. "My mom says hi."

"Did you tell her?"

A flush crests across her cheeks and nose. "No. She was going on about her one-year chip, and I didn't want to overshadow her big news."

Darla's concern for her mother makes me grin. I don't know everything about her childhood, but I know enough to understand that it wasn't good. But Grace is making up for it now, and that's what counts. Like Darla says, better late than never. Her mom is a real sweet lady.

Darla's gaze sweeps across the horizon. "I can't get over how beautiful it is."

The ocean waves come up to shore and break on the sand, but I can't take my eyes off her. How the wind rustles her hair and the way the blue of her eyes matches the sky. "Neither can I."

Her excitement is infectious. I've been to every body of water the world has to offer. I've swum in the crystal waters of the Aegean Sea and gone scuba diving in the Great Barrier Reef, but witnessing the Atlantic Ocean through Darla's eyes is the greatest sight I've ever seen.

I wanted to take her somewhere more tropical. The Maldives or Fiji, some place lush where we could be alone, but when all was said and done, my pretty girl chose to go to the Florida Keys. It's close and easy, a getaway without going too far.

She smiles, turning toward me. "Did you tell your parents?"

Pursing my lips, I shake my head. As soon as my father was sworn in, I quit working for him. That man dictated enough of my life. I opted to put some space between us and start a life of my own that doesn't involve being a Masters. It hasn't been easy, but I'm finally free to chase my own passion, starting with the woman beside me.

Suffice it to say, things have been strained. When I first brought Darla home, he barely spoke to her. He's softened up a bit, but I'm not sure things will ever be the same between us. I'm too happy to let him bring me down. He's too close minded, and I'm hoping to ride this wave as long as I possibly can.

My mom and Darla hit it off instantly. The "sweet girl from the restaurant" doesn't serve her lunch anymore, but they go out to lunch whenever she flies in to visit. Taking care of our parents is an endless job, but it's easier now that we do it together.

"Well, Mrs. Masters, what do you want to do first?" I ask. This is a trip solely for her, and I want to do everything I can to make it memorable. I want to give her the world, show her that every opportunity is now available to her. She's always had the drive, what she lacked was the money. What's mine is hers now. She still fights me on that, but I'm hoping the ring on her finger changes things. I'm tired of living hers and mine. I'm ready for it to be ours. Our life, our home, our future. Together. We sealed the deal yesterday. It was a beautiful ceremony. Just her and I on the beach at sunset. The last secret between us before we share it with the world.

Rising from her seat, she tugs at the belt on her robe. It falls open, revealing the satin nightie I bought her before we left. It hugs her body in a dangerous way. After more than a year together, my body reacts as if it's new. She straddles my lap and threads her fingers behind my neck. "I don't know if I'm on board with that Mrs. Masters shit, though."

I grab her hips and pull her in. She gasps. The heat of her arousal floods the thin fabric between us. "I don't care what you go by, as long as you're still my wife." The word alone stiffens my cock. My wife. Sure, she's unconventional, but I'm the luckiest guy in Texas. "You're mine now. Till death do us part."

She cocks her head. "Thank you for all of this."

"For what?" I cross my body to reach up to entwine our fingers, the gold bands touching as we come together.

"Bringing me here. Forgiving me for the sins of my past. Loving me in spite of all of it."

"I should be the one thanking you."

She grinds on my erection, whispering in my ear. "Think we'd get caught if we made love out here?"

I run my hands over the globe of her ass and under the thin string of her panties to push them aside. "I don't give a shit who sees us."

A salacious grin rolls across her lips. "Fuck me like you hate me?"

"Long as I call you pretty while I do it."

"You're the worst," she says with a giggle. "But I love you anyway."

"I love you, too, pretty girl." And I seal that promise with a kiss.

Loved Dylan and Darla?
Subscribe to my monthly NO SPAM newsletter, and receive a bonus epilogue to this story, in addition to an exclusive novella FREE. My way of saying thank you for signing up!
https://bit.ly/PSYTW_Epilogue

If you want even MORE bad boys of Hell's Bend, one-click
Baby, You're Mine
at a special discount now.
https://janeanthonyauthor.com/ps-bym

———

USA Today Bestselling Author, Jane Anthony, delivers a swoon-worthy, second chance romance with passion, heart, & steam. Secrets are spilled when Hunter Laval—a broody bad boy from out of town— meets back up with Shyanne Delaney—a jaded single mother with a guarded heart —on their road to happily ever after.

P.S. Baby, You're Mine

SHYANNE

THERE'S A KNOCK ON my door just before it opens. I crane my neck to look, but I already know it's Summer coming to start her shift. Her blue tipped hair is pulled into a messy bun similar to my own, except I'd never have the stones to change the color. Red is part of my bloodline. It's one of the only things tying me to the family that cast me out years ago.

"Hey!" I greet, wiping the remainder of Savannah's breakfast off her face. She squirms in her seat, dying to get to her babysitter to play whatever game Summer has in store for her. The girl is a godsend – that is, if I believed such a thing existed. I wasted so many years praying to a deity that's done nothing but screw me over. If there was a God, he'd be number two on my shitlist.

"Morning, Shy," she sing-songs, then lowers to Savvy's height. "Hey, Pumpkin." A nickname I always found ironic since Savannah is the only Delaney for generations with black hair. She got it from her father, along with her smile, but her eyes are mine, which is the one thing I'm thankful for. I'm not sure if my heart could handle looking into those bottomless brown eyes every day knowing he isn't around to see them.

I snatch my bag off the couch and throw it over my shoulder. "I should be home at the normal time. Call me if you need me."

Summer offers a two-finger salute. "Have fun."

"Right," I reply with a snort. Running back and forth with plates of food all day isn't exactly my definition of fun, but it pays the bills. I should be on my way to graduating college, paving the way to a better future, but fate had other plans. When I found out I was pregnant, my priorities changed. Everything I do now is for Savannah. My happiness relies on hers.

Bending down, I sweep her into my arms and lift her off the floor. "Give mama a kiss, my sweet girl." She throws her chubby arms around my neck and pushes her damp face into my cheek.

I must have cried for nine months straight. The day she was ripped from my body, I felt like everything I loved about being young was ripped from my body at the same time. Then they dropped her in my arms, this tiny helpless little creature that looked up at me with the face of innocence. I never thought I'd love again until I saw that face, and now I can't imagine a life without her in it.

"All right, I gotta run." I set her back down and head for the door.

The beat-up Dodge sits in my driveway. When I yank on the handle, the door lets out a shriek as it falls open. Someday soon this thing is going to give up on me, but until that happens, it's my only means of transportation. It has almost two hundred thousand miles and no air conditioning, but it's the only car I was able to afford on a new waitress salary. There's no public transportation in Hell's Bend. It was either this or drive my baby around on the seat of my bike. Until then, I've been saving up for something newer. Something that's at least all the same color and not Frankensteined together from other car parts.

The Texas heat blasts me in the face as I fall into the driver's seat. The cab is an oven; I feel as if I'm baking inside it. I roll down the windows and let the stagnant air flow out as I pull away from my house and head down the main road.

The Red Drum Country Club isn't too far. It's just after the imaginary line where my town ends and Red Drum begins, but inside is a high school reunion of Hell's Bend alumni. My best friend, Darla, made it tolerable, but she got herself fired and left me here to rot.

Okay, I'm exaggerating. It's not that bad. The boss is cool and never gives me a problem when I need a day off to take Savvy to the doctor or whatever. It helps that he, too, grew up in Hell's Bend. Our kind sticks together.

"Mornin', Angel," I say as I saunter inside. Angel Ramirez has been here almost as long as I have, one of the few on wait staff that I call an actual friend.

He turns at the sound of my voice and smiles as I punch my time card. "Girl, I'm all a twitter this morning."

"Why now?" I smile. Angel is such a drama queen, I swear.

"Eddie hired a new busboy . . ." He pauses for dramatic effect, tipping his face to the sky as if thanking God himself. "So hot. He has this swarthy outlaw vibe that has me all flustered." He fans his face with his checkbook, but the only part of the story I lock on is busboy. Hot is of no interest to me.

"He actually loosened the purse strings to hire some help around here? I'm shocked."

"Word on the street is Eddie's doing the guy a solid because he was friends with his mom or something. I dunno. You know how shit flies around here."

"That I do." I secure my apron around my waist and head into the main part of the kitchen to check the board for my assigned side work. "Salad. Great." I sigh. People don't generally realize there's more to being a server than bringing food. There's a whole world of things to do behind the scenes: setting tables, taking out the trash, etc. Salad duty is my least favorite of them all. It means I have to chop the vegetables and make sure the station stays full throughout the shift in addition to taking care of my tables. And let me tell you, these rich people love their overpriced greens. It's a little ridiculous. A head of lettuce is, like, two dollars at the general store, but these idiots line up to pay eighteen plus bucks a plate. Sickening.

"I got setting," Angel taunts.

"Lucky."

I turn on my heel and head for the refrigerators to gather the fixings that need to be cut. Armed with a colorful array of veggies, I step back toward the sink to get started. I wash everything, including my hands, then set it all on the cutting board. With one chop of my knife, the head of lettuce splits in two. I dive into the job, barely registering the sound of footsteps creeping behind me until Eddie's voice cuts through my concentration.

"And this is Shyanne, our head waitress . . ."

At the sound of my name, I twist on the ball of my foot, the knife still lodged in my fist. Eddie's lips move, but I can't make out the words. My mind goes blank.

I can't hear.

I can't think.

I can't breathe.

All I can do is stare into the soulful brown eyes in front of me, eyes colored with the same look of shock I imagine is plastered across my own features.

The knife clatters to the floor at my feet. My knees give out from under me. I fall back against the cutting board for support. Seconds pass like hours. When I find my voice again, the only word that slips from my lips is a name I've refused to say for the last four years.

"Hunter."

Acknowledgments

Special thanks goes to...

Paramita Patra & Samantha Morgan for all your words of encouragement to make this story the best it could be. I don't think I could have gotten it done without you. Mad love for ALL of your help, guidance, cheerleading, and support.

Also - props to Perrin from The Author Buddy. No shit, you are amazing. Thank you so much for all your awesome insight and excitement!

Summer Graystone, Robin Wane—best betas ever!

Dani Rene — holy shit, girl. I'm just gonna leave it at that ;)

Photographer Michelle Lancaster and model, Ben A. for the amazing cover image and Kate Farlow at Y'all. That Graphic for knowing how to make it shine.

Amazing editors, Candace Royer & Jenny Sims for slogging through my horrid first draft, and my slightly less awful second draft.

Bloggers, ARC readers, and Rebels, y'all are the cat's pajamas and I love you!

Books by Jane Anthony

P.S. I Hate You

P.S. You're the Worst

P.S Baby, You're Mine

Last First Kiss

Blue

Kade

Pretty Reckless

Lawless

Off Limits Collection

Secret Promises

Chasing Casey

Pictures of You

About The Author

Jane Anthony is a USA Today best-selling author of contemporary/new adult romance & women's fiction. A reader proclaimed "queen of angst", she approaches tough subjects with a gritty voice that tugs on your heart and leaves you breathless.

Jane gives a bit of herself and her quirky knowledge in each novel by incorporating her love of music through a book-specific playlist and adding things uniquely Jane to the plot, like her crazy family or '80s trivia. When she's not busy being mom or Mrs. A, you'll find her at a concert, lost in a book, or watching horror movies with her husband.

Find Jane Online

The best place to interact with Jane is by
joining her Facebook reader group:
Jane Anthony's Romance Rebels

Other ways to stay in touch:
www.janeanthonyauthor.com
TikTok @JaneAnthonyWrites
Facebook @AuthorJaneAnthony
Instagram @JaneAnthonyAuthor
Bookbub @JaneAnthony
GoodReads

Printed in Great Britain
by Amazon